Sunny Skies Ahead

Published by Aspen & Ivy Press

Cover Design: Yummy Book Covers

Editing and Proofreading: Kelsey Gay

1st Edition published in April 2025

eISBN: 978-1-965506-08-0

Paperback: 978-1-965506-09-7

Dedication

For every military spouse who wasn't believed by their partner's chain of command, or had their abuse swept under the rug: I believe you.

Also by Hallie Anne

Watford Sweethearts Series
Under Pink Skies
Sunny Skies Ahead
Through Stormy Skies [Nov 2025]
Anthologies
Love in Appalachia

Content Notes

Sunny Skies Ahead deals with heavy themes. There are on page references and discussions of suicide, parental death, domestic violence (past, not between main characters), emotional abuse, physical abuse, alcoholism, and biphobia, though there are no graphic on page depictions of any.

There are extended discussions of past domestic violence situations in Chapter 15, where a survivor tells their story to a trusted loved one. Please reach out to the author with any questions. Feel free to DM me on Instagram, or send me an email at hallieanneauthor@gmail.com. Take care of your mental health!

Playlist

- Vertigo – Griff

- Cinnamon Girl – Lana Del Rey

- favorite crime – Olivia Rodrigo

- Now That We Don't Talk (Taylor's Version) – Taylor Swift

- making the bed – Olivia Rodrigo

- Into The Walls – Griff

- Guilty as Sin? – Taylor Swift

- Risk – Gracie Abrams

- run for the hills – Tate McRae

- The Prophecy – Taylor Swift

- Matilda – Harry Styles

- Say Don't Go (Taylor's Version) – Taylor Swift

- better wild – Sierra Spirit

- You're Gonna Go Far – Noah Kahan

- You Are In Love (Taylor's Version) – Taylor Swift

- Dog Days Are Over – Florence + The Machine

Listen on Spotify

Chapter One
Imogen

G rowing up, my father had a theory about hell.

He was fascinated with the notion that hell meant something different to everyone else. For some, it might be standing in a line at an amusement park that never moves, or sitting in a waiting room and never having your name called.

I decided that for me, my personal hell was standing in the doorway of a bridal salon, drowning in a sea of white.

White lace, white pearls, and so, so much tulle. To my eternal horror, there were even white feathers.

I didn't like to dwell on thoughts of my marriage. I'd worked tirelessly to leave that behind; to distance myself from the memories.

But standing in this bridal salon in Brighton while the nice woman at the front desk ran to find my best friend, Abbie, I wondered what it would have been like to wear a dress like this. To stand in front of God and everyone I loved and swear to love the person beside me until the end of my days.

As a child, I thought marriage meant a happy ending. As a teenager, I thought marriage was my ticket out of a bad situation.

I couldn't have been more wrong. I'd been foolish and naive, just like everyone warned me.

I turned away from the front desk towards the entrance to the store. The tall glass windows framing the busy streets of Brighton reflected my brown skin back to me, shoulder-length black curls framing my round face. I gazed at my reflection for the briefest of moments, toying with a stray curl that never seemed to lay where I wanted it.

"Good afternoon!"

I startled, whirling to face the woman. It was a different woman this time, dressed in the same solid black attire, but with a name-tag that read *Diana*.

"You're here with Abbie Collins, right? She's right this way."

Diana led me towards the fitting rooms. I kept my arms tucked in firmly to my sides as we slipped through the overfilled racks of fluffy white. The back of the store had four fitting rooms, two on each side, divided by a center hallway that ended with a curved mirror and a pedestal in the middle.

"Thank God you're here!"

I turned around to face my best friend, painting what I hoped was an excited expression on my face.

"I'm here."

"I was nervous you were going to bail last minute."

I gasped in mock outrage.

"This is your final wedding dress fitting we're talking about here. I would never bail on you. I'll be the only voice of reason here, if those feathered monstrosities in the show-room prove anything."

Abbie shook her head, but her eyes shone brightly with affection. She walked towards the pedestal, fiddling with her hands before smoothing them down the front of her dress. I recognized it as the reception dress she'd picked out several months prior. Simple satin draped elegantly over her curves, a long slit cut to her upper thigh from ankle-length, and two thin straps crisscrossed in the back for an added detail. It was everything her ceremony dress was not, and that's what made it so special.

"All that aside, a bridal boutique is kind of the worst place for a commitment-phobe to be," Abbie teased.

I rolled my eyes. I might be commitment-phobic now, but I hadn't been at eighteen.

Diana appeared behind me as Abbie stepped onto the pedestal, turning around to view the dress from the side. I stepped forward to ensure that all the adjustments had been made, seamlessly transitioning into the role of maid of honor. Diana gave us both a warm smile.

"Can I get either of you some champagne or sparkling water?"

I hesitated for a moment and then shrugged.

"Sparkling water would be great, thank you."

The stylist disappeared from the fitting room area, leaving Abbie standing alone on the pedestal, twisting to get a look at the back of the dress.

"Everything look okay?"

"Yes," Abbie said, her voice a bit too bright. I met her eyes in the mirror and waited for her to elaborate. She crossed her arms over her chest before continuing.

"This all feels a bit much. I mean, two dresses?"

"You won't be able to move at the reception without changing into a simpler dress," I said, nodding to the open fitting room door and the puffy, overflowing ballgown that was spilling out of its garment bag. "You're getting to have your princess moment, and your hot moment. It's a match made in heaven."

Abbie pressed her lips together and cocked her head slightly to the side, as if she couldn't believe she was really standing here.

"Just like you and Connor," I added quietly, watching as the corner of Abbie's mouth twitched, the barest hint of the smile that wanted to break free.

I knew nothing about wedding dress shopping. When my ex-husband and I had gotten married, I was barely out of high school. He was a newly minted United States Marine who had graduated mere weeks before we strolled into the courthouse. No, I didn't even get a nice dress out of the horrible experience that was my marriage.

"Remember when we used to watch *Say Yes to the Dress* as kids, and the bride would put on that one dress and immediately start crying happy tears?"

I nodded, remembering the many summer afternoons we spent indoors with our dream wedding albums, searching through thousands of wedding dresses and hairstyles and Pinterest flower arrangements to build our binders. I probably still had mine somewhere. I was surprised Abbie hadn't mentioned her album yet.

"It just feels surreal," Abbie murmured as she stepped down from the pedestal, heading for the fitting room where her ceremony dress hung. "Like if I snap my fingers or click my heels together, it will all be gone."

Her words caught me off guard. Not because I was worried that Abbie was having second thoughts about the marriage, but because her words hit me like a blow to the chest. Because that's exactly how I'd been feeling since my return to Watford. I spent most of my days looking over my shoulder, wondering when my past would catch up to me.

"I know what you mean," I said quietly, following her inside the room. "And you already know what I'm going to say."

"You're going to tell me that my tendency to overthink is the real thief of joy," Abbie looked at me with a wry expression as she waved me over to help with her zipper. I laughed, but obliged without further comment.

Once she was out of the dress, I carefully hung it back on the wooden hanger and zipped up the garment bag before turning my attention to the very, *very* large dress that took up most of the space in the room.

Abbie unzipped the back and pulled the skirt out. I let out a low whistle.

"Let's get this party started," I said, fake rolling my non-existent sleeves up my forearms. Abbie shook her head as I helped her step into the dress.

"Wait, hold on," I said, grabbing her veil off one of the other hangers. "I need the full effect."

I sprinted from the room, shielding my eyes so I didn't see the full image of Abbie done up completely. I'd already seen the dress—I'd actually been the one to pick it out, a point which I proudly proclaimed to Connor, Lucas, and Kameron the night we'd returned from dress shopping—but I hadn't seen her fully done up yet.

I slumped down in one of the velvet armchairs opposite the pedestal and called out, "Ready!"

Tears welled in my eyes within seconds of Abbie walking out of the fitting room.

The dress was just as perfect as I remember it being. An off-the-shoulder neckline framed the beginning of a lace bodice that flared into a full tulle ballgown right at Abbie's waist, cascading down her body and accentuating her curves in all the right places. Intricate floral patterns adorned the top layers of tulle, culminating in a stunning design encircling the hem of the dress. It was the epitome of fairytale princess, and based on the way Abbie's eyes sparkled as she stepped onto the pedestal, it was exactly what she wanted.

"It's perfect," Abbie whispered, turning around for a full spin. She clasped her hands together in front of her with a girlish joy that made my heart hurt.

"Is it everything you dreamed it would be?" I asked, already knowing the answer.

"Yes," Abbie said, a smile slowly spreading on her face as she wiped away her tears.

"I trust everything is to your liking with the alterations?" Diana asked, and Abbie turned from side to side once more, the full skirt swaying delicately as she did so.

Abbie nodded, and I stood, wrapping her in the biggest hug.

"Are you saying yes to the dress? Again, that is?"

Abbie swatted at my arm, but her grin told me she was happier than she had been in a long, long time.

A short hour later, we were sitting down at a booth in our favorite pizza restaurant in Brighton. After a closer examination of the dress, Abbie had signed off on all of the alterations. The deed was sealed with one last swipe of Connor's credit card and an embossed "refer us" card slipped into Abbie's purse. After trying—and failing—to gently lay both gowns in the backseat of my tiny Camry, we were finally sitting down in the pizza parlor. We ordered a large pepperoni and mushroom pizza to split.

"Looking back, I should have known you'd be the one to find the dress," Abbie said after taking a sip of her water. I smiled smugly.

"Not to toot my own horn here, but I know you better than you know yourself most days."

"Can't deny that," Abbie said, shooting me a grin. "I'm grateful to have the truest of friends in you."

"You deserve to be happy, Abbie," I said earnestly. "I know I had my reservations at the beginning of this, when Connor came back into town, but I really am happy for you. You've more than earned this."

Saying I had reservations about the two of them would be putting it lightly. I was the one who had helped Abbie through the darkest time of her life, the weeks after her mother died and Connor had left town without so much as a note. I'd held her while she sobbed until she was sick, convinced she'd never make it out of Watford and achieve her dreams, because her father's alcoholism wrought havoc in every area of her life.

Abbie had always been convinced there was more to the story of Connor leaving, and it turned out she was right.

Now, the man looked at her like she hand-painted every star in the night sky. Based on my conversations with Kameron, Connor's best friend and boss, it sounded like he'd always done that. That kind of all-encompassing, reckless love is all I had ever wanted for her.

Abbie reached across the table and squeezed my hand, her blue eyes meeting mine.

"You deserve to be happy too, Imogen."

I waved her hand away, taking a sip of my water. I didn't want to talk about myself.

"I am happy, Abs."

"I know," she said, her eyes still shining softly.

"Abbie," I warned, raising my eyebrows. "Don't say it."

"You can find happiness without being married, you know," Abbie said, and I let out a loud exhale.

"I love you, thank you, but I don't need a relationship lecture," I cut in, voice strained. "You need to focus less on my non-existent love life and focus more on preparing for your wedding."

Abbie narrowed her eyes, and I knew this conversation was far from over. Abbie was like a bulldog with a bone. I wouldn't categorize her as a traditional person by any means, but she was still stuck in the love-struck, honeymoon phase of being with Connor and all the bright, sunshine-y promises of the future. That was her path to happiness, and she wanted everyone to experience that love. I didn't fault her for that.

Even if it was like a knife being twisted in my gut every time she brought it up. She knew I didn't want to talk about my future potential for love. Truth be told, it wasn't at the top of my mind. *Ever.* I had my hands full with the homestead, and now with my brother, Kevin, taking over as the manager for the general store Abbie and her father owned, there was a lot going on.

Our pizza arrived, and I sighed as the aroma of melted cheese, fresh tomato sauce, and buttery garlic crust enveloped me. *Heaven.*

Abbie slapped a slice onto a paper plate and pushed it towards me. I took a bite of the cheesy goodness and closed my eyes.

"This is *good.*"

Abbie laughed, the sound bright and airy.

"You look like you need some privacy."

"Hush," I said, and wiped my mouth with a napkin. "I'll update the wedding prep spreadsheet now that everything is set with the dress. Now we need to discuss the flower arrangements."

Abbie's smile widened, and she leaned in, launching into her very detailed vision on what the floral arrangements would look like. I didn't have the heart to tell her we'd already discussed the vision at length, and I just needed to update her on what the vendors had to say, but I let her talk, her hands waving animatedly as she outlined the image in her mind.

Abbie had grown up wanting to start her own flower farm one day, and while she wasn't sure if that dream would ever come true, she could certainly pour every ounce of that passion into planning her wedding.

I smiled and pulled out my phone to take notes. I was surprised when I had a text from Kameron, Connor's best friend and boss.

Kameron Miller

> **Please tell Abbie to text Connor back**

> **He's moping like a sad puppy because he wants to be married already and it's gross**

I smiled to myself before tapping out a brief reply.

Me

> Aw, poor baby, having to put up with that. Need a hug?

Not knowing where exactly that response had come from, I made to put my phone away, but his reply came quicker than I'd expected.

Kameron Miller

> I'll happily take one if you're offering

My heart stuttered strangely.

Abbie and I had widened our social circle to encompass the three men. Lucas and I had immediately bonded over our shared love of country music. Kameron and I had fallen into step as friends too, but he distracted me in a way I wasn't used to. The two of us hadn't really talked to each other at length, at least without Abbie or Connor present, but there was a natural kinship there that unnerved me.

When Kameron conversed with someone, he gave them his full attention. He actively listened, and somehow always knew the right thing to say. Every time I talked to him in person, it felt like I could stay there all day, telling him about my life.

Which is why I actively tried to avoid having lengthy conversations with him. I kept my past close for many reasons.

Kameron, of all people, could understand why.

"What do you think about white daisies instead of baby's breath?"

Abbie's question pulled me from my thoughts.

"Sorry, I'm going to need you to repeat whatever you just said."

Abbie did so, but there was a twinkle in her eyes that told me she had her suspicions. Not that they mattered.

Because the one thing I hadn't told anyone, not even Abbie, is that I made a promise to myself after my divorce.

A promise I wouldn't break, and certainly not for a man who had his own baggage to handle.

Needless to say, there would be no more relationships for me.

Chapter Two

Kameron

As I stood at the top of the farmhouse stairs at Winding Road Farm, watching my two best friends attempt to maneuver a couch down the narrow, rickety stairs, I couldn't help but smile.

"Lift it up, Morales," Connor barked.

"I'm the one with my back to the stairs. I can't lift it any higher," came the muffled reply from Lucas, who was taking each stair carefully.

"If I may—"

"You may not," they both said, and I held my hands up in mock surrender. After Lucas let out another string of curses, I took my leave from my makeshift observation deck and headed into Connor's now empty bedroom, taking in the barren space.

It was strange to see this place so devoid of Connor's personality. For the last year, it had been the three of us, figuring out how to make this farming and non-profit business endeavor work. Connor and Lucas had taken my dream and run with it.

The people you spend time with on active duty are the people you become closest to. I was lucky that I scooped up two of the most confident Marines I'd worked with and had them work for me as civilians.

I crossed my arms over my chest and heaved out a long sigh.

As much as I'd been a rock for Connor to lean on in these last few years, he'd been one for me, too. It was going to be weird not having him here full time.

A loud thud followed another string of Lucas's colorful curses, signaling that they had successfully put the couch in the living room. I descended the stairs quickly, jumping down to the first floor once I'd reached the last step.

Lucas was now laid out on said couch, and Connor returned from the kitchen with two bottled waters, handing one to Lucas.

"Who puts a couch in their bedroom," Lucas muttered after a long swig. "And how did you two get it up there in the first place?"

Connor and I looked at each other and burst out laughing.

Connor stated, "Certain secrets are not meant for sharing."

I took a seat next to him on the couch opposite Lucas and rolled my eyes.

"There was plenty of cursing. Connor and I didn't talk to each other for the rest of the day. Trust me, you didn't miss much."

Lucas downed the rest of his water bottle before turning his attention back to Connor, lifting the empty bottle in a mock toast. "How are you feeling about moving back to Watford, big guy?"

Connor shrugged. "It feels right, for now at least. Abbie and I have been talking about selling the condo and buying a house somewhere between Winding Road and Watford. Since Kevin's doing a trial run with store management, Abbie wants to be close in case he needs something."

"How's Abbie's father?"

"Malcolm's doing alright," Connor said with a shrug. "Some days are easier than others. Right now, he's struggling to find an outlet that works for him. Woodworking is too triggering for him right now, because it reminds him of Abbie's mom. He hasn't taken a liking to anything else he's tried, but I'm confident he'll find something."

Malcolm had struggled deeply with his alcoholism the last few years, and had just finished an intense in-person recovery program at a holistic health center off the Oregon coast. I'd helped him get connected with resources to maintain his sobriety, even though we primarily worked with veterans and first responders at Winding Road. I couldn't help but want to keep tabs on his progress, especially after the events of last autumn, where Malcolm was in a serious car accident after a particularly bad bender. He and Abbie's relationship was mending, but it was a slow-going process, for obvious reasons. You couldn't simply flip a switch and undo years of neglect and abuse.

"It's going to be weird not having you around here, man," Lucas said. "How will I possibly get my day started without you glaring at me over your coffee cup when I'm coming back from my morning run?"

"It's not like I'll never see you again." Connor leaned back against the couch. "I'll still be here after the wedding."

"I figured you'd want to work remotely," I said.

"For the first week after my honeymoon, I'd like that," Connor said, and Lucas gagged. Connor glared at him. "But I'll be here when the next cohort starts. There are some things you can't do from behind a computer screen."

"True," I replied. "That means a lot, dude. Thank you."

"Of course," Connor said.

"I can't believe you're going to be a married man in just a few short weeks," I said, shaking my head slightly.

"Me neither," Connor said, a slow grin forming. "But there's no one else I'd rather be walking down the aisle to."

My heart twisted painfully in my chest, and I shoved all thoughts of that aside.

Deep down, I could admit I was jealous of what they'd found in each other.

I'd seen what love could do to people—how it could destroy them in the end. I'd watched my mother fade into a shell of her former self after my Dad's death. Abbie and Connor's reunion reminded me that love is terrifying. There was never a sure way to protect yourself from life-altering heartbreak.

I promised myself a long time ago I'd never allow myself to get that attached to another human being. And yet, that didn't stop me from wanting it.

Connor and Lucas were now engaged in a heated conversation about something sports related, despite neither of them being big sports fans. I slid my phone from my back pocket. I wasn't surprised to see four unread emails sitting in the Winding Road inbox, but I swiped the notifications away. I'd deal with work stuff later.

I *was* surprised to receive a text from Imogen. Imogen had sent it directly to me, instead of to our group chat.

Imogen Phillips

> Abbie and I would like to come by the barn to finalize the design work for the flowers—will you guys be there this weekend? :)

I smiled beside myself. Our text conversations tended to be brief and sometimes stilted. To be fair, the latter had more to do with my propensity to overthink things, especially when it came to written communication.

Me

> I won't be here this weekend, but Lucas will be. Just come to the farmhouse and he can give you the barn key.

I was annoyed because I had to miss *another* wedding planning day for a conference I had been asked to attend months earlier. Imogen and I's schedules rarely lined up these days, which made it pretty difficult to do any joint planning on the wedding. Considering I had intricate knowledge of the venue and Imogen was Abbie's unofficial wedding coordinator, who had most of the details on Abbie's vision, we needed to have more conversations than we currently had bandwidth for. Most of what Imogen and I had accomplished so far had been through text message.

And as someone who wasn't gifted with written communication, that made things incredibly difficult.

I told myself I was annoyed because it made coordinating things harder, not because it involved missing several chances to see Imogen.

Sounds good, thank you!! :)

My stomach did a weird jump at the presence of two exclamation marks *and* a smiley face emoji. I did my best to ignore it.

I had a tendency to overthink, and nowhere was that more obvious than when Imogen Phillips was involved.

Chapter Three

Imogen

It's hard to pinpoint exactly when Wednesday night dinners became a tradition at the farmhouse.

What had started with a single dinner, where Abbie brought Connor and I together to break bread and make amends, had turned into a once a month tradition where Kameron, Lucas, Abbie, Connor, and sometimes Kevin and his girlfriend, Kyrie, came over to share a meal together.

We started out with rotating chefs, but after the fiasco that was Lucas Morales trying to cook in my kitchen and almost burning the house down, I put my foot down. Only Abbie and I were allowed to cook.

The boys could help, but only with supervision, particularly around the stovetop and sharp tools.

After spending a long Saturday afternoon at the Winding Road Barn with Abbie and Lucas finalizing the design details for the flower arrangements, I was exhausted. Kameron hadn't been there, which had proven to be more of an issue than I'd expected. Lucas had many gifts, none of which involved his ability to embrace a grander vision.

He was the most practical person I knew. Asking him to imagine what the barn would look like decked out in string lights and daisy garlands was like pulling teeth.

The first time we'd toured the venue, it had been far from finished. But now the barn was stunning. Exposed wood beams and high vaulted ceilings, gorgeous windows, and a lofted space that provided additional storage.

Kameron had taken his dream of a multipurpose venue and run with it. The barn would be a gorgeous place to host weddings, but I also knew there were many conventions and organizations that would love the space, too.

The pasta sauce bubbled at a low simmer on the stove. My phone sat on the counter, mocking me. I'd been procrastinating on calling my sister. We'd sent out wedding invitations weeks ago, and while Cassie and Abbie had never been close friends, I'd hoped my older sister would see my best friend's wedding as important enough to come back to Watford for. We hadn't received her RSVP, but we also hadn't received a note saying she couldn't come, either.

I took a deep breath and dialed. Only one way to find out for sure.

"Hello, this is Cassie."

I rolled my eyes at the formal greeting.

"Hi, it's me. Your sister," I added emphatically, just in case she'd forgotten she had one.

There was a brief pause, followed by shuffling in the background, as if she'd pulled her legs up to her chest like she so often did when we were kids.

"Hi, Im. What's up?"

"Are you coming to Abbie's wedding?"

There was a long pause. I probably should have minced my words, given that this was the first phone conversation we'd had in months, but I was exhausted by always being the one to chase her down.

"Imogen, you know I would love—"

"Don't do that," I snapped, slamming the spoon down on the counter. Tomato sauce splattered against the back-splash and I cursed softly. "Don't use the fancy divorce lawyer speak on me, where you twist what I'm saying. Just talk to me directly."

"Alright," Cassie huffed. "I just took a new job, Imogen. I'm putting my condo on the market. I can't just drop every-thing in Seattle to come home."

"The wedding is still a month away," I argued. "We sent out the invitations months ago. You can't put in a paid time off request?"

"When I received your invitation, I told you I was chang-ing jobs. I know you don't understand—"

"Oh my *God*, Cassie, you can be such an ass sometimes. I know you're a lawyer and you're busy. I'm not some hick that's never left Watford."

The words stung harsher than I meant to, and guilt churned in my gut at Cassie's sharp inhale.

I *had* left Watford. And ruined my life in the process.

Cassie didn't know all of it, not in the way Abbie did. There was a part of me that didn't want Cassie to know just how bad things had gotten.

If I was honest with myself, it was easier to be angry. I could hide behind the anger. It was the embarrassment of knowing that Cassie had seen who my ex-husband was long before I did. Cassie had tried to warn me how men could be; that marriage wasn't something to rush into.

I'd gotten married anyway, convinced that my older sister and my best friend were wrong to have misgivings about him.

Anger, I'd learned, was far easier to deal with than self-hatred. Which is probably why I didn't hesitate to launch into berating Cassie for choices she could make as a grown woman. It was also why Cassie and I's relationship was fraying. She was angry at me for not listening to her, and I was angry because if I had listened to her, maybe, just maybe, what happened next wouldn't have occurred.

"The answer is you could come home. You could, but you're choosing not to. I wish you would just be honest instead of throwing around excuses."

Another lengthy pause. I set my jaw forward and turned off the stovetop, moving the saucepan to the middle burner.

"Why are you harping on this?" Cassie said. "This new job is at a huge firm. It's important for my career, and I just started it last week, Imogen. I understand how important this is to you, and I'm so happy for Abbie and Connor. I'm glad the two of them found their way back to each other. While I can't be there in person, I'll make every effort to show my support in other ways."

More corporate lawyer speak. That was all I got from my sister these days; roundabout answers that led nowhere, pretty words that added up to nothing.

"Don't worry about it," I said, more harshly than I meant to. The timer went off for the garlic bread in the oven. "We'll catch up another time. I hope you have a good week."

"Imogen—"

I ended the call and tossed my phone onto the countertop. I didn't have time to deal with Cassie's crap today. I'd taken a risk by calling her, but I'd hoped a direct conversation might change her mind.

Cassie had been someone I looked up to my entire childhood. Her work ethic was something I wanted to emulate. My parents rejoiced when she was admitted to law school after college. And when she moved away, I'd naively thought things would be the same between us.

They had never been the same. The more time passed, the further the distance between us grew. When I told her I was marrying Jacob, she'd told me not to, and laid out all the reasons I should tell him to kick rocks.

Cassie's lack of effort to come home for Connor and Abbie's wedding didn't surprise me. I'd expected that answer when I'd picked up the phone. But her 'no' still cut deeply, mainly because she hadn't been home in years. Nothing was ever important enough for her to come back here.

Not even me.

Cassie had always set her dreams on Seattle. She'd always wanted to move out of Watford. I shouldn't be mad at my sister for achieving her dreams. Especially not when she wasn't the person I was truly mad at.

Everyone around me kept moving forward while I was stagnating. I had the homestead, but it wasn't the same anymore. I did the same things day in and day out. While such a rhythm used to be calming, these days, it wasn't.

"Trouble in paradise?"

I spun around to find Kameron Miller standing in my kitchen with a paper bag in his hand. The skirt of my sundress swung with the motion, and Kameron's eyes tracked the movement before averting his eyes.

Kameron had gotten his haircut recently. The low fade of black hair contrasted with his beard, which was longer than usual, but still neatly trimmed. He had cuffed the sleeves of his crisp, linen button-up shirt at the elbows, boot cut jeans that clung to his body in all of the right places. He was always so put together, steady and unflappable, in the way he dressed, and the way he carried himself.

I sometimes suspected someone sent this man here to tempt me. Kameron was dark-haired, but not the stereotypical, over-the-top, brooding type. He radiated authenticity and generosity. He was honest and kind, and that was a dangerous combination for me.

I turned away, turning off the oven timer and grabbing a potholder to remove the pan of garlic bread. If there was one thing my grandmother had taught me about feeding a crowd, it was that spaghetti and meatballs were the easiest, cheapest way to do so. The latter was less of a concern with everyone pitching in, but I wasn't the person who wanted to spend the day slaving away in the kitchen.

"I wouldn't call dealing with my emotionally detached older sister paradise."

Kameron hummed in acknowledgment.

"I don't have any siblings, so I can't relate on the sister front, but I do have experience dealing with emotionally detached people."

I shrugged, placing the hot pan on the side of the oven not currently covered by a saucepan holding marinara or spaghetti. The meatballs had finished cooking just before I put the garlic bread in and they were now resting on the counter beside the stove.

"What can I do to help?" Kameron asked.

I lowered the heat on the saucepan even more and grabbed the pot of spaghetti, preparing to strain it.

"Could you grab plates, please? They're—"

I blinked twice as I watched Kameron stride confidently over to the navy blue cabinet that held the plates and glasses. As he pulled down a stack of plates to set the table, I was reminded once again that Kameron, Connor, and Lucas had somehow embedded themselves in our lives. Abbie and I already had a history with Connor, having spent all of high school with him, but Kameron and Lucas fit in our lives just as well.

The five of us all had our individual struggles we were working through, but we also got to experience things that most kids our age might not ever get to do. The military had a way of making kids grow up early. The unique demands and trials of military life extended not just to service members, but to their families as well.

I drained the spaghetti and returned the noodles to the pot, adding a dash of olive oil to keep them from sticking together. I grabbed some spoons and tongs for the pasta, and pulled the parmesan cheese out of the fridge. Growing up with siblings, I learned early on to keep the pasta and toppings separate. Even at this dinner table, with only adults, there were still some picky eaters with strong opinions.

I grabbed some glasses and filled a pitcher of water, walking over to the dining room table to help Kameron finish setting up. A few moments later, the doorbell rang, signaling the rest of our group's arrival.

"I'll get it," Kameron said, striding towards the front door. He barely made it three steps before Lucas was stomping past him.

"Next time, you're picking me up," Lucas said, stalking straight for the fridge. "I am *not* carpooling with them again. I'm sick of it. *Sick* of it, do you hear me?"

"Of what?"

"Of *love*."

I couldn't stop the snort that escaped me, and I quickly clasped a hand over my mouth to keep some semblance of composure.

"I hate to say it, but I think we're the outcasts here," I said. "With our damaged hearts and all."

"Damaged hearts club forever," Lucas said, extending a fist for me to knuckle bump him. I did so, rolling my eyes. I wasn't sure the damaged hearts club was something to be proud of, but I was grateful to have found such a loyal friend in Lucas.

Sometimes I felt like I should talk to someone about everything that happened. I'd seen a therapist for a few months after I first moved back to Watford, but eventually stopped going. In some ways, rehashing the same events over and over made the recovery worse. Then again, maybe I just hadn't found the right therapist, or I hadn't given it enough time. Although Lucas's experiences differed from mine, he, like me, was estranged from his soon-to-be ex-wife. Slighted spouses shared an undeniable sense of camaraderie.

"Sorry for the delay," Connor said as he, Abbie, and Kameron appeared in the kitchen, shoving his long blond hair back from his face. Abbie's pink-tinged cheeks told me everything I needed to know. I walked over to embrace my best friend in a hug.

"I don't want an explanation," I said quickly as I pulled out of Abbie's embrace a few moments later. "I don't want to know. We're happy you're here now. Even though you traumatized poor Lucas by screwing before you picked him up."

I met Kameron's eyes over Abbie's shoulder. Kameron smirked, and to my eternal shock, my stomach stirred.

Maybe I wasn't entirely honest with myself about the way Kameron made me feel. What had started as a fascination with the man seemed to have grown into a small crush. For most people, a crush was nothing notable.

That wasn't the case with me. Wanting to know Kameron Miller was a new and distracting feeling.

I smoothed down the front of my dress, quickly shoving those thoughts away as I turned to address the small crowd gathered in my dining room.

"I made spaghetti tonight. You all know how I feel about cooking big, intense meals, so no complaining."

"We would never complain about a home-cooked meal," Lucas said, swooping into action and bringing the now cooled pot of pasta into the dining room. I smiled fondly, remembering the conversation he and I had several months earlier about how much he'd missed cooking when he was on active duty.

Abbie, Connor, and Kameron followed his lead, each grabbing a separate pan or container to bring into the dining room. We all sat down to eat, Abbie and Connor sitting next to each other, Kameron at the head of the table to my left, and Lucas to my right. Everyone began dishing out food onto their plates. Keeping the sauce and meatballs off the spaghetti had indeed been a good idea, as all five of us ended up with a different amalgamation of toppings on our plates.

"So, about the wedding—"

I groaned as Kameron opened the conversation with something work-related. I could have sworn he blushed a little, and the sight had my heart quickening its pace.

"I think some people are a little burned out on wedding discussions," Connor said with a pointed look at me.

"I think it's just me," I replied, stabbing a meatball with my fork and swirling it around to pick up some extra sauce. "And I hope you both know how much I appreciate you. But let's not talk about the wedding tonight. Please?"

The Google Drive folder full of spreadsheets detailing correspondence with various wedding vendors seemed to whisper to me from my closed laptop. There were many moving parts, and the pressure of making sure my best friend's wedding was insanely perfect was getting to me.

I needed one night where I could exist with my friends without thinking about it.

Abbie smiled and reached across the table to squeeze my free hand.

"Of course," she said, and I squeezed her hand back before she pulled away. "Let's talk about you then. How are things on the homestead?"

Oh, the homestead.

I loved this place dearly. I had since the first time I visited this farmhouse when I was old enough to remember the smell of yeast and rising bread wafting through the open space from the kitchen, how exciting it was to look out the guest bedroom window and see cattle grazing in the pastures beyond, how my grandmother had taught me all the practical skills school and my parents would never teach me.

My parents were gone a lot when I was a kid. My father was a businessman, always seeking his next idea, and my mother simply wanted to follow him wherever he went. She hated Watford, and didn't want to spend any more time here than necessary. That 'necessary' time involved dropping her children off with their Nana and heading back to the big city to be with her rich husband.

"Things are going," I said, somewhat nervous about having this conversation with everyone present. I took a big sip of water in order to buy myself time to figure out what to say. "Since the festival, things have really picked up. I've been sending some of my products to a local farmer's market in a neighboring county with the help of another local farm. It's been sapping more of my time and energy than I'd been expecting."

I felt bad that I was even complaining about this, because six years ago I'd been desperate to make a living that didn't involve selling my soul and every hour of my day to a corporate job. The woman I was six years ago wouldn't have been able to comprehend the level of success the homestead has achieved now.

But that itch to try something new remained.

I had needed the healing space this farm had provided for me after I left my ex-husband. I'd needed a place to come and unpack everything, to heal. I'd needed to work with my hands and dig in the dirt and feel the grass and mud underneath my feet, to nurture plants and livestock, to look around and understand that the world was still a good place, although bad people existed.

"Are you thinking of moving?" Lucas asked in between bites, quirking an eyebrow towards me. I shook my head fiercely.

"Well, I couldn't sell it soon, with the amount of work that it needs done," I said with a small laugh. That was the understatement of the century. This house not only needed cosmetic updates to bring it out of the eighties and into the 21st century, but there were many structural updates I'd been putting off, like replacing the air conditioning unit and much of the plumbing. Only the kitchen had been modernized.

"Besides, this is the only thing I have left of my grandmother and her influence in my life. I love this house and everything it has been to me over the years. But I am thinking of selling some livestock and minimizing operations back down to where they were before the festival. I think I got caught up in what could be, especially after the festival, when so many people were interested in partnering with me for various business opportunities. I expanded more quickly than I could handle."

There were also financial considerations with the house; not that I was going to declare that to everyone.

I'd spent a good part of my meager savings on starting my homestead operations. Purchasing my livestock, constructing buildings to house them, buying feed every month, vet visits, general upkeep. . . the list was long and expensive.

My savings were dwindling, and the more time I spent in this house, the more I felt suffocated by that realization. The homestead's profit margins had widened in the months following the Founder's Day Festival, but I feared the growth wasn't sustainable.

The fact remained that if there was an emergency, either in the farmhouse or outside of it, I wouldn't have enough money to fix it. And that was terrifying.

Kameron nodded, and I focused on him as I tried to calm my panicking heart.

"We have our own experience with that. If we weren't able to hire farmhands to come in and help us take care of most of the daily upkeep tasks, I would have sold part of our herd off a long time ago."

"That's exactly where I'm at," I said. "With the farmhouse needing repairs, it's coming to a point where I either need to bring in more help or change the way I'm doing things."

As if I could afford to hire paid help. A few of the local high school FFA students shadowed me after the festival, wanting to gain more hands-on experience with homesteading and learn more about what it actually takes to make this place run daily.

It was scary to admit that out loud, even though I was among friends.

Such was the nature of having your trust broken at a young age. It made it uncomfortable to be vulnerable with others.

I'd already started overthinking what I'd shared when the conversation moved on after Lucas brought up some random news headline he'd read earlier in the day. I relaxed slightly, hunched over the table as I finished my spaghetti. With the spotlight now off me, I could focus on doing what I did best: taking part in the conversation from the sidelines.

Dinner wrapped up as it always did, with everyone carrying their plates to the kitchen, knocking any leftovers into the compost bin before setting them on one side of the sink. I took up my post as the dishwasher as everyone filed into the living room to continue their conversation. This was one element of our family dinner that I looked forward to the most—having a task to focus on while I mulled over my thoughts.

"Thank you for dinner," a voice said from behind me.

I jumped back, my heart lurching into my throat as I spun around to face the person, every part of my body going into overdrive at the unexpected presence of someone behind me.

I relaxed at the sight of Kameron holding the rest of the dirty dishes, pressing a hand to my chest to calm my racing heart.

"Sorry, you startled me."

"Don't apologize. I shouldn't have snuck up on you like that."

I forced a smile as best I could and turned back towards the sink, finishing rinsing the plate I'd been holding. Kameron came to stand beside me, laying the dirty dishes down on my side of the sink and rolling his sleeves back up to his elbows.

"You rinse, and I'll load them into the dishwasher," he said, gesturing for me to hand him the clean plate.

I opened my mouth to protest, but he shook his head.

"You cooked. It's only fair we help clean," Kam said, jerking his head toward the dining room table, where the others had finished clearing the table before taking their seats on the couch.

We fell into a comfortable silence. The repetitive action of scrubbing each plate, followed by a quick rinse, and the handoff to Kameron, was soothing in a weird, domestic way that was foreign to me.

"Come work with me."

The plate I'd been holding clattered into the sink. I winced at the loud clash of ceramic against steel, a shiver crawling up my spine. I swallowed tightly, steeling myself against the rising tide of memory.

If Kam noticed, he didn't say anything.

"What?" I finally said.

"Come work with me at Winding Road," Kam said sheepishly as he took the banged up plate from the sink and finished rinsing it before placing it in the dishwasher. "Since the festival last year, things have really picked up. We received hundreds of applications for our most recent cohort, and even more emails and phone calls from people who want to support us. Unfortunately, I am not gifted with anything remotely administrative, and I'm scared stuff is falling through the cracks because I can't keep up with it all. Abbie tells me you love a good spreadsheet."

I smiled and shrugged my shoulders like it was no big deal.

"You don't?"

Kam's laugh could only be described as beautiful.

"I don't. And I won't lie to you. My life is a mess. But I would love if you came to Winding Road and helped me get my life organized into a spreadsheet."

I chewed the inside of my cheek.

"So, like an administrative assistant?"

Kameron shrugged. "Primarily, yes. Administrative work would be really helpful, but if you wanted to do something more creative, like helping us make social media posts, that would be really helpful too. The pictures on your homestead social media are stunning."

I pressed my lips together to hold back a smile.

"I didn't realize you'd been looking at my page."

I could have sworn Kameron's cheeks went slightly pink.

"Market research and all that."

"Right," I said, unable to stop the grin this time. "Market research."

Kameron's expression softened, and something in my stomach flipped as his gentle gaze fixed on me.

"I know what it's like to feel adrift, trying to figure out what your next move is in life, but not sure how you're going to get there. I know I'm biased, but Winding Road is the kind of place where people find themselves again. And obviously you wouldn't be coming to the farm to be part of a cohort, but. . ." Kameron blew out a breath, wiping his hands off on a spare towel before crossing his arms over his chest.

"I'm rambling. The point is, we could use your help. I could use your help. Most of my energy is going towards filling out grant applications to secure additional funding."

My stomach twisted. The thought that Winding Road was going through financial difficulties similar to me was devastating.

"I thought Connor had invested in the farm?"

"He did," Kameron said. "But I'm trying to think long term. Connor's investment will sustain us for at least another year, hopefully longer. There's so much I want to do, but I'm hesitant to do any of it because I don't want to put the nonprofit in a tight spot."

"So, an administrative assistant. My primary goal would be to ease the pressure off of you so you can focus on grant applications," I said, wanting to make sure I understood. Kameron nodded, his expression lighting up in a way that had me ducking my head.

He was beautiful in a way that unnerved me.

"And you'd be my boss?" I asked, although I immediately regretted how forward and presumptuous the question was.

Kameron just shrugged again. "Technically, yes."

He said it so nonchalantly, I almost convinced myself us working together in close proximity wouldn't be an issue.

"But really, Imogen," Kam said, taking a step closer to me. My breath hitched, and I fought the urge to lean in closer. This is how it had always been between us—this magnetic push and pull, a never-ending dance.

The feeling of Kameron's steady presence at my side last fall flashed through my mind. The night of the fall festival, we'd attended a party in Abbie's honor at the Roadhouse, Watford's local bar. I'd been worn out by the day's extroverting, and being surrounded by a bunch of drunk party-goers wasn't my idea of a good time. Kameron had been there, steadying me without even really thinking about it.

We hadn't discussed it. I honestly wasn't sure he remembered it. But I remembered how comforting his touch had been, how safe I'd felt knowing that he was there, and the relief I'd felt when I hadn't needed to ask for him to step in.

"It's far less about the work, and more about giving you the space to figure out what you want. I know what it's like to outgrow something you once loved with your whole heart. It's painful and, frankly, terrifying, to wake up one morning and realize something you've dedicated part of your life to is no longer serving you."

A lump formed in my throat, and I swallowed tightly. My stomach twisted uncomfortably. That's exactly how I felt about the homestead, and judging by the sincerity in his tone, that must have been how Kameron felt about leaving the Marine Corps.

As I glanced towards the living room, where Abbie and Lucas were engaged in a rather heated debate over what board game to play, I felt that familiar sensation of guilt rise within me. I didn't deserve what Kameron was offering.

Kameron's eyes met mine, and my heart stumbled for an entirely different reason this time.

"I'd need to figure out what to do with the homestead. And home repairs, because I'm honestly scared to leave the house some days for fear that a wall is just going to collapse."

I still felt guilty. It felt weird to accept what seemed like an objectively good deal to help me figure out my next steps in life.

Kameron smiled softly, and my knees threatened to buckle.

"You could work remotely most of the time," Kameron said. "I'm not an expert, but I imagine you could handle most administrative tasks, like checking emails and scheduling content, from any location."

He was right. Aside from the initial setup, like getting the lay of the land at Winding Road, I could do most of my work from home during the week.

Which was good, because the idea of doing all of those tasks near Kameron Miller felt like I was signing up for danger.

Because when he looked at me the way he was now, gentle blue eyes fixed entirely on me, like nothing else existed, I felt the urge to break my promise to myself.

"There's no pressure either way," Kam said, angling his body towards the sink to continue loading the dishwasher. "Just something to think about."

"Thank you," I whispered, forcing myself to look away from his face. I picked up the long forgotten plate and turned the faucet back on, wincing as it sputtered for several long seconds before the flow resumed.

I chewed my bottom lip as we finished rinsing the dishes in silence. Kameron turned the dishwasher on and headed back towards the living room. I leaned back against the stove, watching all of my friends in the other room. My conflicting desires warred within me. On the one hand, this was the perfect opportunity for me to do something different and make a sustainable, steady income.

But then I remembered the way my heart flipped when Kameron trained his attention on me, and I felt myself slipping.

I couldn't afford to get my heart broken a second time. I wouldn't survive it.

That, I was sure of.

Chapter Four

Kameron

I don't know what had possessed me to ask Imogen to come work at Winding Road.

Sure, I'd been thinking of it for the last several weeks. It was clear, based on our conversations after the festival, that she felt like something had shifted for her the last few months. She no longer felt that same connection to homesteading, and Lucas and I really needed some help in the administrative department, especially with Connor about to become a revolving door.

Given what I knew of Imogen's history—namely that she'd left town to follow her now ex-husband shortly after graduating from high school—I knew she was attached to this place. It's hard to let go of something that had been a haven for you after one of the worst times in your life.

Regardless, I felt like an idiot for ambushing her the way I did.

One heated game of Catan later, Abbie was yawning and leaning into Connor's shoulder. Even Imogen, as determined as she was to kick everyone's ass at her favorite board game, was fading.

"Ready to head out?" I asked Lucas. Lucas made a dramatic show of yawning and stretching his arms above his head.

"Might as well."

We packed up the rest of the board game and shared sleepy goodbyes before heading out the front door. I made my way to the driver's side door of my truck, taking a moment to look out at the stars above.

Watford was gorgeous. It was a small town, for better or for worse, but the view of the beautiful night sky, clear and undeterred by light pollution or skyscrapers, felt like a balm for my soul. I'd always known I belonged in the mountains, and when I'd found the little stretch of land that eventually became Winding Road, I knew in my heart I'd made the right decision.

"You good man?" Lucas asked, and I shook my head, pressing the unlock button on my keys.

"Yeah, I'm good."

"Kam!"

I spun around to see Imogen jogging down from the porch.

"Everything okay?" I asked, suddenly concerned that something was wrong.

That was how it had always been with Imogen, though she wasn't a woman that needed my protection. I didn't feel this way about Abbie, or any of the women I'd dated in the past. It was scary to acknowledge that there was something about Imogen that felt different from anything I'd experienced before.

Which is why I didn't dwell on it.

Most of the time.

"When do you need an answer by?" Imogen asked, tucking a stray black curl behind her ear. Something about the simple gesture soothed an ache in my soul. God, she was gorgeous. "About the job, I mean."

"Take as long as you need to think things over," I said, waving a hand noncommittally, feigning a nonchalance I didn't feel. "The offer stands."

Imogen pressed her lips together in that way she did when she was deep in thought, and I felt like I might pass out.

"If you take the job, we can be roomies," Lucas said. I scowled at him, not having realized he'd climbed over the center console to stick his head out of the driver's side window like some kind of feral creature. Imogen's laugh was bright and beautiful, even in the night's darkness, lit only by the faint orange glow of her porch lights.

"There's no way in hell I'll be moving into your house," Imogen said with a shake of her head. "But I'll think about the job offer. Thank you."

"For what? Besides the job, I mean."

Idiot. She obviously meant thank you for the job offer, and nothing else.

Imogen hesitated, as if considering the answer to that question herself.

"For caring enough to offer me a place to figure things out. That's more than most people get in their lives. It means a lot."

I wanted to say more, but Lucas Morales honked the horn with his ass as he climbed back over into the passenger seat, letting out a string of expletives and "sorry, sorry."

I sighed heavily, flashing Imogen my best attempt at an apologetic smile.

"I better go handle that."

Imogen clasped a hand over her mouth. I put one hand on my hip and pointed an accusing finger in her direction.

"This is no joking matter, Imogen Phillips. I've got an hour long drive with this man child in the car."

"I'm twenty three!" Lucas cried, indignant.

"I'd never laugh at such a horrifying prospect," Imogen said, removing her hand and revealing a smirk that was equal parts the cutest and sexiest smile I'd ever seen on a woman.

"Talk soon?"

Imogen nodded. "Talk soon."

I slid into the driver's seat and pinned Lucas with a glare. I cranked the engine to life and headed towards the backroad that would lead us out of Watford and back towards the farm.

"Look, I'm not trying to be in your business."

"So don't be," I said, trying to keep up the appearance of nonchalance.

I was the chill guy. I had always been the chill guy. I was the guy who kept it together, even when everything else was falling apart. I was the guy people came to when they needed someone to help shoulder their problems. I did all of that and more, and I did it gladly, because it really felt like my mission in life most days.

"You and Imogen. . . are you into her?"

Something strange and foreign twisted in my gut.

"Are you?" The question was more defensive than I meant it to be, but Lucas laugh took me by surprise.

"Good Lord, no. I can honestly say Imogen and I are far better friends than we would be lovers. Although we discussed it one time."

"What?" I said, my knuckles tightening on the steering wheel. Glancing towards the passenger seat, I saw the classic Morales smirk and knew I'd exposed myself.

"Imogen and I have never once talked about sleeping together, but you seem rather put off by the idea that we had."

"I'm not talking about this with you."

Lucas fell silent for a minute, and I braced myself for whatever he might say next.

I couldn't remember the last time I'd been interested in someone the way I was interested in Imogen. I'd had a series of what I considered serious relationships during my time in the Marine Corps, but the women I'd dated always wanted something different. They didn't see me as a long-term option. Many of them had dated military guys before, and they looked at me and saw the same thing most people do: a hot guy in uniform.

Good enough to hook up with, fun to date for a while, but not someone to trust with long-term plans. Part of that was my fault: I'd never seen myself as a white picket fence kind of guy, and I kept my past locked down tight. Neither of those things were conducive to a long-term relationship.

"I won't sit here and tell you not to pursue her. I think it's obvious to everyone but the two of you that there's a connection there. But the two of you should level with each other before you do anything crazy."

"Level with each other?"

"Talk about your pasts. We saw that shit play out with Connor and Abbie, and let's be honest, no one wants a repeat of that."

I smiled fondly when I thought about Connor and Abbie, the love they had lost and then found again. But Lucas was right: that wasn't something I was keen on experiencing myself, nor did I want to put Imogen through that. We were both adults who had been through some serious crap. We owed it to each other to talk about the things that had impacted us so deeply.

If we wanted to date, that is. Which, from where I was standing, was an option Imogen was not interested in.

"Imogen's ex-husband really screwed her up. He was. . ." Lucas' voice trailed off. "If I ever see that man again, I'll kill him."

I let out a small laugh to diffuse the tension now present between us, but I knew he spoke true. Lucas was the class clown, but he didn't screw around when it came to the people he loved. It was the thing I admired most about his personality.

We spent the rest of the drive back to Winding Road in contemplative silence. Lucas handled the music, and I kept my eyes on the road.

I ignored the pain in my chest when "Take Me Back to Eden" by Sleep Token came on over the speakers.

Chapter Five
Imogen

Abbigail Kaitlin Collins was a bridezilla.

I'd always suspected this would be the case, but watching my best friend about to lose her mind over one singular flower arrangement being wrong when the florists were still setting things up had me clamping a hand over my mouth to stifle my laughter while also wanting to be an emotional support for her.

The last four weeks had been a flurry of phone calls, meetings, and last-minute conversations ensuring that everything was in order for the wedding. I'd confirmed every detail, down to 15-minute windows of each vendor's expected arrival. The spreadsheets were updated. I'd taken to setting an alarm on my phone to remind myself to eat.

I was in my zone. Abbie should know better than to freak out now, when the finish line was in sight.

The Winding Road Barn was a dream wedding venue. A spring wedding had been the perfect choice. There was the ceremony space outside of the barn, where a wooden arch adorned with white daisies and greenery was staged in front of rows of log benches. Delicate burgundy accents were woven throughout the decor, the deep red designed to be a tie in with both the bridesmaids' dresses and Connor's dress blues.

It was rustic and earthy and everything Abbie had wanted.

Kameron was with Connor in the men's dressing room. I idly wondered if Connor was also freaking out.

"You're freaking out," I said, handing Abbie the water cup. She took the cup from my outstretched hand while looking at me with panicked eyes. I stifled another small laugh. "Your lipstick is waterproof. You're safe."

Abbie downed the whole cup in a single gulp. I took it back from her and set it on the table before taking a seat in the chair opposite her.

"Is this what cold feet feels like?" Abbie whisper-yelled. We were the only ones in the room now, the artist having moved on to do Kyrie's makeup in the next room down.

I rolled my eyes.

"Don't roll your eyes at me!"

I let out a long sigh, turning to face my best friend, who was staring herself down in the mirror. I'd found the hair and makeup artist we'd hired on social media, and she was well worth the money. Abbie's dark blue eyes were striking beneath a delicate smokey eye, her long brown hair pinned delicately into an elegant and intricate braided bun on the back of her head.

"You're freaking out," I said again, keeping my voice even. I faced the mirror, placing one of the pearl studs in my ear. I'd rummaged through my Nana's jewelry box to find something suitable to wear with this dress, and as soon as I'd laid eyes on these, I knew they'd be perfect.

The makeup artist had worked magic on me, too. I couldn't remember the last time I'd done a full face of makeup. Dark, thick lashes, golden sparkles and shimmering tones, which complimented my brown skin and brown eyes.

When paired with the beautiful shade of burgundy that Abbie had chosen for everyone in her wedding party to wear, I felt beautiful. My dress was a-line and sleek, with off-the-shoulder straps that accentuated my upper arms and neck. I felt confident, if not a little sexy.

The last time I had been this dressed up had been the last Marine Corps ball I'd attended with Jacob.

I quickly cleared that train of thought away. Those memories had no place here.

"It's going to be okay, Abbie."

"Can you go check on Connor, please? Make sure he's still here?" Abbie said, finally getting up from her chair and turning towards the dress hanging on the wall behind us. My eyebrows rose.

"Are you sure you'll be okay in here by yourself?"

Abbie nodded her head. "Yeah. I could use a few minutes to myself, actually."

I wasn't going to argue with that. I glanced at the clock on the wall and muttered under my breath. It was just under an hour until the ceremony started, and I needed to get a move on. I slipped out of my sneakers and reached for my heels.

Yet another thing I rarely wore. I stood on slightly shaky legs, adjusting my dress so it wasn't wrinkled. Abbie let out a low whistle and her jaw practically hit the floor.

"Miss Imogen," Abbie said, shimmying her shoulders seductively. "You look ravishing."

I rolled my eyes and ducked my head to hide my heated cheeks.

"I'll go check on your beau. I'm also sending Kyrie in here to help you into your dress while I make sure everything is set up correctly. You don't have to worry about a thing," I said. Abbie looked like she might cry, and I stood there awkwardly for another heartbeat while I waited to see if she would burst into tears or not.

"You're the greatest best friend in the entire world," she said, eyes still welling with tears.

"Love you too," I said, blowing her a kiss as I opened the door to step into the hallway, closing it just as quickly, so no wandering eyes saw the bride before her big moment. I turned down the hallway heading towards the center space to check on the table and seating arrangements. I fiddled with my right earring, rounding the corner and running smack into a very solid, very muscular body.

I gasped and jumped back.

"Whoa," the man said, reaching out his hands to steady my shoulders, and I immediately slumped forward in relief as I recognized the person in front of me.

"Jesus Christ, Kam," I muttered. I met his eyes, surprised to find his attention fixed entirely on me. His gaze swept over me slowly, as if he was taking in every inch. He took me in, his eyes darting to my lips and then down, past my hips and my thighs. I fought the urge to squirm under his gaze.

When his eyes snapped back to mine, there was a fire there that made my heart race.

"You're the one who came flying around a blind curve," Kam said, his lips curling into a smirk that had my knees weakening. "How are we doing?"

I barely heard the words come out of his mouth. I was too focused on the crisp white button down that was only halfway buttoned, the burgundy tie hanging loosely around his neck, and the sight of his muscles flexing under his shirt as he adjusted his cufflinks. Kameron looked glorious in his usual lightweight button up and jeans combo, but Kameron in formal dress was *devastating*.

It took several seconds for my brain to catch up and give me words to respond with.

"She's freaking out."

"Oh good, he's freaking out too."

"He got his hair cut, right? He better have gotten his freaking haircut."

Kameron laughed and shook his head.

"Connor wouldn't dare get into his blues with one hair out of regulation, even though he loves his long hair."

"What's the plan?"

"Speed this process up so these two chronic overthinkers get to the altar as quickly as possible."

"Agreed," I said. We stepped aside to allow the catering staff through.

"I'll check on the music and the chaplain, you check on the catering and seating arrangements?" Kam offered.

"I need to find Kyrie and send her in there to keep Abbie company," I said, grimacing. "I'm worried she'll do something drastic like steal Memphis, grab Connor, and ride off into the sunset." Abbie loved that Tennessee Walker horse so much.

Kameron's laugh eased some of the built up tension in my shoulders. I felt slightly ridiculous, standing there in the hallway of this beautiful wedding venue, having all manner of inappropriate thoughts about the groom's best friend while my best friend—the *bride*—had a mental breakdown several doors down.

"Good point. You find Kyrie and check on the table arrangements, and I'll check on everything else. And remind her that it's just friends and family here. Everything will be fine."

The guest list was smaller than a venue like this typically called for. Abbie and Connor both had a short list of people they wanted to invite. Most of them were friends and fellow business owners in Watford, and then Kevin and Kyrie. There would be less than thirty people here today, but that's exactly what they wanted: a small, intimate ceremony focused on just them, and celebrating the love they'd lost—and then found again.

"Right," I said, though I took those words and tucked them away for me rather than Abbie. The minute she saw Connor standing down at the front of the barn in his dress blues with his gloved hand outstretched towards her, I knew she'd be fine.

I turned to walk away, but a hand circled my wrist. I turned around to face Kameron once more, my breath hitching in my throat when I realized we'd somehow gotten a lot closer to each other. If I leaned just a few inches forward, my chest would brush his. I willed myself to relax, though that mantra wasn't doing me much good at the moment.

"How are you?" Kameron asked, voice earnest and soft in a way that had my stomach doing a strange flip.

"I'm okay," I said, putting on my best smile. I would *not* let Kameron Miller distract me on the day of my best friend's wedding. I would sort my crap out later.

Right now, I needed to focus. And not on the gloriously muscled body in front of me.

"I'm glad I can be here for this. What they have is extraordinarily rare, and I'm excited to celebrate it with them. With all of you."

Kameron's eyes shone with something I couldn't wrap my head around. He released my wrist a second later, and the absence of his skin against mine bothered me more than I wanted to admit.

"Tell me if something comes up and you need a break, alright? This is not a one woman show."

This time, my smile was genuine as I stepped away.

"It's always a one woman show when you're with me, Miller."

Abbie and Connor's vows had everyone in tears, though I expected nothing less.

Everyone filed in to sit on the log benches overlooking the mountains, with the barn at their backs. Kyrie had taken up the helm of flower girl because we didn't know any girls under the age of ten and there was no way I was entrusting such an important responsibility to a grumpy teenager. I followed her, taking my place on Abbie's side of the arch. Kameron had followed behind with the rings, with Lucas and the groom himself shortly behind.

Abbie took everyone's breath away, naturally. She was every bit the fairytale princess as she came down the aisle, her eyes shining with nothing but love for the man in front of her. I was only slightly shocked when I noticed Connor's eyes were misty, too.

It had all come together perfectly. Not that anyone was surprised, once Abbie mentioned I was the one in charge of planning. My spreadsheets were immaculate.

As I strolled up to the dessert table at the reception, I found Kameron sitting at a table close by, nursing some kind of fruity mocktail. I grabbed a chocolate glazed donut—Lucas's request—and sat down in the empty chair next to him. Most of the crowds had cleared out, citing the long drive back to Watford, and the only people that remained were the bride and groom, Lucas, Kameron, and I. I was pretty sure Kevin and Kyrie were also still here somewhere, but I wasn't going searching for them. There was no telling what I'd find.

"We pulled it off," I said, taking a bite of the donut and damn near moaning at the taste of buttery chocolate against my tongue. Kam's eyes snapped up to mine. Even with the sun going down and the venue being lit primarily by candlelight, I swear his eyes darkened as he took my figure in again. I would tease him for the way he stared at me to deflect the way my body warmed at the idea, but I couldn't be sure that was why, so I kept my mouth shut.

"You pulled it off," Kam said, taking another sip of his drink. "The rest of us were just along for the ride."

"That's generous of you," I said, finishing my donut and grabbing Kam's napkin to wipe my fingers off.

"Take credit where it's due," Kam said, a teasing lilt to his voice. "You pulled all of this together. All we did is offer support."

I shrugged and turned my attention back to the dance floor. Connor and Abbie were dancing alongside Lucas, and the sheer joy on everyone's face filled me with an immense sense of pride. Kevin and Kyrie re-appeared from the far hallway to join them on the dance floor and I rolled my eyes.

That pride must have emboldened me, because the next words out of my mouth were, "I'm surprised you and Lucas aren't in uniform."

I wanted to smack my head into the table.

Kameron's answering smirk told me I had definitely exposed myself.

"It's an unspoken rule that you don't wear your dress blues to another dude's wedding, unless they ask you to," Kam said, still smirking, like he knew exactly why I'd asked that. He drowned the rest of his drink and put the cup down. "Wouldn't want to steal the spotlight."

I glanced down at his arms one more time like the selfish fool I am, and I swore he flexed his muscles. I averted my eyes quickly. It was one thing to have a small crush on your friend—it was another thing entirely to openly ogle them in public. At someone else's wedding, no less.

This wasn't like me. Then again, I couldn't remember the last time I'd looked at a man and seen something like what I saw in Kam. I couldn't pin it down. I was comfortable around him in a way that emboldened me to let my guard down. To flirt, even.

My brain quickly shied away from that train of thought. I'd once been comfortable with Jacob, too. And I'd been lucky to walk away from that relationship alive.

Kameron seemed to sense my change in demeanor and cleared his throat gently, giving me a reassuring smile.

"The two of them were made for each other."

I smiled at the image of Connor and Abbie, their smiles wide and bright enough that we could see them, even on the opposite side of the wedding hall.

"That they are."

"I know you had your misgivings about him when he first came back to Watford."

"Abbie and I have seen each other through some really hard times," I said honestly. "When I first heard he was back in town, I was angry, because Abbie had worked so hard to work through things. She wanted to move forward without the past holding her down. And then he waltzed back into town like nothing had happened. But Connor had changed since leaving Watford; I was wrong to assume otherwise.

And I was wrong to assume that his leaving Watford had anything to do with Abbie."

Kameron nodded, slouching back in his chair. He'd undone another button of his shirt, and there was far too much sun-kissed skin on display.

Maybe that was why he got under my skin so badly. He was distracting.

"My feelings about Connor had more to do with my issues than anything else. The night everything fell apart with my marriage, I drove right back to Watford, practically on autopilot. I went right to Abbie's door and collapsed in her arms. Even though we'd been distant, she was there. Even though we hadn't talked in weeks at that point, she knew I needed her."

I felt Kam's eyes on me, and blew out a long breath.

"All that to say," I said, letting out a breathy laugh in a futile attempt to lessen the tension in my throat, "I love that girl. She is so special to me in so many ways, and for so many reasons. I might have been overprotective of her. But if anyone deserves this kind of happiness, it's her. I owe her everything."

"I'm sure she'd say the same about you."

"She'd be lying," I said, and I meant it. I could never repay Abbie for the way she helped me put my life back together after I divorced Jacob. The sacred space she held for me while I healed, physically and mentally.

"Thank you for telling me this part of your story, Im. I never want to push you, and I'll never ask you directly, because I know what it's like to have things from your past you don't want to talk about. But I hope you know you can always come to me with those things. I want to know more about you."

A door in my mind slammed shut, reflexively defensive at letting anyone close to me. My fingers itched for a drink, despite the fact that I hadn't drank in months. When Abbie got sober because of her father's struggles, I did, too. I hadn't been a big drinker before—one of the many things Jacob thought was unbecoming of a woman—but I'd wanted to support her.

"I appreciate that. I do. But I don't enjoy talking about the past. I'm not sure why I said any of that," I laughed, trying to brush it off as if it was no big deal. Kam looked hurt almost, and I felt a pang of shame deep in my stomach.

Kameron wore his heart on his sleeve in a way so few men did.

I was damaged goods. I had been for a long time. As much as I blamed Jacob for what he did, my track record with self-doubt and poor decision making went back even further than our marriage. Keeping Kameron far away from the chaos that was my inner world was the safest possible thing for everyone.

Which is why I wanted to smack my head into the table once again when the next words out of my mouth were:

"I want the job."

Kameron's eyes widened. "Really?"

I nodded. "It's the perfect opportunity. I get to do something new, dial back the homestead operations while also focusing on repairing the farmhouse, and I get to help you guys run Winding Road more efficiently. As long as you're okay with me working from home during the week, I'm in. It's a win-win for everyone."

"You're really saying yes," Kameron said, his shock slowly transforming into an excited grin.

"Calm down, cowboy," I said, unable to stop myself from returning his smile. "We still need to iron out the details."

Kameron's answering laugh settled deep within my bones, and I realized with a jolt of awareness that I could listen to that sound forever.

Chapter Six

Kameron

"**C**onnor Harvey. Married. I never thought I'd see the day," Lucas said.

Connor shoved another pair of shorts into an already over-stuffed duffle bag. Lucas flopped down on the far side of the bed to continue eating his chips. I stood in the doorway, shaking my head fondly at the two idiots in front of me. It was the day after the wedding, and there was a flurry of activity at the farmhouse getting things ready for the honeymoon drop off.

"I don't know what you're on about, Morales. Connor was the most likely out of us to find love."

Lucas shrugged, popping another hot chip into his mouth as he gestured to Connor, who was muttering to himself about what he might be forgetting.

"I've watched you shove flip flops, wool socks, board shorts, and jeans into that bag. Where the hell are you going?" I asked, realizing I'd never gotten the full details from Imogen.

Connor looked up, and I laughed at the terror written into the man's face.

"Imogen planned the entire honeymoon," Connor said, voice strained. "Abbie wanted a surprise honeymoon. It was part of her dream for her wedding. Said it would have stressed us out to plan it ourselves, which is insane, just so we're clear. I couldn't narrow down the destinations, even after she sent the packing list. Hence, the pants *and* shorts."

Lucas let out a low whistle, and I clapped a hand over my mouth. This was Connor's worst nightmare: being thrown into a situation with no way to prepare for all the variables.

It was yet another reminder that there was only one person in the world Connor Harvey would ever make this many sacrifices for.

"At least you know it's international," Lucas said, gesturing to Connor's passport tucked into the front of the duffel. I shook my head.

"Not necessarily," I said, smiling. "There's a good chance it's a domestic destination and Imogen asked them to bring their passports in order to throw them off the scent."

"I trust that she's picked somewhere Abbie will love," Connor said, waving a hand. "The two of them have been planning their weddings since the dawn of freaking time. At the end of the day, that's all I care about."

I smiled while Lucas made a gagging noise.

"You're going to have to get used to it," I said.

"The two of you keep dropping like flies," Lucas whined. "First, it was Connor and Abbie. Now, you and Imogen keep circling each other. It's only a matter of time. Soon enough, I'll be the last man standing."

My eye twitched. "I think you're mistaken."

"Oh, he's not mistaken," Connor chimed in. When I gave him a look, Connor just grinned at me. "Abbie might have let it slip about your, uh, job offer."

I pressed my lips together. I had been meaning to tell the two of them, but with the wedding and everything that came after, I hadn't found a good time to do so.

"It's a very part time arrangement."

"Right," Connor said, a smile playing on his lips.

"Look, we need the help. None of us have administrative skills. All three of us would much rather be in the great outdoors, doing literally anything else. Imogen thrives with organizational stuff. It seemed like the perfect fit."

"And it just so corresponded with her quarter life crisis."

I was going to smack Lucas one of these days. I could feel it in my bones.

"Yeah, it did," I said, feeling more like a petulant child than a grown man. "I know I should have run this by the two of you, but with Connor splitting his time between Watford and the farm, we need someone here to pick up the slack. Imogen is that person."

"I'm not mad about it," Lucas said. "Imogen's been talking for months about how she needs a change of pace from the homestead. I think it'll be good for her. And you're right, we need the help, especially because your focus needs to be on grant proposals."

"So, why are you worried?" I asked, somewhat exasperated.

"Because of what we talked about in the car," Lucas answered, giving me an uncharacteristically serious look. "Don't screw with people's feelings."

"He wouldn't do that," Connor said, zipping his bag shut and pinning Lucas with a glare. "You haven't known him for as long as I have. Kameron's the most honest of the three of us. He wears his heart on his sleeve. He wouldn't lead Imogen on like that."

I didn't need Connor to defend me, but it was nice to have someone step in on my behalf sometimes. Lucas set his jaw forward.

"You're right. I shouldn't have dug at you like that. Imogen has been a really good friend to me these last few months. We've shared a lot with each other. I don't want her to get hurt. That's all."

Something about Lucas's tone got under my skin. I didn't know if it was the insinuation that I would somehow intentionally hurt Imogen, or Lucas's clear perception of something worth exploring.

I'd really screwed myself.

On the one hand, this new proximity would give Imogen and I more of a chance to get to know one another, instead of doing this weird back-and-forth text message exchange where we somehow talked about everyone else but never ourselves.

"Ready to head out?" I said, standing to my full height as opposed to slouching in the door frame.

That smitten glint returned to Connor's eyes as he grabbed the duffle bag and slung it over his shoulder.

"Hell yes," he said.

I felt that odd, familiar feeling twist in my gut when I saw how excited Connor was to see Abbie again. Connor had been parted from Abbie for less than two hours, and he was already tripping over himself to get back to her.

I shook my head, unable to reconcile the thoughts swirling in my mind.

I had seen the ways love could destroy people. I had seen my mom become a shell of the woman she'd been when I was growing up. When my dad died, a light in her went out forever.

Things were better now. Strained, but not broken.

But I'd never forget the dark years I spent trying to find a way to bring that spark back to life. They'd made a mark on my soul. Those years were what drove me to swear love and connection off in the first place.

Yet deep down, I was realizing that I still wanted it for myself.

I wanted to experience that kind of all-encompassing love.

Even if it broke me the way it had broken my mother.

Chapter Seven
Imogen

Dropping Abbie off at the airport for her honeymoon was a full circle moment.

When I'd handed her the tickets for Amsterdam, alongside a folder full of information about what farms and tulip fields to visit for the best view this time of year, she burst into tears.

The moment I'd realized that early May was one of the best times of year to see the sprawling tulip fields in the Netherlands, I'd known it was the ideal vacation destination for Abbie.

Couple that with how Amsterdam wasn't a bustling city in the way New York or Paris was, and I figured it was the perfect honeymoon. Their rental was nestled in a quieter part of the city, close to beautiful waterscapes and historic sites. There was something for both Abbie and Connor there.

Abbie's blubbering 'thank you's' and Connor's misty expression told me my instincts had been right on the money.

After our excursion to the airport, I'd come back to the homestead, eager to hand the reins of every day operations over to Kevin. He met me in the driveway of my farmhouse, hands in his pockets as he leaned against the side of his truck.

"How was the send off?" Kevin asked as I approached him.

"It was perfect."

"Of course it was. I'm guessing you picked the right destination?"

I puffed my chest out with mock pride.

"Of course I did. You should have seen the two of them. Abbie was completely beside herself with excitement. I thought Connor was going to sink to his knees with utter relief that I wasn't sending them to a huge city."

I let out a long sigh, kicking at a piece of stray gravel on the ground.

"You sure you're still okay to manage both the homestead and the store while I focus on renovations and figuring out what the hell I'm doing going forward?" I asked. "It's a lot for one person to handle. I know you'll have help from the FFA kids, but. . ."

Kevin gestured for me to give him the keys. I narrowed my eyes and cautiously handed them over.

"I've got this. The farm is in excellent hands."

"If you need something over the next two days, please call me," I said. "I mean it. Don't try to figure it out by yourself. I promise I won't make fun of you."

Kevin's raised eyebrows told me he didn't believe me.

"I'm planning to be back on Thursday morning."

"Take your time," Kevin said. I didn't miss his smirk. I put one hand on my hip and pointed the other in his direction.

"What's your deal?"

Kevin shrugged, tossing the keys up in the air before catching them again.

"I should ask you the same."

I tamped down the urge to stomp my foot and demand, for the thousandth time, that people stay out of my business.

"It's a special opportunity," I said. Kevin shrugged.

"It is."

"Spit it out, Kev."

Kevin sighed, shoving his hands into the front pockets of his jeans once more.

"You deserve good things, Imogen."

Kevin's words, and the sincerity with which he spoke them, momentarily surprised me.

"Okay," I said, scrunching my nose in confusion.

"This is an excellent opportunity. It's one Kameron and the other guys made specifically for you. You're smart, and talented, and you should know that."

I sniffled. Kevin rolled his eyes.

"Think whatever you want," Kevin said as he opened the driver's side door of his truck. "Doesn't change the facts."

"What's that?"

"That you can lie to yourself, but you can't lie to your family."

My heart twisted as Kevin closed the door behind him, cranking the truck engine to life.

I stood in my driveway long after the dust had settled, mulling things over.

You can't lie to your family.

I had to assume he was talking about himself and Cassie.

The insinuation that our family might also include the Winding Road trio was too much for me to take in.

I realized when I pulled out of my driveway the next morning that this was the first time I was traveling to Winding Road by myself. I'd only been a handful of times, but even then, those visits had been in a wedding capacity.

This time, I was going there for myself.

I'd double checked my laptop bag before I left, making sure I had all of my sticky notes, notebooks, laptop and charger, the pencil for my tablet—everything a brand new administrative assistant could need.

As I pulled up to the charming white farmhouse, I let out a small gasp at the view beyond.

I'd been too distracted in the few times I'd been here, including the wedding, to really take in the scenery. I was certain I'd never seen a farm as gorgeous as this one. The lush pasture stretched out into the valley, the Washington mountains in the backdrop. I knew the barn was just down the hill opposite the pasture, and that it overlooked a gap in the forest that showed the mountain passage in all its glory. The three therapy horses—Memphis, Chesty, and Reckless—were grazing in the pasture nearest the farmhouse.

I slowly got out of my car, transfixed on the horizon beyond. To my right, the chickens squawked merrily in their fenced-off area.

Watford was gorgeous, but in some ways, it had nothing on Winding Road. How Kameron was able to snag this perfect piece of land would remain a mystery.

"You made it!"

I whirled around to see Kameron descending the steps of the farmhouse.

Oh, sweet Jesus.

Kameron was wearing his classic jeans and t-shirt pairing, but I'd either forgotten how good he looked in green, or simply hadn't prepared myself for what the sight of him was going to do to me. I looked down at my denim overalls and white t-shirt, feeling slightly overdressed.

Couple his incredible physique with the excited grin on his face, and I was really about to lose it.

I didn't know how I'd convinced myself doing an overnight here would be fine.

With Kameron looking like that, and my head a jumbled mess of feelings I couldn't untangle, the night was sure to be a disaster.

"Hi," I said, smiling back at him. "Thanks for letting me come by for a few days."

"I'm glad you're here," Kam said. "It'll be good for you to see everything before you work remotely most of the week."

I smiled and adjusted the strap of my bag over my shoulder, hitting the lock button on my keys.

"So, am I sleeping in the farmhouse?" I said, gesturing to my bag.

"About that," Kameron said sheepishly. He scratched the back of his neck awkwardly. "I might have made another small infrastructure investment."

"An infrastructure investment?" I repeated. Kameron nodded, gesturing for us to turn around. There was a small natural incline built into the hill that descended past the chicken coop.

"Trust me," Kam said, heading down what felt like a natural staircase leading down the hill. It was only a few more steps before the tiny house appeared. My jaw hit the floor as I took in the structure and I whirled towards Kameron, who was blushing.

"You built a tiny house?" I practically squealed. Before leaving Watford, and before I knew my Nana had left her land to me, including the farmhouse, I'd dreamed about building a tiny house in my Nana's backyard. I loved the appeal of living in a small, minimalist space where every design feature, every nook and cranny, had a purpose.

"Ta-da," Kam said weakly, pulling a small key out of his pocket. I took it from him, my face still shell-shocked as we walked towards the front door. The house had wooden paneling with black accents, a small front porch, a black door, and several windows, including what looked to be a skylight on the far side. I opened the front door and gasped.

The interior was something out of a Pinterest dream. We entered the kitchen, which was surprisingly spacious for a tiny home. A lofted bed rose above the living room seating area with a built-in desk along the far wall. There was a small couch, and just off the kitchen was the bathroom, complete with a small shower.

And, to top it all off, the small wall behind the small vertical fridge boasted a built-in book shelf. I walked over to it, my eyes immediately scanning the titles.

"I originally had the idea to install a tiny house when Abbie and Connor got back together," Kameron's voice brought me back to the present moment.

"I figured they might want more privacy than the farm-house can provide. So, I reached out to a local builder, and now we have this guy," he said, knocking his knuckles against the wooden shelves. "The idea was to rent it out as an Airbnb eventually, but right now, it's yours."

"What?" I said, still running my fingers along the wooden bookshelves built into the wall of the home.

"You can spend the night here, as opposed to the farm-house, if you'd like."

"It's. . . Kameron, this is beautiful."

Kameron stood against the wall, leaning his full weight into it.

"I'm glad you like it. I thought of the books you and Abbie read all the time, so the bookshelves were a necessity."

I turned to face him, unable to find the words to explain what I was feeling.

What was happening?

He didn't build this house for me. I knew that, and yet I also couldn't stop the torrent of emotion rising within me at all the details he'd thought about. Details that were connected to *me*.

"So, I figured I'd give you some time to settle in here. Whenever you're ready, come back up to the farmhouse. I've got a pot roast going. We can eat lunch and discuss things."

"You cooked?"

Kameron shook his head, a teasing grin on his face.

"Need I remind you that Lucas is the one who is inept in the kitchen? I'll have you know I can cook just fine."

"I'll be the judge of that."

"So you will," Kameron said, smiling as he turned to leave. I turned my attention back to the loft above the small living area. The house couldn't have been over 350 square feet. This house was a fraction of the size of my farmhouse, with its long ranch style hallway and small bedrooms, but it was every bit as cozy.

I climbed the ladder to the loft, lying down on the bed and groaning at the softness of the duvet and mattress beneath. I rolled over onto my back, exhaling deeply.

When I opened my eyes, I realized I was looking up at a skylight.

By the time I returned tonight, I knew I'd have an unobstructed view of the Washington night sky.

When I entered the farmhouse a while later, I was surprised by how soft and restful the space was. I'd only ever been on the porch of the house while waiting for Lucas to get back with coffee. With three young military veterans living here, I had assumed the place would be disgusting.

The opposite was true.

It still had that rustic charm every older farmhouse naturally possessed, and the mostly thrifted and second hand furniture only elevated that feel.

Kameron was in the kitchen grabbing bowls from the cabinet above the sink. There was a red slow cooker next to him.

I inhaled deeply and almost choked on the nostalgia. The scent of roasting potatoes and carrots in delicate and cozy homestyle spices reminded me so much of the days I spent in the kitchen at the homestead with my Nana.

I remembered all of the times she pulled the step stool close to her soup pot so I could stir whatever delicious meal we were cooking up that day.

"Hey," I said as I walked towards the kitchen, trying to shake the grief from my bones.

"Oh good, you're here," Kam said. "Everything okay at the tiny house?"

"It's perfect," I said. "You really thought of everything."

"You're the first person to stay there, so if something comes up tonight, just text me and I'll come fix it. Hungry?"

Kameron held a bowl out to me, and I nodded gratefully.

"This smells amazing," I said earnestly. "My Nana used to make the best pot roast in the world."

Kameron's light laugh skittered over my skin. I'd never heard a laugh as beautiful as his.

"Well, I'm certain this roast won't be as good as your Nana's, but my mom used to make this for my dad after he worked the night shift on a holiday. And we both thought it was pretty good."

Kameron ladled some of the roast into his bowl before handing off the spoon to me. I followed suit, and we both took a seat at the dining room table.

"Did your dad work a lot of night shifts?" I asked, thinking the question was innocent enough.

Kameron coughed uncomfortably. "He worked nights pretty much my whole life, until he passed."

I almost dropped my spoon onto the table.

"I'm so sorry," I sputtered. "I shouldn't have—sorry."

Way to go, Imogen. Bringing up his dead dad at the first meal.

"It's okay," Kam said with a shrug. "It was several years ago."

I knew better than to ask what happened, despite my natural curiosity. When Kam was ready to give me that information, he would. I took a bite of the roast and let out a pleased hum. Kameron choked on his next bite.

"This is really freaking good," I said, quickly scarfing down another spoonful. "Your mom knew what she was doing."

Kameron smiled, despite still trying to catch his breath after swallowing his bite wrong.

"She certainly knew her way around the kitchen," Kam said.

We settled into a comfortable silence and ate the rest of our meal. When we were both finished, I grabbed my notebook and a pen and returned to my seat at the table.

"Let's talk about job stuff," I said. Kameron nodded and sat back in his chair.

"Now that the wedding is over, I need to focus all of my attention on securing additional grant funding. Connor's investment will sustain us for the next year at least—hopefully longer. But ensuring the long-term success of Winding Road means securing additional funding so we can keep up with our expenses and also build up our savings."

I nodded, jotting that point down.

"With daily operations, what are your biggest pain points? Tell me all the crap you don't want to deal with so you can focus on grant proposals."

"Email," was Kameron's immediate response. "I hate that thing."

I tried to hide my smile as I wrote it down.

"Also, social media. I'm not gifted in that department. I feel bad, because our page really took off after we posted some snapshots of the Founder's Festival, but I don't want to keep up with it."

"Duly noted," I said. "You're in luck, because I love both of those things."

"I don't know about your email skills, but if the way you handle your homestead's social media is any indication, I'd say we're in good hands."

Again, that weird, butterfly-esque feeling sparked to life in my stomach.

"Here's what I'm thinking," I said. "You hand over the reins to the Winding Road emails, both for the farm and the nonprofit. I'll take both of those things over full-time so you don't have to worry about them. If something comes up that needs your decision or input, I'll text or call you.

Email is a great task because I can handle it even when I'm in Watford."

I paused, feeling a rush of excitement as the wheels started turning in my head in earnest. "For social media, I want to focus on short form video content. I'd like to spend at least a day or two here every week so that I can create content here. This place is like a gold mine for content ideas. You guys have a really good following, but we can do more to keep them engaged. You never know what opportunities might come your way, with a robust social media presence."

I stopped myself, smiling awkwardly. Kameron was staring again, the fork in his hand long forgotten as he looked at me from across the dining table.

"If that's too much, then—"

"You're amazing," Kam said, and it felt like the chair had been taken out from under me. I would never understand this man's ability to disarm me with only a few words.

"It's what I'm here for," I said, shrugging.

But Kam didn't look away. He *never* looked away.

"What?" I murmured, looking back down at my plate and stabbing a carrot with my fork. I didn't like being scrutinized. I had always been the wallflower type.

"I want to kiss your brain."

I let out a choked laugh, fumbling for my glass, gulping down some water in an effort to clear my throat.

"I'm surprised you get that reference," I said, still laughing.

"Connor is the grandpa here. Just because I don't like content creation doesn't mean I don't like to scroll."

"Fair enough," I said, my laughter finally dying down. "I needed this. Thank you for the meal, and for the laugh. And the job. For everything."

I blew out a long breath.

"I'm glad you're here, Im."

"Well, this is surprisingly romantic."

I whirled around in my chair, a loud high-pitched sound that was very close to a scream escaping my lips. Kameron stood from his chair with a loud scrape. Standing in the front door was no other than Lucas Morales.

"Jesus Christ, Lucas," I gasped, pressing a hand to the center of my chest to slow my racing heart. "You can't sneak up on people like that!"

"You told me you were taking the day off," Kameron muttered.

"I took the day off. And now I'm back at my house, because I want to sleep," Lucas said, strolling into the kitchen and yanking the fridge door open to peruse his dinner options.

Kameron sat down in his chair wearily.

"You let your guard down," Lucas said, looking at Kam. "You should have seen me come in. Were you, perhaps, distracted?"

"Take your grumpiness elsewhere, Lucas," Kam said, shaking his head. "You're welcome to join us."

"Thank you for the meal," I said, smiling apologetically as I stood to leave. "To be honest, I'm still running a sleep deficit from the wedding the other night. Is it okay if we resume everything tomorrow? I could use tonight to rest."

Kameron opened his mouth to say something else, but Lucas cut him off.

"See you in the morning."

I kept my smile plastered on my face until I had stepped through the door, immediately sinking into the relief of the cool mountain night. The path back down the hill to the tiny house was well-lit, and the sound of the trees and grass rustling and the crickets chirping was a comfort to me.

I made my way inside the tiny house, locking the door behind me before I put my phone on the charger and flopped down on the couch. There weren't many windows in the house, a detail I was grateful for. Too many windows would have made me feel exposed.

Just like with everything Kameron had a hand in, there seemed to be a perfect balance.

I drummed my fingers along the edge of the couch, parsing out my next move. My mind was far too active for sleep, full of ideas for how to streamline Winding Road's operations.

And maybe a few thoughts about the intensity of Kameron's stare.

I shivered, wrapping my arms around myself.

I poked around the tiny house for a few more minutes, exploring the bathroom—surprisingly spacious, considering the overall size of the house—before I climbed the ladder up to the loft. I laid down on the bed, looking up through the skylight.

I fumbled for the remote to dim the lights, opening the small nightstand drawer. The dimmed lights, leaving only a faint glow from the downstairs kitchen, illuminated the full night sky visible through the skylight.

It was breathtaking.

I went to return the remote to its rightful place in the nightstand when my eyes landed on a book. Not just any book, but my favorite book of all time.

The book that I'd re-read over and over while I was clawing my way out of an abusive relationship.

The book I saw so much of myself in.

I saw this book on your shelf at our last Wednesday night dinner, and it was the only copy on your shelf you had annotated. I figured it might be one of your favorites, so I bought you a copy to have here, over the summer.

— Kam

Butterflies took flight in my stomach once more as I ran my fingers over the embossed cover of the book.

Was this something that friends did for one another?

I'd almost managed to convince myself that these feelings were one sided. But this was on another level. A fresh copy of my favorite book, that I hadn't even told him about—he just happened to notice it was the most well-loved copy in my home library?

The reality of my life up to this point came crashing over me.

I was the girl who had jumped at the opportunity to run off with a man she'd barely dated for a year, right after graduating from high school.

I knew nothing about love or romance. The only true friend I had was Abbie, and even then, I felt like I could never measure up to everything she'd done for me over the years.

I didn't know what to do.

As I read over the note once more, Kameron's rough scrawl etched into the paper, tracing the words again and again, I realized I might have completely misread those stares.

I groaned and flopped back against the pillowcase, unable to sort my thoughts out. This was the harsh, realistic aftermath of escaping an abusive relationship.

Your ability to trust your instincts was diminished, to the point where you spent most of your time overthinking, rather than living your life.

That, perhaps, was the most egregious theft of all.

Chapter Eight
Kameron

After Imogen had left the farmhouse last night, I'd cleared the table, put the dishes in the dishwasher, and walked upstairs without saying a word to Lucas.

His sour attitude had spoiled what had been a really nice meal with Imogen.

And yes, perhaps he had been right about the romantic tilt to the evening.

But truthfully, I'd been happy to listen to her talk about her plans for Winding Road.

Winding Road was my pride and joy. The work we did with veterans and first responders was my life's passion in every sense. Knowing that Imogen could see the vision I had for this place meant something to me.

It meant *everything* to me.

As I walked downstairs the next morning, I fired off a quick text to Imogen.

Me

I've got coffee and eggs ready, if you're hungry.

Imogen Phillips

You're a saint, I'm walking up now

I smiled and tucked my phone back in my pocket before grabbing another coffee cup and pulling out a plate. Imogen came in the door a few minutes later, wearing a green sundress that had me swallowing my tongue.

"Good morning," Imogen said, smiling when I extended the full plate to her. She sat down at the kitchen table, and the sight of her, shoulders relaxed and well-rested, made any residual misgivings about our arrangement fade entirely. She took a bite of her eggs and considered for a moment.

"Good?" I said, sitting in the chair across from her.

"The eggs from my chickens taste better."

I let out a disbelieving laugh.

"What are their names?"

"Pam, Jim, and Michael Scott," Imogen said smugly.

"Let me guess, someone named all of them after characters from *The Office*?"

"How did you guess?" Imogen said, ever the deadpan humorist. "Do you have a themed name for your chickens, too?"

"Oh yes," I said, scooping some more eggs onto my fork. "I think Old Gram and Rambo would take issue with your claim that your eggs are better, though."

Imogen threw her head back in a full body laugh that made my skin break out in goosebumps. Beautiful. The word was on a constant loop in my head every time she was around.

"You did not name one of your hens *Rambo*. You wouldn't torture her like that."

"Guilty as charged. If it makes you feel better, she barely tolerates my crap. She much prefers Lucas."

Imogen laughed again, and I scrambled for something else to say to make her laugh again.

But, naturally, Lucas decided that was the perfect moment to make his grand entrance downstairs. He looked like crap, as if he'd spent the entire night tossing and turning.

"There's eggs on the stove, and some potato hash."

"Thanks," Lucas said without his usual tone or humor. Imogen frowned and walked over to the stove.

The two of them talked in hushed whispers, and I only caught every other word. The words "ex" and "wife" came up often enough that I assumed yet another roadblock had come up during Lucas's attempt to divorce his ex-wife. Imogen was the one person he confided to about his marriage. They seemed to have common ground there.

I trusted that when the two of them were ready to share more with me, they would. Even if it was hard to wait it out. I wouldn't consider myself a nosy person by default, but when the two of them did things like this—talk in hushed tones when other people were still in the room—it made things awkward. Imogen ended the conversation by hugging Lucas before coming back to the table.

"Today I thought I could show you around the farm," I said, taking a sip of my coffee. "Give you the lay of the land, so you can go wherever you want as ideas come up for you."

"That would be great," Imogen said, her smile bright as she pulled her tablet and pencil out from her bag. "Before we go, will you sign into your email? I use an app that aggregates everything for me so I only have to check one inbox, but if you're not comfortable with that, I can do things a different way."

"Nope," I said, gesturing for her to hand me the tablet. "Email is the bane of my existence. Do whatever you need to do to make things easy for you."

Imogen smiled and handed it to me. I quickly signed into both the nonprofit and farm email and handed it back to hear with an overdramatic sigh.

"I feel lighter already."

Imogen just shook her head and smiled.

After breakfast, I tugged on my boots and grabbed my keys. Lucas was frowning over some documents at the kitchen table.

"Do you need anything?"

Lucas met my eyes, his expression tired.

"Nah, I'm good. Thanks though."

"I know better than to ask if everything's alright, so instead I'll just say that you don't have to do this on your own. Whatever you're carrying, Connor and I can help. We all can."

Lucas gave me a stunted smile.

"Thank you, Kam. I really appreciate it. I promise I'll let you know if I think of anything."

I nodded once before heading out the door. Imogen was already at the bottom of the stairs, staring out at the sprawling farm before us. A gentle breeze blew by, rustling the grasses of the pasture and kicking up dirt along the gravel road.

"Ready to go?"

"Yes," Imogen said. "If I had a view like this, I don't think I'd ever leave my house. It's stunning."

I gestured to our left, where a gently sloping path led down past the venue barn towards the back of the horse pasture. Imogen came to walk beside me, and we set off down the path.

"You have a pretty similar view out the kitchen window of the farmhouse."

Imogen shrugged and readjusted the strap of her bag over her shoulder.

"I suppose so. I guess it's different for me, since I practically grew up in that house. My Grandma would stand at the kitchen counter all day, cooking and preparing meals, teaching me about the most random topics."

"She sounds wonderful," I said.

Imogen smiled fondly.

"She was. Growing up biracial in a small town, even one like Watford, is hard. My relationship with my family is complicated, but my relationship with my Nana was unshakeable."

Imogen shook her head. "I miss her a lot. Living in her house the last few years has hit me harder than I expected. Everywhere I look, I see her. And in some ways, it's a reminder that I really haven't done much up to this point in my life."

I pressed my lips together to hold back a frown.

"I get not being where you want to be. I think you and I are similar in that way. We want to achieve all our goals and we're not willing to make as many concessions as other people are. But you have done things, Imogen."

I stopped in front of the horse pasture, hopping up onto the first wooden rung of the fence and whistling for Memphis to come over. Reckless was grazing further back in the pasture, but he rarely came when called anyway. Chesty was an old soul who liked to hang out near the barn. Memphis, on the other hand, loved himself some pets. The horse trotted over to us.

"You're right," Imogen said, dropping her bag and hopping up on the fence next to me. "I'm just at a weird point right now. If I'm melancholic or distant, don't take it personally."

Imogen sighed, regarding Memphis as he pressed his head against my chest. I responded in kind, stroking his neck.

"I think maybe I don't know the person I am right now. I'm a stranger to myself. And that scares me."

"Yeah," I murmured. "I get that."

Imogen reached out, and Memphis nuzzled her palm with his nose, snorting in approval. Imogen's soft smile undid something in me.

"You know who you are, don't you?" Imogen said, stroking Memphis's mane. "Maybe you can help me figure out who I'm supposed to be."

Memphis merely pressed his forehead to hers. Imogen gasped softly, but didn't pull away. She continued to stroke his mane, and I stood there, transfixed by the beauty of the moment.

I'd seen this interaction so many times, but seeing that connection with Imogen truly stole the breath from my lungs.

Horses had a way of connecting with us on a primal level. Horses saw us as more than the sum of our past experiences and trauma. They had a way of showing love and care, even to those who felt undeserving of such love. I'd seen Memphis and Reckless march right up to grown men who felt like they would never be whole again, and watched as they held these horses and sobbed, clinging to them as if the world would disappear beneath them.

For many, this moment was a bridge to the next part of their life. It was an opportunity to break from the past and step into a new future.

"Thank you," Imogen whispered, pressing the softest of kisses to Memphis's muzzle. The horse snorted softly before trotting away, back to the middle of the pasture where he'd been grazing earlier.

I didn't say a word as we stepped down from the fence. Imogen grabbed her bag, wiping swiftly at her eyes before I continued down the path.

"We can walk around the far side of the pasture, and I'll show you the orchard and the crop fields."

I looked back to see that Imogen was still standing near the fence, looking out at the pasture. I walked back towards her, and she gave me an apologetic smile.

"Sorry. I know I came here with the purpose of learning more about Winding Road, but. . ."

"You can be honest with me," I said, offering her a small smile. "You can tell me that interaction with Memphis brought up a lot for you, and you'd much rather go back to the tiny house where you can have a cup of tea and curl up with a book and take a few hours for yourself before you get on the road."

Imogen looked at me, pure shock written on her face.

"There's no way you've deduced all that in a matter of hours."

"We've known each other for months," I reminded her gently. "You can keep your secrets, Imogen Phillips. But that won't stop me from trying to untangle them."

Imogen gave me a coy smile.

"As much as a day in that gorgeous tiny house sounds enticing, I do need to head back to Watford tonight, so unfortunately that relaxing staycation will have to wait until this weekend."

I tried not to perk up at the promise in her statement.

"Glad to know I haven't run you off entirely, if you're already making plans to come back."

Imogen simply brushed past me, looking back at me over her shoulder. I saw it then, the moment she slipped back behind that mask she wore. It was the mask I'd put on myself after a vulnerable moment, where I wasn't sure how to act or what to say to the people who'd seen me unguarded.

"You coming, cowboy?"

I rolled my eyes, even as heat flared beneath my skin.

Two could play at this game.

Chapter Nine
Imogen

My day at Winding Road was largely uneventful after we toured the pasture. Kam showed me the orchard and some of the crop fields, and took me to visit the hen house, where I got to meet Old Gram and Rambo in the flesh. I still couldn't believe Kameron would name one of his hens Rambo, but when I thought more about the company he kept, I supposed it made sense.

Kameron and I parted ways at my car, with me promising to text him when I left on Friday night to head back here. We'd worked out a schedule where I'd spend the weekends here at Winding Road, and most of the work week back in Watford. Given that this was supposed to be a part time position, and that most of the work that needed doing around Winding Road took place on the weekends, that arrangement made the most sense.

The moment I walked in the door of my farmhouse, I dropped my bag, flopped onto my couch, and let out a long sigh of relief.

It was good for me to get a change of pace. But nothing compared to the comfort of this couch, and being back in my safe place.

I only had a few minutes of peace before my phone rang. When I saw it was Abbie, I quickly sat up, smashing the answer button.

"Hi Abbie!"

No answer.

"Abbie?"

Just as I was about to panic, believing my friend had been kidnapped in a foreign country, I heard the faint rustling of sheets in the background.

"Hellooo," I said, rolling my eyes when I heard giggling in the background.

"Hi, sorry," Abbie said, out of breath.

"I know you are not calling me while you're in bed with Connor."

"We just woke up!" Abbie insisted. "I know it's getting late there, and it's almost time for your evening 'me time.' I wanted to hear your voice before you went to sleep. How are things?"

I smiled, leaning back against the couch cushions.

"They're good. I just got back from Winding Road a few minutes ago, actually."

"Oh?" Abbie said, intrigued. "Did you have fun?"

There was a muffled sound against the receiver, as if she'd covered the speaker phone with her hand while discussing something she didn't want me to hear.

I let out a long sigh.

"I'm there to work, Abbie. As nice as it is working for friends, I do still have to work."

"Of course," Abbie said. "I don't mean to downplay that part of it. I guess we're all still adjusting to the change in dynamic."

"What do you mean?"

"I mean, not to get too deep into the romance novel weeds here, but isn't Kameron technically your boss now?"

Something in my body flashed hot, and I shook my head, even though Abbie couldn't see me.

"Technically, yes. I didn't realize how much these guys hated checking their email. The Winding Road inbox is seriously neglected."

"And. . . you're okay? Outside of work, I mean."

I pressed my lips together. Abbie didn't mean anything negative by it. I knew she was asking out of genuine concern for my wellbeing. It also made me feel icky, to know she was on her honeymoon and still worried about me. Like I was back in the mental state I was years ago, unable to be alone with my thoughts and memories.

"I'm doing great," I said earnestly. Even if I hadn't been fine, there's a good chance I would have lied to Abbie. At the very least, I would have tried. The last thing I wanted was for her to be thinking about me while she was supposed to be enjoying newlywed bliss with the love of her life. "Did you know about the tiny house Kameron built at the farm? It's stunning."

Another pause stretched between us.

"Well, honestly, Kameron didn't make plans to have the house put in until after you accepted the job."

That brought me up short. "What?"

"He always had plans to put a tiny house or two on the property, thinking he could eventually rent them out if we ever needed extra cash, but that project was put on the back-burner after the festival," Connor explained, his voice louder than Abbie's, like he was calling out from another room. "After you took the job, Kameron went back to the builders and gave them the green light to build the first one. They just installed it in the last few days."

My heart squeezed in my chest. My mind spiraled into thoughts of why Kameron would do that. They all came back to one answer I couldn't wrap my mind around.

He wanted me to have a place. A place that wasn't the farmhouse. Where I could be alone without the presence of other people bothering me.

I quickly shoved that thought of my head. Not only was it egotistical and completely ridiculous to insinuate that Kameron had literally built me a house, but it also didn't help my tendency to overthink things when it came to my friends.

Connor coughed to clear his throat, and I remembered it was my turn to talk.

"That's nice," I said weakly.

"Go away," Abbie said. "I need to talk to my best friend for a minute. Alone."

Connor made a noise that sounded suspiciously like a whine, followed seconds later by the closing of a door. I smiled to myself. The three of us liked to poke fun at Abbie and Connor for being lovesick idiots, but I didn't blame them. They'd spent years apart, and had a lot of time to make up for.

"How are the Netherlands?"

"Gorgeous," Abbie said. "We're visiting one of the tulip farms later today, and I am buzzing with excitement. Thank you for organizing this trip, Imogen. It's been so nice to be able to actually enjoy my honeymoon without overthinking everything. I would have been stressed the whole time if I had planned this."

I smiled, slouching back on the couch, and picking up the remote to scroll through my various streaming apps to find something to watch.

"I'm so glad everything's gone smoothly. I tried to pick a mix of activities that I thought you and Connor would both enjoy."

"You've done a great job," Abbie said.

There was a pause while Abbie considered her next words and I continued my scroll to find something interesting to watch tonight.

"How is Lucas?"

"Weird," I sighed. "The divorce proceedings are stalled yet again. He's going back to Seattle at the end of this month for another meeting. I don't know. It's complicated and I don't really understand it."

Abbie let out a low whistle. "She has to be running out of things to do to stall it. Based on what I know, all evidence points to her being the instigator here."

I shrugged, ironically landing on a docuseries about crazy exes and murder. I hesitated briefly, wondering if it might be too triggering for me, before I hit play. Screw it.

"Yeah. She doesn't seem like a very nice person."

"And Kameron?"

"He's fine," I said, far too quickly. "He's done surprisingly well with Connor's absence. The two of them are like peas in a pod."

Abbie let out a loving chuckle. "Yeah they are. I'm glad things are going well. We miss you guys and are looking forward to being home."

"We miss you guys, too. Be safe. Don't do anything I wouldn't do."

"I'm not dignifying that with a response," Abbie said. "Love you."

"Love you," I replied before ending the call.

I made myself a bowl of popcorn and a cup of hot chocolate—my go-to comfort snack, much to Abbie's horror—and settled into the couch. I reached for my favorite fuzzy blanket, draping it over my legs as I hit play on the docuseries.

Nights at home truly were my favorite thing. But tonight, I wondered what it would be like if someone was here beside me, curled up next to me with their own mug of hot chocolate and an extra bowl of popcorn.

Chapter Ten

Kameron

I spent the next three days filling out three separate grant proposals. Connor's investment and our existing grant funding secured us for the next year, but I was planning for the future.

I didn't want to put our nonprofit in a bad spot if we weren't able to get the farm off the ground, or if we ran into any emergencies.

I'd worked so damn hard to build this place.

I wasn't about to let mismanagement take it away.

On Friday, I spent the entire morning and early afternoon decidedly not listening for the sound of Imogen's car pulling up in the gravel lot next to the farmhouse.

I told myself I was excited for her to arrive because I had new ideas about outreach opportunities I wanted to run by her, and not because I was excited to have her close to me again.

I idly wondered if this was how Connor felt those first few days back with Abbie in the fall of last year. Abbie and Connor had a lot more history between the two of them compared to Imogen and I, but I couldn't help seeing some parallels.

And that was a rather terrifying thought.

Right as I put my head down to continue writing objectives, my phone pinged.

Imogen Phillips

Don't hate me for what I'm about to say

Me

I could never hate you.

What's up?

Imogen Phillips

There's a lot of stuff going down at the farm. We need all hands on deck.

Is it okay if I work remotely this weekend?

Me

Yeah of course. Is everything okay?

Imogen Phillips

Yeah. Mostly my control issues rearing their ugly heads

Me

Should I laugh?

Imogen Phillips

More like you should prevent me from killing Kevin

Me

Why are we killing Kevin?

Imogen Phillips

I appreciate that you didn't immediately come for me

Or say that violence wasn't the answer

Me

That was kind of my job for six years

I'm the last person who should be judging threats of violence

Imogen Phillips

Touche.

My brother has gotten it in his head that he is God's gift to mankind because he's been tasked with managing both the general store and my homestead

His ego is the size of Washington State right now

Me

Is he doing a bad job of it?

Imogen Phillips

That's the PROBLEM

He's doing a great job of running both of them.

It's like he was born for management.

It's made him insufferable

Me

What's bad about that?

Imogen Phillips

He's trying to show me up!!

He's trying to prove to everyone that he can take something that I built from scratch and do it better than me

#middlechildproblems

I didn't have siblings, and couldn't speak to the exact sibling dynamic of being the middle child sandwiched between two individuals that had their life together, and feeling like the odd person out, because you didn't.

But I had been in the Marine Corps for six years, and I did know how it felt to be the one person who hadn't hit their peak yet.

Me

Are you stressed about having to go back?

Imogen Phillips

No, I'm stressed about the fact that eventually I'm going to go back and everyone is going to be so used to doing things a certain way, that everyone is going to forget what it's like when I'm here

Sorry for the rant

Me

Don't apologize. I think I get it now.

Being away from Watford was causing Imogen anxiety, but not in the way I'd originally expected. I'd accepted the fact that the conversation was over, which is why I jumped when my phone started vibrating and Imogen's contact picture appeared on my lock screen.

It was a self-portrait she'd taken on the back porch of her farmhouse a few weeks earlier. She was sitting on a wooden bench, legs crossed, holding a bundle of yellow tulips near her face that obscured part of her smile, and matched her yellow sweater perfectly.

It was artsy, and cute, and so damn attractive. That yellow sweater haunted my dreams, because it perfectly encapsulated who Imogen was: sunny and bright and creative.

I forced myself to get a grip as I swiped to accept the call. I put it on speaker while I continued to scan the document in front of me for typos.

"Hi," Imogen said, sounding out of breath. "Sorry for dumping all that on you out of nowhere."

I couldn't help the smile that overtook my face. "It's no problem. Sometimes you've gotta let it out."

Imogen chuckled. "True, but enough about me. I want to talk about your email inbox, sir, and the state that you gave it to me."

I let out a disbelieving laugh and slouched back in the seat.

"All right, hit me with it. Tell me all of the ways I screwed up."

The shuffling of papers on the other end of the phone told me Imogen was all too delighted to dive in.

"First of all, I've already established a new email specifically for grant proposals. I know you're working on a couple for the Winding Road nonprofit, and I want to make sure that we don't miss any important communication. I'll text you the details so you have them. Secondly, I have gone through the extensive effort of color coding every single one of your folders and organizing all of your existing emails into said folders."

I shook my head. "I promise you, Imogen, if you ever leave us that inbox is going to go right back to where it was, and all of your hard work will be for naught."

"You wouldn't dare disrespect my hard work like that."

I couldn't help the grin that spread across my face. At this point, my smile was permanent wherever Imogen was involved.

"It has nothing to do with how much I appreciate your effort, but unfortunately, I'm not built like that."

"You're saying I'm built different."

"I'm saying you're built different," I agreed, a grin still on my face. We settled back into conversation about Imogen's plans to expand the Winding Road photo feed. I was grateful we were on the phone, and not in person. Imogen was incredibly distracting on a good day, and it was hard to focus on anything she was saying when she had a very focused, very cute expression on her face.

"With all that said, since I can't be there in person, would you or Lucas be willing to take some pictures of the property and send them my way? I really want to take some good pictures and video of the venue so that we can start promoting it. The photographs and video are due back from Abbie and Connor's photographer towards the end of this month, so hopefully we'll have that as well. They've already given the okay to use pictures from their wedding promotional materials for the venue."

I stood from the table and headed into the kitchen to pour myself a fresh cup of coffee.

"I'd be happy to oblige."

"You have my thanks," Imogen teased. "I've got to put out some fires here, but call me later if you need anything."

"Will do," I said, and hung up the phone.

I rubbed the back of my neck and ran the cover letter and objectives I'd written up through my grammar checker one more time.

I'd get Imogen to read over it before I formally submitted it. The objectives sheet would stay the same for most of the grants I was applying to, but the cover letter would need to be adjusted and tailored for every organization.

I was about to close my laptop when my phone buzzed again. I glanced at the screen. My heart dropped when I saw the caller ID. I accepted the call with shaky fingers.

"Hey, Kameron, it's Gail," the woman said, sounding tired. I immediately sat up straighter in my chair.

"Hey, Gail. What's wrong?"

"Sorry to call you out of the blue like this," Gail said. "I'm calling to let you know your mom had another episode."

I closed my eyes, tightening my grip on the phone.

Gail was the director of the Laketon nursing home where my mother resided. More than that, she was a close family friend who helped my mother and I navigate life after my father's death. I owed so much to her.

"How bad was it?" I asked, already dreading the answer.

"We're on day four now," Gail said quietly, and my heart sank. "You asked for us to let you know if things progressed with her memory loss. Unfortunately, I think it's time for us to discuss moving her to a higher echelon of care."

The words clanged through me. My chest tightened, and I fought to keep my breathing even. I'd first noticed the dementia signs in my mother years ago. It was little things, like her forgetting a story she used to tell about her and Dad, or that she couldn't remember I'd joined the Marine Corps after high school.

"How often is she lucid?" I said, the words tasting like ash in my mouth.

"On a good week, maybe half the day? On weeks like this, where she's struggling. . . less than an hour, if that."

I inhaled sharply.

"I'm sorry, sweetheart," Gail murmured. "You have no idea how badly I wished this wasn't the case."

"You always told me it was a possibility. I guess I'd just hoped we'd have more time."

"Can you make it out to Laketon sometime this month? I'm sure she'd appreciate a visit, and we can discuss her care going forward."

"Yeah, of course," I said, wiping a hand down my face. "Let me get in contact with my assistant and figure out a time."

"So things are going well at the farm, then? If you've hired an assistant," Gail said. If my heart wasn't actively breaking at the knowledge that my mom's health was declining, my chest would have swelled with pride.

"They are," I mumbled. "Thanks for updating me, Gail. I'll call you."

"Take care of yourself, honey."

I hung up and let my phone clatter to the table as I put my head in my hands.

When I'd helped my Mom move into the center in Laketon, I'd done it because she needed more mental health support than what I could give her. It was right before I'd received orders to an extended training course at Pendleton. I didn't want her alone in the house Dad and her had bought when they found out she was pregnant with me.

I'd convinced her to sell the house and move into the Laketon facility because they had a tiered system of care, meaning she could live as independently as she could manage, and they'd adjust her care plan as needed. I'd never been more grateful for her government pension than I was when I got the first bill from Gail's facility.

Over the last few years, she needed less mental health support, and more health support. Her dementia was progressing.

My mother was never the same after my father died. She never fully recovered.

Yet, hearing that her memory loss was progressing felt like I was losing a parent all over again. It would be a different kind of pain, watching my mother fade mentally while she was still with me physically, but no less poignant.

I stared at the front door, wishing more than anything that Imogen was coming this weekend. Her presence calmed me more than I cared to admit. My phone buzzed with a text from her.

Imogen Phillips

Objectives and cover letter look good to me!

When she was around, I felt like I could navigate the toughest battles.

And entering this new chapter with my mom would be the toughest battle I'd fought in a long time.

Chapter Eleven

Imogen

The fires I mentioned to Kameron may have been metaphorical, but the overwhelming sense of dread was not.

While re-caulking the guest bathroom—a task I'd deemed easy enough—I'd noticed mold lining one side of the bathtub. I tried to control my spiral upon noticing it, but its presence in the bathroom was troubling.

I'd called Joe, who was known as Watford's handyman and a complete know-it-all when it came to everything building related.

I stood in the doorway of the bathroom, nervously fidgeting with hem of my shirt. Joe crouched down next to the tub, running his gloved fingers along the caulk.

"How does it look?"

Joe didn't respond. I tapped my foot impatiently, already anxious about the findings.

"I'm going to need to peel back some of this tile," Joe finally said. "I'm worried that the mold behind the caulking is the least of your worries."

"You think it's in the walls?"

Joe met my eyes in the mirror and shrugged. "Only one way to find out."

When he'd removed one of the tiles in the middle of the shower to find the entire backside covered in black mold, my heart stopped.

"Let's talk in the living room," Joe said, placing the tile mold-side up in the tub. I headed for the living room, palms sweaty and stomach churning with anxiety. I knew mold was bad, but how bad, I wasn't sure. Joe went to the kitchen first, washing his hands twice before he returned to the living room.

"You're going to need a full mold remediation on this house," Joe said, never one to mince words.

"You're kidding," I said, but I knew he wasn't. "You're saying every room in this house probably has mold in it? How long would that take? How much would that cost?"

"I know a guy in Brighton that owns a home repair business. I'll ask him to draw up a quote for you," Joe said. "It'll be expensive, but I'm telling you Imogen, mold isn't something you want to mess around with. If it's in the guest bathroom, there's a high likelihood it's in other places, too. No home renovator is going to come within a mile of this house once they uncover mold, and you're damn sure not going to be able to sell the place unless it's fixed."

I rubbed my temples. I still hadn't decided whether I was going to sell the house or not.

"You'll need to find somewhere else to live while they do the remediation," Joe said. "For a case like this, I'd estimate they'll need at least a week, if not longer."

"A week?" I exclaimed. Joe handed me a business card with Dillon's information on it.

"Dillon can give you more information once he draws your quote up," Joe said. "I'm sorry, kid. I wish I had better news. For your health and safety, promise me you'll sleep somewhere else tonight?"

"Yeah," I murmured, blinking back the sting in my eyes. "I will. Thanks for coming, Joe."

"I'll give Dillon a call and tell him my findings. Let me clean things up in the bathroom and I'll be out of your hair."

I nodded and swallowed tightly, heading for the kitchen to make myself a cup of tea.

"Take care of yourself, kid," Joe called when he returned from the bathroom, waving at me from the entryway.

"Will do," I called back, sighing as I heard the front door open and close. I knocked my head back against the cabinet, feeling the weight of the financial implications of a full remediation on my shoulders. It was going to happen—if for no other reason than for my health if I decided not to sell the house.

I picked up my phone to call Abbie. She and Connor had just gotten back into town after their honeymoon, and as far as I knew, Connor was working from home organizing the next cohort and Abbie was checking in on things at Watford General.

"Hey, Abs," I said when she picked up the phone. "Got a minute?"

"For you, always," Abbie said. "Kev, can you take over the register for me? I'll just be a sec."

I poured the hot water over my chosen tea bag and took a seat at the dining room table.

"So, there's mold in my bathroom," I said, cutting straight to the chase.

"What?" Abbie screeched. She whispered a soft 'sorry' to whoever she'd scared. "How did you find that out?"

"Long story, but Joe Sakis just confirmed it. He gave me the number of a guy in Brighton that has experience with remediations, but I'm pretty sure it's going to take a few days."

"Jesus, Imogen, I'm so sorry," Abbie said. "I'm sure that's stressful."

Understatement of the freaking century.

"I'm the worst friend for even asking this of you when you literally just got married, but can I stay with you tonight? I was supposed to be at Winding Road this weekend, but I canceled so I could focus on renovations here since I was feeling motivated, and now . . ."

"Why not just go to Winding Road like you originally planned?"

"Ouch," I muttered, though she had every right to say no. It was a strange thing, your best friend getting married. On the one hand, they were the same person they'd always been. But every so often, I was reminded that things were different now. There was another person to consider in the dynamic. It was no longer just Abbie and I against the world.

That meant there was a distance there that I couldn't quantify. Our friendship wasn't in question, but things had shifted, and rightfully so. True friendships evolved and changed with life's seasons, and as Abbie entered this new chapter, so would I.

That didn't make it any easier to navigate the gap.

"Not that I don't want you here," Abbie responded quickly. "It's just that, if Kameron was already expecting you, it might be easier if you reverted to the original plan."

"Right," I said. "I guess I could bring myself to text him and grovel."

Abbie's laugh brought a smile to my face.

"I doubt you'd have to do much groveling. In fact, I'll bet you ten bucks you make his entire weekend by telling him you can still come."

My stomach did a weird twist that had nothing to do with my anxiety over the mold situation.

"I don't know about that."

"Guess there's only one way to find out," Abbie said teasingly. "I've got to get back to the register, but call me if you still need a place tonight. But I doubt you will."

We exchanged I love you's and hung up. My fingers hovered over Kameron's contact. I had just canceled on him less than three hours ago.

Was I really about to ask if he could just disregard my inability to be professional?

Then again, the whole job setup we had going for us was strange. Most administrative assistants probably weren't living part time in a tiny home their boss had constructed on their property.

What was supposed to come first here? Professionalism or friendship?

This was *exactly* why overthinkers like me shouldn't mix the personal and professional.

Even so, I swallowed my pride and pulled out my phone.

Me

At the risk of sounding like a complete ass for going back on my word. . .

Is there any way I can still come to Winding Road tonight?

Kameron's reply came before I'd even put my phone down on the table.

Kameron Miller

Please do

Come to the farmhouse and grab a bowl of soup before you head to the tiny house.

It's my night to walk the grounds for evening checks, but I'll see you in the morning

My heart skipped and my skin flushed, and I knew for a fact that my body's reaction had everything to do with the speed at which he'd responded. Kameron didn't wait by the phone for anything, much less a text from me.

Yet I couldn't deny that there was something girl-ish about the excitement that a boy responded to your text quickly.

Kameron Miller gave me freaking *butterflies*. The realization stunned me.

Me

I'll text you when I'm on the road. See you soon :)

Was the smiley face overkill? Maybe. But something told me Kameron wouldn't mind.

A few hours later, I'd gotten a full quote from Dillon for the mold remediation, and I'd almost swallowed my tongue at the total listed at the bottom of the invoice. It was estimated to take a week at most, during which time I needed to be out of the house. As I packed a full suitcase full of clothes and a week's worth of necessities, I realized I was going to pull a classic "ask forgiveness later" when I rolled up to Winding Road with a full suitcase and an intention to hang out on the property for a full week.

I realized thirty minutes into the drive to Winding Road that I now owed Abbie Collins ten dollars.

Chapter Twelve
Kameron

For the first time in six years, I woke up with a scratchy throat, an aggressive cough, and a pounding headache. I was freaking sick.

Imogen had texted me to say she arrived late last night. I'd been upstairs in my bed, trying and failing to take my mind off of the phone call with Gail. Around midnight, I finally forced myself to stumble downstairs and take some decongestant meds. It was spring, anyway. Didn't people usually get sick in the winter?

After a night of tossing and turning, I returned downstairs. I opened the screened window in the kitchen to rotate some fresh air through the living space, futilely hoping that the soft smell of mountain pine would clear my sinuses, to no avail.

Around 8 a.m., Imogen strolled through the front door of the farmhouse. I tried to raise my hand in greeting and failed miserably, letting out a weak "hi" from where I was curled up in the fetal position on the couch.

"What's happening right now?" Imogen said, shrugging off her laptop bag and laying it on the dining room table.

"Hurts to talk," I sniffled.

Imogen's confused expression morphed into one of pure delight.

"Kameron Miller, are you ill?"

My silence was damning.

"You *are* sick," Imogen said, crossing her arms over her chest and shifting her weight to one foot. "The man who always jokes about his perfect immune system is *sick*. In the middle of spring, no less."

"Don't be mean," I mumbled, meaning it as a joke. Imogen's expression softened.

"I'm sorry," Imogen said softly, coming to kneel in front of the couch. She reached out and swept my hair off my forehead. I closed my eyes, savoring the feeling of it. "Do you think it's just a cold?"

I opened my eyes again, just a fraction, so as to not aggravate my headache with a sudden onslaught of sunlight.

"If I say yes," I croaked, coughing for emphasis, "will you make fun of me?"

Imogen's laugh was sudden and breathtaking as she threw her head back with the force of it. Even though the sudden noise made my skull rattle, I didn't say a word, content to watch her just as she was. Stunning. Effortlessly so.

"I will keep my judgements as internal thoughts."

"Thanks," I said, my usual dry, mocking sense of humor falling short as another cough rattled my body.

"Alright champ, you stay here."

"I can rally, just give me a few minutes," I said, moving to push the blankets off me and stand. Like hell was I going to let a cold make me miss out on a day with Imogen, especially when I'd resigned myself to a weekend without her. Not to mention that I dreaded checking the grant proposal email to see if there were more rejections.

God, I'd forgotten how much being sick sucked.

"No rallying for you," Imogen said, placing her hand on my shoulder and pushing me back down towards the couch. "You need to stay horizontal."

"But, the grants—"

"I'm here to help," Imogen said gently, stroking her fingers against my cheek once more. The touch sent shockwaves through my body. "Let me go make myself some coffee and then I'll sit with you. We can go through the emails together. I'll read the important ones aloud and you can tell me how you want to proceed. Okay?"

I shuddered, but not because of the fever. Because Imogen was far too caring and too kind. Imogen, who had every right to make fun of me for being a man-child about having a cold and feeling under the weather, but instead was choosing kindness.

"You're a nice lady," I mumbled. Imogen looked stunned for a moment before she let out another twinkling laugh. My heart stopped and restarted in my chest. I wanted to hear that sound every damn day. Knowing that it was my stupid quips and comments that often made her make that beautiful sound drove me wild.

"Thank you. I think you're nice too, for what it's worth."

Imogen took a step away from the couch, but I snagged her wrist before she could go too much farther.

"Thank you for staying."

The words were rough and sticky in my throat.

There was a reason I'd prided myself on my inability to get sick these last few years. Being sick reminded me of the dark days with my mother's depression, where I was sick a lot, and my mother wasn't present to take care of me. The two of us had spent many days laid up on the couch with the house a wreck, moldy dishes in the sink, dust mites gathering in every corner and crevice. My lungs rattled with the force of my coughs and my mother—

My mother just sat there with me, a vacant stare on her face as she glared at the wall. Day in and day out. I finally mustered up the courage to ask one of my friend's moms to drive me to urgent care so I could get something to ease the pain. I had to come up with the most elaborate cover stories to dissuade the present parents from calling CPS on my mom.

My mother isn't mean, I remember myself saying. *I love my mom. It's just been hard since my Dad died.*

I squeezed my eyes shut tighter, unable to deal with the torrent of memory washing over me. I wasn't a sickly, scared, grieving child anymore. My mother was better now. She would never be the person she was when my father was still alive. That ship had long since set sail. But she was healthier. She was still alive. She had people who cared for her.

Even if she couldn't remember it.

I swallowed down my nausea as Imogen reappeared.

"Talk to me," she said. She gestured for me to sit up, sitting down on the couch and letting me lay my head in her lap as she got comfortable. My head was swimming from the sensory input of my cheek pressed against her warm thigh, and the wave of memory threatening to drown me.

"I hate being sick," I whispered. Imogen put her freshly brewed coffee on the end table and laid her hand on my head. She stroked my scalp with her fingertips, and I bit my tongue to keep an embarrassing moan from escaping. Imogen's hands in my hair was surely a conjuration of my illness-addled brain, but I intended to savor every moment.

"Is this okay?" she murmured, running her hands through my hair. As if she needed to ask. I nodded, and she continued to rub my head as I found my next words.

"I hate being sick because it reminds me of my mom."

Imogen's hands didn't falter. She made a low hum in her throat, a gentle encouragement for me to continue. I inhaled deeply, letting the scent of jasmine and citrus ground me.

"My dad died by suicide when I was a teenager."

Imogen exhaled, long and steady. This isn't really how I'd wanted to tell her about my dad. As important as my father's story was to the mission of Winding Road, I didn't enjoy talking about it so openly. Mostly because people don't know what to say or how to act when you tell them you've lost a parent to suicide. For most people, it's so gut-wrenching that their only response is "I can't imagine." Others try to cover up their own discomfort by offering meager platitudes like "they're in a better place" or "at least their suffering is over."

To someone who is grieving an earth-shattering loss, that's about the least helpful thing you could say. Add in the fact that I was barely a teenager when it happened, and you had a perfectly reasonable explanation for why I didn't like to talk about it.

Imogen didn't say anything, and I knew it was because she was processing the information. She was controlling her own reaction to the news because she cared for me, and she knew how important it was to regulate your own reaction before opening your mouth to say something, particularly when someone shared about their trauma. My chest tightened at the realization.

"I was barely fifteen when it happened. I was at school when I got the call. And there's a lot of shit that happened afterward, but the long and short of it is that my mom never fully recovered. My parents were the ideal couple. They were obsessed with each other. My childhood was perfect because of them. My dad went to work, and my mom stayed home with me. But when he died, a part of her died, too. We were never the same after that. Our family was irrevocably severed."

I stopped then, painfully aware I'd already said too much.

"Thank you for telling me," Imogen murmured. "I don't know what to say, but I'm here for you."

"That means more than I can express."

It did. I should have known Imogen would understand that it was sometimes more damaging to try and come up with something to say, instead of just sitting with the discomfort of it, of processing. I'd been sitting with this knowledge for years. I'd heard a lot of crap from people, everything to I'm so sorry or that's awful, as if I don't know how awful it is, having lived that experience first hand.

"Sorry for dumping that on you," I murmured. "Being sick makes me sentimental, apparently."

"There's nothing to apologize for," Imogen said, voice still soft as her fingers scratched my scalp gently. "I recall you once telling a shy girl at a wedding that you'd be there to hear her story whenever she was ready to tell it. I'm grateful that you trusted me with part of yours."

Damn if my heart wasn't putty in her freaking hands.

I felt it in that moment, the growing feeling I couldn't keep denying.

I was falling for her. Not in the big, grand gesture, lovey-dovey way, but in the raw, real, heartfelt way.

In the way that you come to adore the small details of your relationship with someone, the small things you look forward to and appreciate about the person in front of you.

I was falling for Imogen Phillips, and as much as the rational part of my brain was telling me to pull back, that we'd both only get hurt in the long run, the more my heart and my body resisted.

"I'm gonna grab my laptop so I can start working," Imogen said, brushing her fingers along my brow. I opened my eyes to meet hers, and I swear, butterflies took flight in my freaking stomach at her gentle gaze.

I knew I had a habit of staring at Imogen. I'd tried my hardest to make people see I wasn't doing it in a creepy way, and half the time, I wasn't even staring because of my growing infatuation.

Imogen's energy was infectious. She was bright and sunny beneath that shy, inquisitive exterior. She brought a warmth to my life that I'd long since written off as nothing more than childhood nostalgia or distant memory. Imogen had been through one of the worst things that could happen to someone—surviving an abusive relationship—and she somehow came out on the other side, still radiating sunshine.

She took my damn breath away.

I said nothing as she eased my head from her lap so she could stand up, grabbing her laptop from her bag and returning to the couch.

"You can stay lying down."

"It's okay," I said with a gentle shake of my head. "I've been curled up on the couch all morning. It would be good to be vertical for a while."

It wasn't technically a lie. I'd been curled up on the couch since in the morning. It was also a convenient excuse to put some distance between the two of us before I did something truly insane like confess my feelings for her.

"Suit yourself," Imogen said, sitting down on the couch beside me. I sat up, leaning my head against the back of the couch. I stared at the ceiling of the farmhouse and listened to the gentle clacking of Imogen's fingers on the keys.

"Anything interesting?"

"Not so far," Imogen said. I looked at her laptop, awestruck, as I watched her deftly archive, delete, and organize the twenty emails sitting in our inbox.

"That will never not impress me."

Imogen shot me a wry smile.

"It's easy to make a system and stick to it. Don't Marines love their organization?"

"The institution does. Individual service members? Not so much. The Marine Corps likes to develop the most convoluted systems that 'make people's lives easier', but the exact opposite is true in practice."

Imogen shrugged. "That makes sense, actually. You can have good intentions, but the impact isn't always what you designed it to be."

I bit the inside of my cheek as a question popped into my head. It was risky to ask Imogen anything about her past, but I needed to know.

"What did your ex-husband do? In the military, I mean. What was his job?"

Imogen stilled, and I inwardly cursed myself for opening my mouth.

"I don't know the MOS number or anything like that. I just remember how much he'd go on and on about how important his job was, how Marines would die without him, yada yada. I think it was water related. Honestly, it's a wonder I remember anything about him at this point. The only things I do remember are the things he used to remind me of all the damn time."

"How long was he active duty?"

"He was a year older than Connor, Abbie, and I, so maybe six years? I don't know how he split his enlistment, what portion of time he spent active versus the reserves. And obviously I don't talk to him now, so. . ."

Imogen trailed off, and I knew we were approaching the natural end of this conversation. There were more questions I wanted to ask, but this morning had already taken a strange turn, between me waking up sick and trauma dumping on an unsuspecting Imogen.

"Oh my God!" Imogen exclaimed, sitting up straighter.

"What? What?" I said, my head whipping towards hers.

"We've advanced to the next round for the Warrior's Grant," Imogen said excitedly. "They've narrowed down the applications to a hundred and the committee is reviewing them. The next step would be a video interview with the grant proposal committee to learn more about Winding Road's mission."

The mention of the Warrior's Grant cut through the sickly haze clouding my mind.

"The Warrior's Grant is the big one," I said, trying to wrap my mind around it. "It's the one I applied to on a whim. I didn't think we'd get it, but then Connor told me I should just apply anyway to see what happens. I barely got the application in before deadline."

"That's the one," Imogen said, beaming at me. "The email says we'll hear something about scheduling the interview in the next week, if we've been selected to continue on. *Kam*, this is incredible."

Imogen excitedly scrolled through the lengthy email. My head was spinning with a new sense of dread.

The Warrior's Grant was the one grant I hadn't expected to hear back from. I'd already received dozens of rejections from various smaller grants, and I'd gone back and forth on whether or not to even apply for the Warrior's Grant, because that's how much of a long-shot it was.

Now, they wanted to know more about Winding Road. They wanted to know more about the work we did with veterans and first responders.

The Warrior's Grant could sustain Winding Road for the next five years, longer if the barn venue took off in the way I hoped. This grant would allow us to expand and do things like build on-site housing for cohorts, which would further reduce the overall financial burden for the non-profit site.

"I might throw up."

Imogen looked at me incredulously. "Kam, this is a good thing."

It's only a good thing if I don't screw it up, is what I wanted to say, but I was too scared to open my mouth for fear that my sickness and anxiety combination would lead me to projectile vomit all over the coffee table.

"You'll have plenty of time to recover."

"Can I pay you to do the interview for me?" I whispered. Imogen shook her head.

"The email specifies that they'll want to talk to the executive director directly. It makes sense, because you have the most intimate knowledge about how everything works."

I closed my eyes against the rising tide of emotion.

This was a good thing. This was a bigger chance than I'd ever had. We hadn't technically moved on to the interview round, but I couldn't stop myself from imagining that we did. The festival last year had put us on the map, but nothing compared to having the support of a massive organization. The connections alone would be worth their weight in gold for a small, start-up nonprofit like Winding Road.

Selfishly, the possibility of a team supporting us also excited me. That was the other part of the Warrior's Grant that made it so appealing: they didn't just cut you a check and send you on your way. They offered consulting on proper money management for nonprofits, offered guidance on planning for the long-term success of the nonprofit, and provided referrals and recommendations to people to partner with for expansion.

So far, everything that had gone into Winding Road had been done because of my or Connor's research. I didn't have any formal education in the nonprofit sector. Before establishing Winding Road, I'd never even been part of a nonprofit. Everything I knew about running a nonprofit came from talking to people more knowledgeable than I, and doing an insane amount of Googling and reading.

"Hey, look at me."

I looked back at Imogen, and she reached for my hand, squeezing it gently.

"We've got this. We'll make sure you have everything you need to smash the interview, and if the journey ends here, we'll keep applying. You're not alone."

You're not alone. How many times had I repeated those same words to various people over the last few years? And how often did I have those words reflected back to me by Connor and Lucas?

Yet somehow, the words felt different coming from Imogen. They felt grounding. Encouraging. Hopeful.

"Thanks, Im."

She pulled her hand back, and I snagged her wrist gently. She blew out a quick breath, lips parting around a gentle gasp.

"Thank you for everything," I said earnestly. "I don't know what we'd do without you. This place would probably fall apart."

I *would fall apart* is what I wanted to say, but I held back. The last thing I wanted was for Imogen to get it in her head that I wasn't serious and write off my comment as nothing more than me being delirious while sick.

Something flashed through Imogen's eyes that looked suspiciously like disappointment, though it was gone too quickly for me to say for sure.

"Always happy to help. It's my job, after all."

Chapter Thirteen
Imogen

We didn't have wait a week. Just a few days after we got the original email, we received notice that we were advancing to the video interview stage. The next week was spent facilitating a watered-down version of media training for Kameron. The selection committee had sent over a list of questions they planned to ask in the interview. Most of them were pretty surface level—questions about the mission and the population served. The interviewers already had the answers to most of those questions in the grant application, and the video interview was designed to put a face to the written proposal.

The day of the interview finally came, and I had never seen a more stressed out man in my life.

"What if the Wi-Fi goes down?"

Kameron was pacing around the kitchen, alternating between muttering to himself and playing the "worst-case scenario" game.

"Then we'll set up a hotspot," I said, pouring the freshly boiled hot water over a bag of green tea. Kameron was pacing around the kitchen, wearing a crisp white shirt, jeans, and boots. The whole ensemble was highly distracting on a good day.

Couple that with the way he kept running his hand through his hair to calm himself down, and I was a goner.

"What if they don't show? Or worse, what if they *do* show up and then they realize that they actually meant to give this opportunity to someone else, and—"

"Kameron," I sighed, putting my mug down on the kitchen counter. I walked over to him and took his face in my hands, unable to bear the back and forth.

"Stop psyching yourself out over this," I said, shaking his face gently for emphasis. "You've done everything you can to prepare. Focus on the questions at hand. Go 'military work mode' or whatever it is you used to do when preparing to do something that stressed you out when you were on active duty. You've got this. You've done everything you can to prepare. It is what it is."

Kameron's breathing evened out, and I patted his cheek.

"I'll be waiting down here when it's over. Whatever happens."

Kameron, to my surprise, enveloped me in a bear hug. He murmured a muffled *thank you* into my hair and squeezed me. I let out a small laugh of bewilderment, trying desperately not to think about the hard lines of his body pressed against mine. Which was disrespectful, considering that he was in an emotionally vulnerable position right now.

This is your boss. This is Kameron. This is one of your closest friends.

Maybe if I repeated it enough times to myself I'd start to believe it.

Ninety minutes later, Kameron came bounding downstairs, exclaiming that he hadn't bombed the interview. In fact, he was pretty damn confident that he nailed it.

"They stuck to the list of questions they sent out earlier. I was expecting at least one curveball, but it never came," Kameron said, slouching down in the dining room chair. I smiled and took the seat across from him.

"So, are you in a place where you can admit that you might have been panicking unnecessarily?"

Kameron waved a hand. "Me? Unnecessarily panicking? Never."

"So, now that the interview is out of the way. . . . what should we do next?"

"We're taking the day off," Kameron said, closing my laptop. I yelped in protest, attempting to remove his hand, but my efforts were futile. "Leave the inbox how it is, and go put your bathing suit on."

I slouched back in my chair, glaring at him.

"Some of us have work to do."

"I thought I was your boss," Kameron said, the ghost of a smile on his lips. Something about the way he said the word 'boss' had my mind sprinting in a direction it should stay far away from.

"In most workplaces, it would be inappropriate for a boss to tell one of their employees to put on their bikini."

"Who said anything about a bikini?" Kameron said, and I swore under my breath, knowing he had me.

Damn him.

"Do I at least get to know where we're going?"

"Swimming," Kameron said, as if it was obvious. "We're going to the lake."

I leaned back on my hands, turning my face to the afternoon sun. The thick clouds provided enough cover that I didn't need to shield my eyes from the rays. I could breathe deeply and focus on the comforting feeling of the warm sun on my face. My legs dangled off the side of the dock, and the dress over my bathing suit rippled gently in the late spring wind. Kameron had cannonball'd off the end of the dock as soon as we'd arrived, and I'd painstakingly slathered myself in sunscreen so I could enjoy my time beneath the warm rays.

"Come on in, the water's fine," Kameron said when he resurfaced, playfully splashing water in my direction.

"I'm not getting in there," I replied with a laugh, dangling my legs in the water. "I just washed my hair."

And I was not keen on repeating the tedious process all over again, regardless of how much Kameron flashed me those baby blues.

Kameron was floating face up in the water, eyes closed as he soaked up the rays. He looked at peace, without the usual tension in his shoulders.

Not that I paid attention to how much tension he carried in his shoulders, because that would be well outside of what was allowed.

I closed my eyes, as if it would quiet the butterflies in my stomach.

It was getting harder to decide what was and was not allowed.

"You're beautiful."

I opened my eyes to find Kameron hovering in the water just a few feet in front of me. The unfamiliar words struck something in me that had long since laid dormant.

"I'm sorry," Kameron said sheepishly. "That slipped out."

I laughed, tossing some of my curls over one shoulder and looking over my shoulder in a teasingly suggestive gesture.

"Thank you. This is my favorite dress," I said, smoothing my hands down the green and white floral dress that barely hit my knees.

"It is a nice dress, but I've always thought that," Kameron said, shaking his head. "Your beauty isn't new to me."

I pressed my lips together, the teasing confidence of earlier vanishing instantly when I looked at Kameron for the first time since he'd jumped in to swim. Kameron Miller had a way of unnerving me when I least expected it, and the sight of him, shirtless and wet and very, *very* close, had my throat closing up.

Kameron swam up to me, pressing both of his palms on either side of my hips. My heart pounded in my chest, my pulse a dull roar in my ears.

"I want to kiss you so fucking bad," he murmured, and I felt like I might pass out. "I tried not to. I've tried for months. But I can't look away from you. I'm always looking for you. Even when I know you're not there, I still hope that you will be."

His blue eyes were fixed on me, and instead of breaking out in a cold sweat, I found myself leaning in. I straightened my dress, and Kameron tracked the movement. A small noise escaped him.

"You with these *freaking* dresses."

My laugh was breathy and somewhat choked, as if all the air between us was quickly disappearing.

This was the line. I'd spent so many nights at Winding Road the last few weeks wrestling with the war in my mind over where the line was. I knew, as Kameron's pupils dilated, that this was the line. If we crossed it, things would get messy.

But Kameron was staring at me with that intensity I craved, and suddenly, I'd never wanted to cross a line more in my life.

"Do it," I whispered as my heart thundered in my chest. "Kiss me."

What I meant to be a dare turned out to be a moment of truth as Kameron surged up, leaning all of his weight into his hands as he kissed me. I moaned into his mouth, shocked by how quickly my body responded to the kiss—to *him*.

The kiss was searing in the most delicious way. Because he was using his hands to balance himself on the dock, I expected an awkward clashing of teeth and tongue, when this was anything but. Kameron slanted his lips against mine at the perfect angle, tasting the strawberry lemonade we'd shared earlier.

I reached my hands out to grab his shirt to have something to steady myself, gasping when my hands met only damp, heated skin. His muscles flexed underneath my touch and warmth blossomed in my stomach, new and exciting and all-consuming.

Kameron didn't waste a moment, tilting his head to deepen the kiss. His arms trembled with the strain of holding himself up, and I broke the kiss with a startled gasp. The spell we'd both be under broke, and I scooted away from him, allowing him a moment to haul himself up onto the dock.

He wiped his thumb over his lip, and I realized I was doing the same. My fingertips hovered over my tingling lips, still swollen and raised from the scratch of his beard and the fierceness of his kiss.

"Imogen."

My name on his lips was the last seal breaking.

"I am so sorry," I blurted before he could speak again. "I shouldn't have—"

"It's okay," Kameron said, though his chest still heaved with the aftershocks of our kiss.

Our *kiss*. Oh no.

I stood quickly, smoothing down the bunched fabric of my dress, keeping one palm pressed to my side as a gust of wind blew past. Kameron was still sitting on the dock, shirtless, and trying desperately not to stare at my legs.

I cursed internally. The wind was not my friend today.

"I'm sorry," I said again, because what else was there to say?

Hey boss, that was the best kiss of my life. Can we please do it again?

Kameron stood, opening his mouth to say something as he reached for me.

I took a step back, and even though he deflated, I stood my ground.

"See you at dinner!" I called, turning tail and doing what I'd always done best: run in the opposite direction of what I'd screwed up.

I wanted to look back. Wanted to pick up right where we'd left off.

But I kept walking, one foot in front of the other, all the way back up to the tiny house. I let the door close behind me, smacking the back of my head against the cool wood.

I'd really done it this time.

Chapter Fourteen
Kameron

I didn't stop thinking about the kiss the entire rest of the afternoon.

I'd lived through a lot of crap in my life. I'd weathered storms that would have broken other people. I'd gotten incredibly good at compartmentalizing when things went south. I could forgive and forget and move on without putting much effort in.

But the feeling of Imogen's kiss was a feeling I didn't think I'd ever be able to forget.

Perhaps more alarmingly, I realized as I walked down the hill to the tiny house; I didn't want to forget. I didn't want to sweep this under the rug as a mistake. It didn't feel like a mistake in the moment, and it didn't feel that way now.

Our kiss felt like a reckoning, a homecoming.

I wanted to do it again. I wanted to do it properly, where I could feel her smooth skin beneath my hands, capture every beautiful, breathy sound, see those curls that drove me wild fanned out against my pillow. I wanted to learn how she liked to be kissed, to give her everything she wanted and more.

I wanted more. That was the simplest way to describe it. I always wanted more when it came to Imogen. I had an unsettling suspicion that it would always be like this.

Unless we found a way to clear the air.

I stepped onto the porch of the tiny house, raising my fist to knock on the door. I hesitated, and in the two seconds I hesitated, the door opened, and I damn near jumped out of my skin.

Imogen had changed clothes. She was wearing a sage green PJ set that looked impossibly soft. The tank top rode up just enough that I could see a sliver of her brown skin, and that desire to kiss her, touch her *exactly* how she wanted to be touched, flared to life again.

"Hey," I said awkwardly, not trusting myself to say anything else. It was embarrassing, really, how freaking awkward I was when it came to Imogen.

Now that I knew what her lips felt like, how she tasted, that awkwardness was even more apparent.

Imogen gave me a soft smile and leaned against the doorframe, her black curls falling over her shoulders with the movement.

"Hey yourself."

Some of the tension leached from my shoulders. She hadn't left the house, nor was she screaming in my face or calling me a creep.

"I wanted to say I'm sorry for earlier," I said, swallowing tightly. "With what happened at the dock."

I wanted to smack myself.

Imogen's soft smile remained, and she shrugged.

"There's nothing to apologize for, Kam."

"I asked to kiss you," I said with a grimace. "I crossed a line, and I shouldn't have. If I made you uncomfortable in any way, you have my sincerest apologies."

Imogen's expression softened even further, and I felt like the biggest dick on the planet. The last thing I wanted was to put her in an awkward position.

"If I'm remembering correctly, I was the one who dared you to," Imogen said. "You're not entirely to blame. And I'm sorry for running."

I let out a small laugh, crossing my arms over my chest with a shrug. If she could be casual about this, I could too. Some of the anxiety dissipated from my body as I looked at her.

"I guess you did."

"As crazy as this sounds," Imogen said, "I'm glad we kissed."

The floor damn near fell out from under me.

Tell me it's not all in my head. Tell me there's something here.

Tell me you've been thinking about our kiss all damn day the way I have.

Tell me you feel it too.

"Now that we've gotten whatever weird thing exists between us out of our system, things can go back to how they were."

Oh.

I tried not to feel the soul-crushing weight of Imogen's dismissal for what it was. It was far better this way, for us to chalk this connection up to a mutual crush that had now run its course. We'd kissed. There was no going back. But we could move forward professionally.

No need to jeopardize our friendships or working relationships over a silly crush.

"Right," I said, feigning a relieved sigh. "Thank goodness for that."

Imogen's smile widened into a grin and she shook her head slightly, as if trying to convince herself she wasn't a complete idiot for letting me kiss her.

I decided at that moment I was going to go back up to the farmhouse and ask Lucas to bury me alive in the backyard.

"I was thinking tomorrow we could head down to the barn and the pasture and film there. I've got a cute idea for a video introducing the horses."

I nodded my head, that familiar smile whenever I was in Imogen's presence returning. I hadn't completely screwed this up. I might not have everything I wanted, but I still had her in my life. It would be enough. I would make it enough.

"Sounds good. Meet you at the farmhouse for breakfast in the morning?"

Imogen nodded and turned to head back inside. She hesitated at the threshold, and that ridiculously hopeful part of me perked up.

But whatever Imogen might have wanted to say, she thought better of it, giving me a quiet "good night" before stepping back inside the house, closing the door behind her.

I mulled the day over as I walked back up the worn dirt path to the farmhouse. I knew Imogen had her walls built high. I knew enough of her past to know that those walls were more than justified.

Selfishly, I could admit that I wanted to know her. She was gorgeous, yes, but more important, she was kind, funny, and adventurous. I felt more myself around her than I did in most places.

I sat down at my desk, drumming my fingers along my closed laptop. Imogen had taken on a lot of the administrative work that I hated—that was the job I'd hired her to do, after all—but relinquishing full control over those aspects of Winding Road had proven more difficult than I'd expected.

Every spare cent I'd made in the last decade had gone towards purchasing this land and establishing this nonprofit.

I was creating the place I'd wish existed for my father.

Because if he had known there was a place where first responders could be in community with one another, where they could be with people who understood all the horrible things they'd seen, maybe things would have been different.

If he'd had someone to share his burden, maybe he'd still be here.

Maybe my mother wouldn't be where she is now.

I let out a heavy sigh, rubbing a hand over my face. I stalked into my bedroom, opening up the windows to let in the cool evening air.

The crickets were already singing their night song, and the distant sounds of rustling trees were a balm to my soul.

It would never be enough.

The next morning came quicker than I was prepared for. I didn't sleep great, spending the first part of the night mulling over everything that happened with Imogen yesterday. I rolled over in bed and took my phone off the charger, groaning when I saw I had five unread text messages, most from Connor.

"It's not even 7A.M.," I muttered.

Big Daddy Connor

> We'll be there around 17:30 tonight. Abbie's making peanut butter cookies.

> Need us to pick up anything at the store?

He'd sent a follow up text less than twenty minutes later.

Big Daddy Connor

> Don't tell me you forgot

"Damn it," I exclaimed, jumping to my feet. The kiss had completely derailed my ability to form a cohesive thought yesterday, and in the chaos, I had completely forgotten that Connor and Abbie were going to be joining us for dinner tonight. There were two more unread messages from Lucas, but I quickly decided I'd deal with them later.

I pulled on fresh clothes, brushed my teeth, and flew downstairs. Imogen was standing by the kitchen sink, a fresh cup of coffee in her hands. She was wearing a lilac dress that hugged her hips in a way that really should be illegal.

This was torture, I decided. Having the woman I craved standing in my kitchen, looking like she walked right out my dreams and into my house, and not being able to touch her was torture.

"Good morning?" Imogen said, glancing around, clearly confused as to why I was panting like I was being chased by a freaking bear.

"Abbie and Connor are coming over for dinner and I completely forgot," I said. Imogen let out a low whistle.

"Well, it's a good thing they're really important grant proposal people and not our best friends. Otherwise we'd really be in trouble."

"Ha," I said, rolling my eyes. "Very funny. I still don't have anything prepared."

Imogen rolled her eyes.

"We have plenty of food here. I'm sure between the two of us we can figure out something to feed the children."

I nodded. Between the two of us, we'd figure something out. Imogen didn't seem concerned, and I decided I wouldn't be either.

"I know we're still waiting to hear back from the interview committee, but I'd really like to grab a few more shots of the property. Your website is pretty good, but I'm working on updating some of the copy and images, so it all looks professional. Do you have any nature trails nearby?" Imogen asked. "We can showcase that as a potential photoshoot location for wedding and event photographers."

I nodded. "There's one just past the barn, actually."

"Let's go then, cowboy."

She really needed to stop calling me that, or I was going to be ruined forever.

Imogen was looking around with her camera in her hands, taking in the full effect of Winding Road in the daytime as we headed towards the barn. The venue had been mostly quiet since Abbie and Connor's wedding, save for a baby shower a few weeks ago. I'd be lying if I said I wasn't nervous about the barn becoming a money pit. So much of Connor's inheritance had gone into the renovations, and the last thing I wanted to do was shirk his gift by making a bad judgement call about the viability of the venue.

Imogen had faith that once we started advertising the space was open for booking, we'd see an increase in overall income. I could only hope she was right.

Believing in Imogen's vision for Winding Road's social media was how I ended up leaning against a tree with one arm above my head, looking forlornly into the distance.

"No one wants to see me like this," I countered, and Imogen shook her head fiercely.

"I promise you, Kam, people want to look."

I scrunched my eyebrows in confusion. Imogen waved me back into position, her face never leaving the viewfinder of her camera.

"Okay, now cross your arms over your chest and look towards me."

"You better promise me that you'll make Connor and Lucas take headshots like this."

"Quit your grumbling and smile."

"So now I'm smiling instead of doing the grumpy vet thing?"

Imogen sighed and held her camera in her right hand, putting her other hand on her hip.

"You are a grumpy vet. All three of you are," Imogen said. "It's part of your appeal. You just happen to hide it better than the other two. I also know you want to do everything you can to make Winding Road a smashing success, so put on your big boy pants and smile for the damn camera."

"Aye ma'am," I muttered, but did as she said. Imogen let out a surprised noise when I stuck my hands in my pockets and smiled.

"Why weren't you doing that the whole time?" Imogen exclaimed, flipping through the pictures. "You look so good here."

"Aw thanks Im," I said, puffing my chest out. Imogen shoulder checked my playfully, but I swore I caught a faint blush dotting her cheeks.

"You know what I meant," Imogen said.

I was about to ask her to clarify what exactly she meant when Imogen jumped back.

"Shit!" Imogen shouted, jumping out from the tree line right as a fuzzy white creature shot from the trees, darting across the road. I instinctively moved in front of her, holding my arm out defensively.

"Did you see that?" Imogen panted, looking around frantically.

"What?" I asked, my heart rate increasing.

"The dog!" Imogen waved frantically towards the dirt path. "It was this scrawny white dog. He ran across the trail right in front of me."

"Oh Jesus," I said, following Imogen down the trail, keeping my eyes peeled for any sign of the animal. Less than a minute later, the dog came from the tree line again, this time approaching us slowly, cautiously, limping slightly on his right side.

"Oh, you poor thing," Imogen said as she took a step closer. I swallowed down my anxiety about her approaching a random dog we found in the woods. There's no telling what kind of disease or pests might be on him.

"Your paw is red," Imogen said with a frown, kneeling down to take the dog's paw in her hands.

I pressed my lips together. "Does he have a collar?"

Imogen shook her head. "It doesn't look like it. Maybe he lost it."

To my complete and utter dismay, Imogen picked the dog up and turned towards me. The dog didn't so much as nip or growl at Imogen, but he was looking at me with malice in his eyes.

I was not a dog person. Everyone in my squad had joked it was my biggest red flag. Connor and Lucas knew this, but evidently I'd forgotten to tell Imogen this key piece of information somewhere along the way, because she continued to approach me with the feral ball of matted fur.

"We need to take him to the vet," Imogen said.

"What?" I said, blinking slowly, as if that would help me comprehend what was happening. "Imogen, we don't know anything about this dog. Please put him down."

"We are not abandoning this dog in the woods, Kameron Miller. He's scared and lost, and he needs help. Now let's go."

I groaned inwardly. My crush was growing. I didn't know how it was possible to have so much respect for someone who cared so deeply about everything—including animals—and also be frustrated by her sheer lack of self preservation.

"His owners could be out looking for him right now," I exclaimed, knowing I was fighting a losing battle. The Winding Road acreage extended several miles back from this spot, and if this dog had managed to get here even while injured, there's a good chance he'd been dumped near the property line. I doubted anyone was coming back for him.

I could practically see the bond forming between Imogen and the dog. Imogen scowled and turned her back towards me, adjusting her camera strap so she could cuddle the dog closer to her chest.

"Don't listen to him," Imogen practically cooed as she continued to check the dog over for injuries as we walked. "He's a grumpy old man."

"I'm not a fan of picking up random dogs we found in the freaking woods!"

Imogen just shook her head and kept walking towards the vehicles.

One very expensive trip to the emergency vet later, I was sitting at my kitchen table trying to figure out how my day had gone this far off the rails.

"What's got you all mopey?" Connor said.

"We have a dog now," I said, taking a swig of my non-alcoholic beer.

"A dog?" Lucas and Connor said in unison.

At that moment, Imogen returned from taking The Dog outside to pee in the backyard. Imogen squealed with glee as The Dog made a beeline straight for Connor and Lucas, and promptly set about sniffing the two of them like he worked for TSA.

"Oh my God," Connor murmured at the same time as Lucas said, "Oh, you mean a real dog?"

"Yes," Imogen said, still beside herself with joy. "And we need your help naming him."

"For the record, I voted against keeping the dog."

At that moment, Abbie appeared, carrying a tray covered in tin foil. She let out a gasp of sheer delight when she saw that said dog was nuzzling Imogen's leg. She immediately thrust the pan into Connor's hands before yelling, "You got a dog?"

Abbie leaned down to let him sniff her fingers, and he promptly decided she was a safe bet as well, rolling over so both women could give him belly rubs. Imogen's giggle did something to me, and I squashed it before I exposed my crush for what it was in front of all my friends.

"He's cute though," Lucas said, sitting on the floor in front of the couch, eagerly patting his thighs. The dog didn't so much as look in his direction. "Does he have a name?"

"Not yet," I muttered. "I wrote Dog on the vet paperwork."

"Very original," Lucas replied.

"I vote we name him Chesty," Connor said.

Abbie and Imogen both groaned.

"We are not naming the dog Chesty," Abbie said sternly.

"Why not?" Connor said, affronted. "You're telling me you found that dog in the woods, injured, and he pulled through? Chesty is a perfect name."

"Hell no," Lucas said, shaking his head. "You infantry guys name everything after Chesty Puller. Get a new bit. We already have a horse named Chesty, for God's sake."

Connor and I both launched into explanations of why Lucas was categorically incorrect, that Chesty Puller was indeed the most legendary Marine to ever serve, and that he held patron saint status among infantrymen for a reason. Lucas covered his ears and shook his head. At that moment, the dog jumped up and began sprinting around the room.

I groaned, knocking my head into the back of my chair.

"He has been doing this all day since the vet got that huge splinter out of his paw. He's supposed to be taking it easy, so he doesn't agitate his paw more," I said, glaring at the animal. The dog didn't seem to mind that he and I weren't best buddies yet, as he continued to run circles around all of us.

The dog weaved in and out of people's legs, much to the ladies' delight, before running headfirst into the open fridge door. Lucas cursed and glanced down. Right as he leaned down to make sure the dog was okay, the four-legged demon took off again, resuming his sprints like he hadn't just brained himself on a fridge door.

"Chill out, Basilone, damn."

Connor and I both turned towards Lucas, who was digging around in the fridge for a non-alcoholic beer. He slammed the fridge door shut, using the bottle opener on the counter to break the seal.

"What?" Lucas said after taking a swig.

"Basilone," I said, and Connor's smile widened. The dog continued to run circles around the living room before slowing down.

"Who is Basilone?" Abbie asked.

"John Basilone is to machine gunners what Chesty Puller is to infantrymen," Connor said.

"I'm not following," Imogen said. "Is this Marine Corps lore?"

"Something like that," was all I said, lest I open a can of worms.

"John Basilone fought at Guadalcanal," Lucas said. "He fought his way through hostile ground in order to resupply the machine gunners under his command. The man ran for days, weaving through the battlefield to ensure his guys had supplies and ammunition to keep up the fight. He was later killed in action at Iwo Jima."

"That was a surprisingly concise explanation," I said, giving him credit where credit is due.

"Unlike you Chesty fanboys, we know how to make our point."

"His nickname could be Bass," Connor said, scratching his chin.

Imogen clapped her hands in sheer delight as Bass finally settled at her feet.

"It's perfect," she crooned, and as much as I was decidedly not a dog person, seeing the joy on her face at the new addition to our chosen family had all manner of emotions mixing in my chest. "Welcome home, Bass."

Something twisted in my chest as I watched her. So rarely did Imogen find herself in a place where she could be unapologetically herself. Where she could embrace every-thing she loved and wear that love on her sleeve, un-abashed, unashamed. The knowledge that she had found that here, at Winding Road, in this farmhouse, in this space that we had cultivated so carefully, brought me a sense of pride I hadn't realized I could feel.

This felt different than receiving an email from one of the veterans we worked with saying that he had made amends with his family and was focusing on their sobriety. This felt more personal: it was deeper, I realized, because this was about Imogen.

This woman who I had so much respect for. This woman that I wanted to know, to cherish.

As if sensing my thoughts, Imogen looked up, her eyes searching mine out. Connor, Lucas, and Abbie were already digging into the casserole Abbie had made, and their con-versation focused on some drama in the country music world I wasn't well versed in.

Imogen held my gaze for a moment before she gave me a soft smile and mouthed "thank you."

God help me if my heart didn't crack right down the middle at how breathtaking it all was.

I wasn't a dog person, but I decided in that moment that I'd get her a dozen dogs, if she'd smile at me like that again.

Chapter Fifteen
Imogen

Watching Kameron slowly warm up to Bass was going to be my undoing.

I knew Kameron's reaction to finding Bass in the woods had nothing to do with the dog itself and everything to do with the fact that Kameron just wasn't a dog person.

Bass wasn't an "ankle biting" dog, as my grandmother would have called them. Bass was a sweet, gentle-hearted lap dog. He fit himself in amongst the five of us, as if he had always been part of our little family.

He loved to run around the farm, and at night, he tucked himself into his dog bed in the living room and slept all night.

I was lounging on the couch of the farmhouse, scrolling through emails after scheduling a few social media posts. I responded to a few basic inquiries, most of which was redirecting folks to the cohort application or our FAQ website page where they could get more information about the farm.

When a new email arrived from the official Warrior's Foundation address, I gasped out loud.

"Holy crap," I shouted, dropping my tablet like it burned me. Kameron whipped his head into the living room from the kitchen.

"What? What happened?"

I was still staring at the email on my upturned tablet when Kam came to stand over my shoulder.

"Winding Road has advanced to the last stage of the grant process," I said, still trying to wrap my head around it. "They want you to come present to the selection committee in person in Seattle next month."

I turned to face Kameron, unable to control my smile as it spread across my face. I grabbed both of his biceps—against my better judgment—and shook him gently, trying to break him out of the trance.

"Kam, you did it. Only three people made it to this stage. Your chances of getting this grant are high. Sky high, because you're amazing at rallying support, and Winding Road is—"

My rambling was thankfully cut short as Kameron stepped forward and picked me up, spinning me around while whispering "oh my God" over and over again. I let out a joyous laugh and squeezed him back, not wanting this moment to end.

Everything he had worked so hard for was coming together. Kameron's energy was infectious. There was no doubt in my mind that when Kameron got into that boardroom and made his presentation, the grant would be his.

Kam put me back down on the ground, but his hands didn't leave my hips.

"Oh," I whispered, staring into his eyes.

I was *helpless*. Absolutely freaking helpless every time this man looked at me with that level of devotion and care.

Which is why I couldn't be blamed for standing up on my tiptoes and kissing him.

Kam let out a sound of surprise, his lips parting on a gentle gasp as he wrapped his arms around my waist, pulling me in close. The gentle scratch of his beard against my jaw set my skin on fire. The push and pull of him, this connection between us, the delicate string that pulled us back to one another like moths to a flame.

It had never felt this good kissing someone. I didn't know a kiss stoke this kind of desire, to be utterly *consumed* by someone.

I never wanted it to stop.

But just a few seconds later, it did, and I found myself still staring, unable to stop myself. There was a flush high in his cheeks, and his eyes were dilated, entirely focused on me.

"Sorry," Kam said, his thumb still hovering over my pulse point. If I could feel my pulse hammering against my skin, I knew he could, too. I was surprised the sound of my heart racing wasn't audible in the space between us. "Got carried away."

"It's great news," I said, my voice still raspier than usual. "I don't mind. We should celebrate this."

Kameron let me go, and I felt the absence of his hands as an ache in my chest. That wasn't normal, right? It wasn't normal to miss someone who wasn't yours. Someone that you couldn't have because things would get messy.

Nope, I thought to myself. Not going there.

"I hope you weren't planning on quitting on me now that the renovations are done, because I'm going to need your help."

I shook my head gently, clearing all thoughts of my negative emotions away. I focused entirely on Kameron, who was reading over the forgotten email.

"They want a bunch of deliverables, mainly graphics about revenue and plans for the next five years," Kameron said.

"Well," I said, sitting down on the couch. "The good news is Winding Road hasn't been in operation long enough to need some of what they're asking for. And lucky for you, one assignment I've given myself over the last few weeks is to organize your shared drive. It might take a while to create the presentation, but it won't be difficult to do."

Kameron smacked a messy kiss on my cheek. I let out a noise of fake disgust, even though my stomach tumbled.

"We're going to need more coffee for this."

I made a promise. There would be no more relationships, because I couldn't trust myself to make the right choice.

It was the *only* promise I'd ever made to myself.

So why did I have this ache in my chest that only disappeared when Kameron's lips were on mine?

As I watched him retreat into the kitchen to brew us another pot of coffee, I realized that maybe the ache in my chest was the weight of the past holding me back.

Kameron returned with two cups of coffee, and I leaned forward to kiss his cheek gently.

"Thank you," I murmured, and I hope he understood all that I tried to convey, but couldn't find the words to speak aloud yet.

Kameron's answering smile told me he did.

Kameron video chatted Connor and Lucas to tell them the good news, and I spent most of the afternoon creating folders for each type of document we'd need. I sorted through everything from invoices to monthly bank statements and correspondence with previous cohorts. I went through our social media accounts and scoured the comments and direct messages for anything we could use as a personal anecdote, and sent messages to those individuals asking for permission to use their statements in our presentation.

It might have been a bit overboard, even for me, but I refused to give Kameron anything less than my best.

This was what we'd all been working towards so hard this spring and summer. If Winding Road could secure the Warrior's Grant, all of Kameron's grand plans for this land would come to fruition. Not only that, but they'd be well on their way to ensuring the long-term success of Winding Road with all the resources the Warrior's Foundation would provide for them.

It was a life-changing grant. For everyone involved with Winding Road, but also for the people that came here to get the help they so desperately needed.

By the time the evening rolled around, Lucas was back upstairs after a full day of farm work. We'd both spent most of the afternoon and evening hunched over our laptops, compiling notes and ideas into a shared document that had the basic outline for the presentation.

Kameron shut his laptop first, and I followed suit.

"Do you have plans tonight?" I blurted.

Kameron quirked an eyebrow. "If by plans you mean the fact that I planned to watch T.V. and goof off on the internet until I collapse, then yes, my evening is booked solid."

I looked down at my lap briefly. Was I really about to do this? It was hard enough for me to throw caution to the wind and stop overthinking for long enough to enjoy something, and what I wanted to do tonight involved more than just living in the moment.

It required vulnerability.

"Do you have plans?" he asked.

I have so, so many plans, I wanted to say.

But there was something I had to do first. If I was going to put my heart on the line, I needed Kameron to know the full story. There couldn't be any more secrets, no more closed doors or hiding from the memories.

"I want to tell you my story," I whispered. "But I need you to promise me that you won't pity me."

Kameron's eyes shone with understanding, and he reached for my hand.

"I don't pity you, Imogen. I never have."

"You're a good listener," I said, zipping the pendant of my necklace along its chain. It was a classic nervous habit I'd never been able to break.

"And that's a bad thing?"

I swallowed back a hysterical laugh. Was I really about to do this?

"It's not a bad thing. But it's not something I'm used to."

"Well, I've got all the fixings for burrito bowls," Kameron said, nodding his head toward the kitchen. "What do you say we fix dinner and talk?"

"Sounds good," I said. The act was innocuous enough; we'd shared dozens of dinners together. None of those dinners had come after a series of kisses, but it would be fine.

Kameron set about making the ground beef and I gathered the toppings, taking time to wash out Bass's water and food bowls before refilling both. Hopefully, he'd want to take a nap during dinner so Kam and I could talk in peace.

The scene was surprisingly domestic. I'd lived by myself for most of my adult life, save for the year I lived with Jacob. That year was anything but domestic bliss, so the ease with which Kam and I moved around each other in the kitchen took me by surprise in the best possible way.

We took our seats at the table, and I let out a long breath.

"Do you remember that night at the party, when Abbie made that joke about my chaotic bisexual energy?

Kam paused with his fork halfway to his mouth as he looked at me. My heart lurched in my chest.

"I just wanted to make sure you knew I'm bisexual. I like girls and guys. Everyone. All."

I might as well dig my own grave.

"I remember," he said. "I don't want to dismiss you sharing that with me, but I also want you to know it doesn't change anything."

I blinked.

"Did you think that would change something?" Kam said, inclining his head slightly.

"No," I said earnestly. "I just. . . . I don't advertise my sexuality, not because I'm not comfortable telling people, but because it's my life. I'm comfortable with who I am and I don't need to open myself up to unnecessary criticism or comments from people."

"Understandable," Kam said. "And if you told me because you're worried that your sexuality might interfere with a romantic relationship, I promise you it won't."

I smiled then. Kam coughed awkwardly as he realized what he said.

"Not saying we're entering a romantic relationship," he corrected. "But if you wanted to, it's a non-issue. I like you for who you are. That includes your past relationships and your sexuality."

He really, *really* needed to stop saying things like that before I fell head over heels in love with no way to dig myself out.

"Since you shared something with me," Kameron said after another bite of his dinner, "I'll share something with you. I don't want kids."

I startled. "I don't know why that surprises me."

Kameron shrugged. "I think many people our age want to do the whole family thing, and I can honestly say that life has never appealed to me. I love my job, and the work that we do here. Bringing a child into this world is something sacred, and I know myself well enough to know that it's not what I want. People have told me I'll change my mind, but I won't. I'm okay with the choice to be childfree."

"I'm the same," I said, trying not to sound too eager. "I decided kids wouldn't be in the cards for me a long time ago. And I'm very much okay with the idea of being Auntie Im."

Kameron chuckled. "How long do you think it'll be before we're visiting Connor and Abbie's little family?"

"I give it a year, tops. They're not going to waste anymore time."

"I hope so," Kameron said with a wide smile.

"The childfree conversation leads me to my last point," I said. I set my fork down and rubbed my sweaty hands along my thighs. "I'm not getting married again."

Kameron paused. If any of the three things we'd already talked about would be deal breakers, it was this one. I told myself it would be okay, even as I waited for the rejection.

"I want to find love," I murmured. "I hope I find someone I can share my life with in the way I deserve. But I can't tie myself to someone in that way again. It's not—it's not something I can do again."

Kameron's eyes softened.

"That's okay," he said quietly, reaching for my hand. "Honestly, marriage has always been a distant concept for me. Something I saw everyone around me doing, but something I couldn't quit envision for myself. For a long time that was because I'd convinced myself I'd never find someone who would love me unconditionally like that, but now. . ."

"Now?"

"Now there's someone in my life who I care deeply about, who doesn't want to get married," Kameron murmured, his eyes never leaving mine. "And it feels right."

I ducked my head, suddenly blinking back tears. There was something about Kameron's demeanor that stripped away all pretenses. He saw me as more than the sum of my past.

My past. The last and final piece of this conversation that needed to be had before we could entertain the notion of a relationship.

"What if we took an after-dinner walk?" Kam said.

I met his eyes once more, searching his expression for any hint that his offer might not be genuine.

"That would be good."

I had spent so much of today psyching myself up for this conversation. I'd drowned myself in prep work for Kam's presentation, but in the quiet moments, I'd snuck glances at him, taking in how adorably his nose scrunched when he was deep in focus.

I loved Lucas and Abbie, but I was tired of only having two people in the world I could go to about my problems. More than that, Kameron and I had gotten closer over the summer. Not just because of what happened at the docks or the living room, but because of all the nights we'd stayed up late talking.

And in all of those conversations, Kameron had given me so much of himself. From his frank conversations about his dad's suicide, to how hopeless he'd felt about being able to help his mom, Kameron had never been anything but open and honest with me.

Guarded, yes, but never dishonest.

I wanted to tell him my story. Not because I felt like I owed to him, after everything he'd shared with me, but because I wanted us to finally be on the same page.

Because if I was going to abandon the promise I made to myself, I needed to be damn sure that Kameron wasn't going to balk at my past. I needed to know beyond a shadow of a doubt that he wanted this, too. That he wanted me for all of me, bruised parts and all, the way I wanted him and everything he was.

Kameron extended a hand, and I took it gratefully, the cloth napkin across my lap cascading down to the floor as I stood to follow him out the front door.

As soon as we stepped into the cool spring night and I felt the mountain breeze tickle my skin, the ache in my chest eased.

"We always seem to end up here, don't we?" Kameron smiled, gesturing towards the pasture. I let out a quiet laugh.

"I guess we do."

I took a deep breath, wringing my hands together as we set off down the dirt path, slow and steady.

"I met Jacob Kilpatrick when I was thirteen years old."

I swallowed the lump that formed in my throat after saying his full name out loud.

"It was our eighth-grade year. His family had recently moved to Watford, and we ran into each other in the lunch line. Literally. He collided with me. I told him to watch where he was going, and then scampered away before he had time to formulate a response. I didn't talk to him again that year. And then we went to high school."

I gritted my teeth against the onslaught of memories, using the rhythmic pace of our walk to keep my focus on the story itself, and not the emotions attached to it.

"We didn't interact much our freshman year, beyond group projects and the occasional presentation. We didn't run in the same circles. I was the nerdy girl who always had her head stuck in a book, while Jacob was on track to become the first star quarterback in Watford history. He wanted to go pro, and everyone in town was convinced he'd get there one day."

I inhaled deeply, allowing the cool evening air and the smell of fresh pines to fill my lungs. Kameron was ever-present, unwavering, standing less than a foot away from me. I looked towards the night sky, smiling faintly at the beauty of the twinkling stars above. It was a stark contrast, the gorgeous navy of the night sky dotted with sparkling white, and the story I had yet to tell.

There's light in the darkness, I reminded myself. One just has to remember to find it.

"Jacob did not go pro. He realized that he didn't want to play football professionally. He wanted to serve his country. He shipped out for boot camp right after graduation. We'd been casually dating when he left—he was a year ahead of me in school, so I had just started my senior year when he graduated. I wrote him letters while he was gone, was there waiting for him with open arms when he got back to Watford on leave.

"It's all a bit ridiculous looking back. When he asked me to go to the courthouse with him and marry him, I didn't hesitate. I loved him. Or maybe," I sighed, shaking my head. "Maybe I just saw him as the most viable option to get away from Watford. Away from my parents. Regardless of why I said yes, we were married at the courthouse, and I was off to Camp Pendleton as soon as I graduated from high school."

I let out a long exhale, focusing my gaze on the stars above us.

"The first time Jacob Kilpatrick hit me was four months after our wedding day."

Kameron inhaled sharply, but didn't say a word. Abbie had been too shocked to say anything when I'd finally told her this part, but Kameron's reaction felt different. Kameron, I knew, was willing to raise all matter of hell for the people he cared about.

I knew without a doubt that I was towards the top of his list.

"He had barely been in the Marine Corps for a year. I dropped a glass while cleaning up from dinner, and it made a loud sound in the sink. I guess it triggered him. He didn't say a word to me that night. I didn't get an explanation or an apology or even an acknowledgement.

"The day after, he went to work, kissed me on the cheek and told me he loved me. I spent most of my day questioning whether I'd made the whole thing up. Jacob always said I had a crazy streak, and I wondered if it was true."

I chewed my thumbnail, feeling like a weight had been lifted off of me, knowing that I could speak freely to someone who wasn't Abbie about what that moment had been like. So why did it also feel like there was a boulder on my chest, squeezing every last breath from my lungs?

"That was the first time, but there were many, many times after that. You're not a stranger to domestic violence. You've probably worked with guys who were either the perpetrators or the victims of D.V., so I won't bore you with the details. I'm sure you can imagine."

Kameron had gone still as death beside me. The only signs of life around us with the soft whisper of grass as the gentle breeze rustled them. I pressed my fingers to my mouth, gathering the strength I had left to finish the rest of the story. It was important for Kameron to know this—not because he wanted the full story, but because I wanted him to know.

I wanted him to understand every time I flinched when he appeared unexpectedly, the reason why I ran from him at the dock the day we kissed.

It wasn't him I was running from. It was the memory of the last time I let a boy get close to me. It was the memory of every time my mother or her friends told me that a boy liked me when I came home crying, talking about how mean he was to me. It was the knowledge that I would always carry this with me. No matter how many therapists I saw, or how much time I spent in nature or with friends, I would never fully outrun the memory of Jacob and his abuse.

The physical scars had long since faded. It was the mental and emotional scars that would never fully close.

I couldn't tell Kameron all of that—not yet. But I could tell him how it ended.

"Everything came to a head at the Marine Corps ball that year. I had one too many glasses of wine, determined to have fun on the one night of the year I was allowed to. I still don't know what I did to trigger him that night, but he grabbed me by the elbow and led me to one of the dark corridors leading to the ballroom. He was damn near shouting at me, telling me how much of a slut I was, how I was making him look bad. It's funny, because he was far drunker than I was, but somehow I was the one making him look bad."

I let out a mirthless laugh.

"He was louder than he intended, because someone from his squad found us. That man saw Jacob pinning my wrist behind me. I don't know whether he saw the fear in my eyes or the bruises that already existed on my skin. It didn't matter, because he stepped in immediately, telling Jacob to back off and get some air. I never knew his name, but I never stopped being grateful. Jacob didn't come back to our hotel room that night. I felt bad about it at the time, but I've long since stopped being ashamed of the relief I felt whenever Jacob found a reason to avoid me."

"Please tell me that was the end of it."

I closed my eyes, taking a deep breath of fresh air into my lungs and holding it until my lungs began to burn.

"I wish it was," I whispered. I finally dared a glance at Kameron, who was staring straight ahead, his hands clasped together in a white-knuckled grip. "Hey."

He turned his head to look at me. I could tell by the look in his eyes he was furious, but I knew somehow that he wasn't furious at me. He was angry at Jacob, at the memory of him that lingered behind my eyes.

"You don't have to hear the rest," I whispered. "It's heavy stuff. I won't blame you for needing a break."

"You've carried this for years," Kameron said, swallowing audibly. "Let me carry some of this weight for you."

I let my hand drop from his face, reaching instead for his hand. He shuddered, but took it, linking our hands together. I didn't realize how much I'd needed that touch, that grounding presence, until I found myself leaning into his chest.

"I didn't see him much that week. Abbie and I texted sparsely, but I kept our conversations to a minimum. That was another thing that could trigger Jacob's jealousy—long phone calls or text message threads with people that weren't him."

"Abbie's your best friend," Kameron said, his body tense. I held him tighter, pressing my face into his shirt, allowing myself this moment of comfort.

He was clearly trying so hard to keep it together for my sake. He wanted this moment to be about me and not him, even if he was infuriated by what he was hearing.

"Two weeks after the ball, they were scheduled to go to the field, so I wasn't expecting to see him that night. When I got home from grocery shopping, I walked in the house to see Jacob sitting at the dining room table. I'd seen Jacob angry so many times. I'd seen him pissed beyond belief. But I'd never seen him so angry he was calm."

I shuddered and pulled away from Kameron's embrace. I wrapped my arms around myself, as if I could stop the cold dread sluicing through the very center of my being.

"Stop," Kameron murmured. "I can't—I want to know this, eventually. But I can't tonight. Because every part of my being wants to find this motherfucker and kill him for ever laying a hand on you."

Some of the tightness in my chest eased at his words.

Whether he asked me to stop for my sake or for his, I didn't know. I also didn't care. I'd spent enough time going over the events of that night in my head. I didn't need to do it with Kameron, too. We could pick this conversation up a different day.

"I think the craziest part about that night is that I still don't know what I did. That's the thing about abusive relationships—once you're out of one, you can spend hours ruminating over every little thing you did, trying to trace your actions to their reactions. I knew most of Jacob's triggers. I did everything in my power to avoid pissing him off. I permanently walked on eggshells around him, even in my own house, and yet when I think about that night, I'm at a loss. What had I done to deserve it?"

"Nothing," Kameron rasped. "You didn't do anything to deserve it."

Something broke in me as I looked at him, the stars twinkling above us.

"I know that now," I said, reaching for his hands. I interlocked our fingers once more, damning the consequences. He needed to feel grounded in the same way I did.

"Imogen," Kameron said. The way he whispered my name as if it was something holy, sacred, was my final undoing. I leaned into him fully, tilting my face towards his and pressing a featherlight kiss to his lips. It was barely there, a whisper, an echo of the fire that blazed between us on the dock that day.

"I can't pretend anymore," I whispered against his lips. "I can't pretend that I don't see you everywhere. That I don't want to feel you everywhere, too. I've thought about kissing you every single day since that day at the dock, and now that everything is out in the open between us, I don't want to run. I don't want to pretend like I don't want you."

Kameron pulled back the slightest fraction so he could look into my eyes.

"Am I dreaming?"

I let out a small laugh, holding his face in my hands, running my thumbs along the black beard growing there.

"Not dreaming," I murmured. "Let's head back."

Kameron's lips tilted up in a smirk.

"Surely you don't mean back to the farmhouse."

I shook my head.

"The tiny house, obviously."

Kameron narrowed his eyes briefly.

"You're going to have to tell me exactly what you want, Imogen."

My cheeks heated.

"I want you," I said quietly, running my hands up the length of his arms, "to stay the night with me."

"And do what, exactly?"

He leaned in, running his fingertips along the column of my throat, a feather-light touch that ended with him cupping my face.

"I'll tell you when we get there."

Kameron turned his face to the sky and let out that loud, thunderous laugh that made my insides melt.

"You and your secrets, Imogen Phillips."

I untangled myself from him, leaving only our hands intertwined, and pulled him towards the tiny house. I'd never been more grateful that the pasture wasn't far from the houses, because as soon as I pushed open the door of the tiny house, Kameron was there, sliding his hands up my arms and pulling my face towards his again. I hadn't realized we were moving backwards until my backside hit the counter, reality clicking into place as I pulled back, chest heaving and lips tingling.

"What about Bass?" I gasped as Kameron leaned down to press a kiss to my jaw, tracing the sensitive shell of my ear as he did so.

Kameron groaned, pressing his face into the column of my neck.

"Tell me you're not asking me about the damn dog when I'm *this* close to—"

"We can't abandon him," I said, cheeks flaming as I cut off whatever dirty talk was about to come out of his mouth.

Kameron pulled back to look at me, that fire still blazing in his eyes. His gaze sent a shiver down my spine.

"I gave him his nightly bone before we went on our walk, and he has a dog door," Kameron said, stepping back and undoing the top button of his shirt. My eyes tracked the movement before snapping back up to his. He paused at the second button, his eyes clearing for a moment as he looked at me. "Unless you mentioning the dog was a polite way to say you've changed your mind."

"Don't you dare leave," I said, grabbing two fistfuls of his shirt and pulling him to me once more, groaning at the feeling of his lips moving against mine. The kiss at the dock had been incredible, but nothing compared to the earth-shattering feeling of Kameron's full attention on me, devouring every breath and small noise like they were his life force.

It's too soon, the voice in the back of my head whispered. *It's too soon to feel something like this.*

But as Kameron's shirt fell to the floor and his fingertips traced the outsides of my thighs before lifting me onto the counter and stepping between my legs, I realized I didn't care. His lips found mine once more, and I wrapped my legs around his waist, keeping him as close as possible, letting myself fall into the feeling of him.

Chapter Sixteen

Imogen

Waking up next to Kameron felt like waking up in a liminal space. Somewhere between reality and a dream. His arm thrown over my waist, his face turned away from me, the sheets having shifted in the night to reveal the long, muscled planes of his back.

"It's nice to be the one being stared at for once."

Heat immediately rushed to my cheeks, and I bit down on my index finger to hide my smile.

"Sorry," I said somewhat sheepishly.

"Don't apologize," Kameron said, the sound muffled as he turned over to face me.

Kameron was devastating on a good day, but I decided this Kameron was my favorite. Black hair tousled from sleep, his beard illuminated by the early morning light filtering in from the skylight, blue eyes that sparkled in the dawn.

"It's nice to wake up next to you," he said, reaching for me. I propped my head up on my hand and extended my other to meet his, our fingers tangling together. My heart hammered in my chest, so full of life and light that I was worried I might explode.

Was this what it was supposed to feel like?

I quickly diverted my thoughts. Leave it to me to complicate a nice moment.

Even if it did feel like waking up to Kameron was inexplicably complicated.

"Did you think I'd be gone when you woke up?"

Kameron paused where his thumb was stroking over the back of my hand. I laid my head down on the pillow to be closer to him, throwing one of my legs over his, smiling when he untangled our fingers and pulled me closer.

"I really hoped you wouldn't be," Kam said.

"The thought didn't even cross my mind," I said honestly.

"It wouldn't have been the first time," Kam said with a weak smile.

"Well, they were idiots," I said, pressing the tip of my finger to his nose. He wrinkled his face.

"Was last night—"

"Perfect? Incredible? Earth shattering? All of the above."

Kameron let out a loud laugh, and I smiled even wider.

"Way to make a man feel proud," he said, eyes shining with something I couldn't place as he looked down at me. "But that's not what I was going to ask."

I held my breath for whatever question might come out of his mouth. I didn't expect this to be a one-night thing. Though, in retrospect, it probably would have been helpful to have that conversation before I had the best sex of my life. The best sex I would probably ever have.

My mind was in the gutter, and I didn't know how I would ever get it out, with the memories of last night now plaguing my every thought.

"What do you want?" Kam murmured, raising his right hand to my face. His thumb traced my lower lip, and my breath hitched.

"That's a complicated question," I said, scrambling for something to give this man that didn't involve a piece of my heart.

"Do you want to do this again?"

"Yes," I said, without hesitating. Kameron smirked.

"I knew it. You just want me for my body."

It wasn't a jab, but something about it made my skin crawl.

"No," I blurted. "I don't. That was the first time I'd—since him."

Kameron's eyes widened. "Really?"

"Yeah," I said, pressing a hand over my mouth to keep from laughing. "Sorry. I probably should have clarified that before."

Kameron still looked vaguely terrified, and I snuggled closer to him, so our faces were just inches apart. I kept my eyes downcast, allowing my fingers to idly trace patterns on his chest.

"What I want," I said, trying to keep this conversation from derailing entirely, "is to explore whatever this is. But I don't want the others to know yet. I have a hard time trusting my judgement in situations like this. I don't want other people in our space until we're in a good place."

The understatement of the century. I didn't trust my romantic judgement at all after the events of the last few years. I was notoriously terrible at reading people's signals. I much preferred data and numbers that could be quantified and organized. Romance and love and being vulnerable with another person was just about the messiest thing one could do. It was never simple, never easily quantified.

But if last night was any indication, I had a feeling the two of us could figure it out.

I hesitantly looked up to meet his eyes, surprised to find him staring back at me with a mix of awe and excitement.

"How does that sound?" I asked, running my fingers along his jaw. I was still trying to convince myself this was real.

"Only if you want to," Kameron said, his fingers tracing delicate patterns along my upper back. His touch sent a shiver down my spine.

"I think I want to," I said. Kameron paused.

"You think, or you know?"

"I don't know how to do this," I confessed, frustrated with myself.

"It's just you and me," Kameron said, kissing my forehead. "We get to make the rules here."

"I wouldn't know where to start," I said, laughing to mask the discomfort forming in my chest.

"How about we start with being honest to each other?"

I sat up in bed, clutching the sheet to my chest and giving Kameron a wry look.

"After last night, I'm not sure I have any secrets left."

Kameron smiled and leaned back, crossing his arms behind his head. His muscles flexed with the movement and I bit my lip.

"That's a good sign," Kameron said, smirking when my gaze met his again.

"Don't get smug," I warned, jabbing a finger into his chest. "The last thing we need is Lucas finding out about this."

"You're worried about Lucas? I'm worried about Abbie."

I shook my head, unable to stop the smile slowly spreading across my face.

"Abbie would be ecstatic. She's been dropping not-so-subtle hints ever since the festival last year. She wants us to get together. Lucas on the other hand. . . he might kill you."

Kameron rolled his eyes. "He wouldn't even try."

"Oh, let's make a bet," I said, amused.

Kameron leaned forward so our faces were only centimeters apart.

"Twenty bucks says I tell Lucas about us and all he does is make a sound of disgust."

I considered this for a moment, inclining my head towards him like I was going to seal the distance between us.

"My money's on Lucas kicking your ass into next week," I whispered, smacking a quick kiss to his lips before sliding off the bed and climbing down the ladder, headed for the bathroom.

Kameron's squawk of indignation had me laughing the entire way there.

After walking Bass in the morning and checking on things at the farm, we returned to Watford that afternoon. The remediation had taken longer than expected, and when Dillon had called me to say that everything was finished, he did have some other concerns to speak with me about. As we pulled into the gravel roundabout in front of the farmhouse, my stomach twisted with anxiety at the sight of Dillon's work truck still parked there. He came down the front steps and waved to us as he put another bag of tools and equipment into the tailgate.

All of the bliss from this morning was replaced by anxiety.

I still hadn't made a decision about the house.

We headed inside, and I was surprised by how normal the house looked. I didn't know why I was expecting it to look like a FEMA site.

"Hey Dillon," I said. "This is Kameron, my. . . friend."

I stumbled over the word and immediately felt my cheeks flush. The whole "not putting a label on it" thing felt good when we were in our tiny house bubble, but I had some work to do. I needed to be able to introduce Kameron as a friend without showing every sign of embarrassment possible.

"Nice to meet you," Kameron said, removing one of his hands from his pockets and extending it to Dillon to shake. The other man took it.

"Good to meet you," Dillon replied. "First off, the mold remediation was successful."

I let out a sigh of relief.

"That said, we discovered a few more issues that will need to be addressed," Dillon said. "I know you haven't decided whether to sell the house or stay, but either way, they'll need to be fixed."

He gestured for us to follow him, and for the next half hour, Dillon explained some issues they'd found in the walls. Everything from pipes that needed to be replaced, to electrical wiring that needed redoing, and even showed me several places on the outside of the house where some of the siding was rotting away.

"The house isn't in good shape," Dillon said honestly. "It goes well beyond the mold issue we found in the bathroom."

"What's a ballpark estimate to get this place into shape?"

"I'm not a realtor, but I can tell you that you're looking at a repair cost that's pushing six figures."

I rubbed a hand over my face, feeling slightly dizzy.

"And if I sold it as is?"

"Depends on whether you sold the land with the house," Dillon said. "The value of the farmland would most likely offset part of what you'd lose on the house. But again, I'm not a realtor. I can put you in touch with a company in Brighton if you need a recommendation."

"No, I can talk to Kelly," I said, knowing Kelly Sakis would have knowledge about how to sell a house like this. The fact that she was a Watford local also brought me comfort, because she would know how much this house meant to me.

"Sorry I don't have better news for you," Dillon said. "It's safe to stay here for now, but I urge you to get some of these structural repairs dealt with sooner rather than later."

"Thanks for everything," I said as Kameron and I walked Dillon to the front door. He waved before climbing into his work truck and setting off.

"Crap," I groaned, knocking my head back against the door immediately after closing it.

"Tea?" Kameron asked, pressing his lips to my forehead. I sighed into the touch, leaning into him.

"Please," I said, the sound muffled against the fabric of his shirt. He took my hand and pulled me towards the kitchen, putting water in the kettle and setting it on the stove.

"It feels like I'm stuck between the past and the future," I muttered as I took a seat at the dining room kitchen. "That doesn't make sense."

"It does," Kameron insisted, sitting down with me while we waited for the water to boil. "For so long, this place represented peace and comfort to you. It's where you grew up. And your Nana gave it to you after she passed. There's a lot of memory and emotion in these four walls. I'm sure the idea of giving it up is difficult."

I looked around at the familiar walls, the kitchen that I had painstakingly remodeled soon after I moved back to Watford. It was the first big home project I'd planned and completed. I loved baking; it brought me so much joy, and the previous kitchen couldn't hold up to how much time I spent there.

"I love this house," I murmured, meeting Kameron's eyes. "But I can't shake the feeling that. . ."

"What?" Kameron encouraged gently after I fell silent.

"It doesn't feel like home anymore," I whispered. Kameron's lips parted. I waited for the anxiety about throwing my feelings out into the open to crush me, but it didn't. Because this was Kameron. After everything we'd shared last night, there was little left to hide from him.

What's more, I realized, is that I didn't want to hide from him.

The kettle whistled and Kameron looked away. I let out a long breath as Kameron stood and made his way over to the stove to remove the kettle from heat.

"What are we in the mood for?" he said, opening the drawer full of every kind of tea one could hope to try.

"The stress relief one," I grumbled. Kameron chuckled but obliged me, placing some of the loose leaf tea into one of the silver strainers and bringing the steaming cup to me. I inhaled deeply and sighed.

"Thank you," I said. "For everything."

"I know that we both have a complicated history with dating," Kameron said, "but I do know that in most relationships, you don't need to thank the other person for making you tea."

I shook my head. "I'm not saying thank you out of obligation, I promise. I'm saying it because I'm grateful for you."

Kameron's features softened. "Then I'll accept it."

I rolled my eyes.

"So, what are we thinking?" Kameron said, gesturing to the living room to our left.

"I think I'm going to talk to Kelly," I said quietly. "I think it's time to let go."

As terrifying as the prospect was, I couldn't deny the way I'd outgrown this place.

"Okay," Kameron said, reaching for my hand and squeezing it gently. "Let's talk to Kelly."

The way Kameron so casually used terms like *we* and *let's* should have had me running for the hills.

Instead, it felt like the most natural thing in the world.

Chapter Seventeen

Kameron

Trying to explore a new romantic relationship while also trying to keep said relationship a secret from your best friends and coworkers was messy.

It was much harder than anticipated, trying to find time to whisk Imogen away. Connor was only at Winding Road on site a few times a week. Most of his work could be done from home, since we were gearing up for the next cohort. Imogen would be the one working from home, and Connor would be here with Lucas and I.

Imogen was also walking through the process of listing the farmhouse. After several conversations with Kelly about the reality of the house's condition and the value of her land, Imogen made the decision to sell.

I knew it wasn't an easy choice, but I couldn't deny how excited it made me. Imogen didn't know where she was going next, and it would most likely be months before she formally moved, but there was a good possibility she'd want to move here.

Add that to my rising anxiety about getting ready for the Warrior's Foundation presentation that was coming up in just a few short weeks, and I was drowning.

It was also getting difficult to keep the situation with my mother under wraps. All five of us had a lot going on, and the last thing I wanted to do was to stress my friends out with my crap.

I also realized that this would be one of the last opportunities for me to visit my mother before the next cohort began, because I was a terrible son, and still hadn't called Gail back to arrange a visit.

With things between Imogen and I so delicate and new, I was nervous to introduce her to this part of my life. Dementia was a heavy thing to walk through, and Imogen was someone I cared deeply about. I also knew Imogen's propensity to take things on where she shouldn't. I didn't want her to feel a sense of obligation to go with me.

And yet, when she approached me the next morning, wrapping her arms around my waist and tucking her face into my neck, the words "I need to tell you something" slipped out before I could hold them back.

Imogen turned to face me, her jaw set in a way that I recognized as a sign of her anxiety rising. The expression made my stomach flip.

"That came out weird," I said. "Sorry. I'm really anxious."

Imogen's face softened. "What's going on?"

"My mother. . ."

Crap. How was I supposed to tell her this? Would she be mad that I kept this from her despite my good intentions.

"My mother lives in a memory care facility in Laketon."

There. It was out there, and there was no taking it back. Imogen's face gave nothing away, and she gave me a subtle nod to continue as she turned towards the coffee machine to make her morning espresso.

"I got a call from the director a few weeks ago. She's not doing well."

Imogen's face fell. "I'm sorry, Kam."

"I want—I *need*—to go visit her. I don't know when things might progress. I'd like to have some memories of her, even if they're hard. I haven't visited her as often as I should have these last few years."

That was an understatement. In the same way that Connor ran from Watford without so much as a text to Abbie, I had run from my mother. I'd found her a place with Gail's facility, helped her move out and sell my childhood home, and then I'd hopped on a flight right back to Camp Pendleton. I hadn't stopped to consider every longstanding implication of her decline, and what that meant for our relationship.

My relationship with Lilliana had been complicated since my father's death. She'd walked through an unimaginable loss. As an adult, I had all the empathy in the world for her. As a teenager, I'd wish I could take that pain from her.

But in recent years, I'd walked the labyrinth of untangling that time in our lives, and realized that her actions had impacted my life in detrimental ways.

She'd been grieving, but I had been a child.

She had just lost her life partner, but I'd lost my father *and* my mother in one crushing blow.

"I'm happy to take things over here," Imogen said as she pressed the start button on the coffee machine. "Take as much time as you need."

I ran a hand through my hair, trying to silence the anxiety roaring within me.

"Will you come with me?"

Imogen's expression morphed into one of shock, though she smoothed it over quickly.

"You want me to go with you to visit your mom?"

Her tone wasn't accusatory, but her words still dug at some wounded part of me. As much as I poked fun at people like Connor and Lucas who kept their secrets protected, I'd always prided myself on being the one person who laid it all out on the field. I didn't hold things back.

Except for my parents. My father's death and my mother's subsequent illness created a gaping wound within me I knew would never fully heal. I was an open book about everything, except for them.

"Yes," I said, my voice rough under the weight of the emotion clogging my throat. "I need you with me."

My feelings for Imogen transcended want. They had for a long time. I was slowly getting to a place where I could admit that if she walked away now, I would crumble. If she met my mother and decided afterwards that all of this was too much, I wouldn't be the same.

I couldn't go back to a life without her in it. It felt insane to say that aloud, considering she and I hadn't known each other that long. We existed in each other's orbits, twining around each other through the festival last year and Imogen's work at Winding Road these last few months.

The thought of losing her made me dizzy.

"Hey," Imogen said, and even though she wasn't a mind reader, she abandoned the coffee machine and strode over to me, holding my face in her gentle hands. I slid my hands up her arms to cover her hands with mine. "I can tell when you're going to the bad place, you know."

I know you can, I wanted to say. You know me too damn well, and it's terrifying.

As if sensing my discomfort, Bass came running through the back door, rubbing against Imogen's legs first before coming to sit between mine. I shook my head fondly at the creature. We'd gotten off to a rocky start, but I couldn't deny how much his presence had grown on me.

"Of course I'll go with you to visit your mom," Imogen said, stroking my cheeks with her thumbs. "I'm honored that you asked."

"Sorry for ambushing you with that," I murmured, focusing on her eyes as the tightness in my chest eased.

"You don't need to apologize, cowboy," Imogen said, and my heart squeezed anew at the term of endearment that was reserved exclusively for her. "Whatever hesitation you sensed on my part had nothing to do with you asking me to come with you, and everything with my own anxiety about meeting your mom."

"She'll love you," I said, even though my mind sped through the various ways this visit could go poorly. If my mother was lucid, things would be fine—great, even. And if she didn't remember who I was, there was little chance she'd be okay meeting someone new. I also knew that there was a very good chance Lilliana would say something outrageous to Imogen if she wasn't fully lucid, and that was the most terrifying possibility out of the three.

"When do you want to go?"

"I just need to call Gail," I said, glancing at the clock. It was only 9 a.m. "It's been a few weeks since she asked me to visit."

"I can be ready in thirty minutes," Imogen said, pressing a gentle kiss to my lips. "I'll get dressed."

She slipped away from me, and I felt the absence of her hands on me like the warmth from a campfire suddenly extinguished. I leaned back against the counter, gripping the edges as I stared at the floor.

"Crap," I muttered. "Crap."

Even while regretting every single one of my life choices up to this point, I pulled out my phone and dialed Gail. To no one's surprise, she was ecstatic to finally hear from me and said we were more than welcome to come to Laketon today to see her.

"She'll be overjoyed to see you," Gail said. "I'll let the nurses know to expect you and your companion."

I didn't miss the way Gail's tone changed around the word companion. I couldn't help the small smile that spread across my face. Gail was the director of my mother's facility, yes, but she had also been a dear friend to her for most of my childhood, especially after my father died.

Imogen came through the front door, having walked down to the tiny house to grab her things. She wore a solid green dress that went just past her knees, a cream cardigan, and her favorite pair of sandals.

"Is this okay?" she asked, throwing her hands out and doing a quick twirl.

"You're beautiful," I said, walking towards her. Her face lit up at the praise, and I didn't hesitate in sliding my hands around her waist and pressing my lips to hers. She melted into me, her hands wrapping around my neck and pulling our bodies closer together. I would never stop wanting this—her curls tickling the sides of my face, the small, breathless noise she made when I deepened the kiss.

When we finally pulled away, her eyes were glassy, her chest rising and falling with the effort of calming her breath. The sight did something to me that felt a lot like a four letter word I didn't dare name, even in my mind.

"You're bad for my health, Kameron Miller," Imogen murmured, and I chuckled, not missing the way her eyes widened and her lips parted at the rough sound.

"You find it irresistible," I said. Imogen shook her head as she pushed past me. She grabbed my wallet off the kitchen counter, tossing it to me. I caught it and leaned back against the door as I watched her grab two to-go cups from the cabinet, the creamer from the fridge, and begin making our cups of coffee. I checked Bass's food and water one last time and closed the dog door. The last thing we needed was Bass terrorizing the chickens while no one was here to supervise him.

I couldn't stop the image that flashed through my mind, of the two of us being like this all the time. No more sneaking off to the tiny house, no more raucous roommates, just the two of us in our little domestic bubble where the rest of the world couldn't touch us. When she returned to my side with two steaming tumblers of coffee, I leaned down for another kiss, which she quickly dodged.

"No sir," Imogen said teasingly. "If you don't get your head out of the gutter, we aren't making it to Laketon before lunchtime."

The words sobered me, and I drew in a deep breath, settling for a forehead kiss instead. Imogen made a small noise of surprise and I tucked that piece of information away for later.

As I opened the door to lead us down the steps and towards my truck, I reminded myself that I could do this. With Imogen by my side, I felt like I could do anything.

As I slid into the driver's seat and Imogen took up residence beside me, I realized it was the incessant pull between us, whatever force kept bringing us back together, that had us both risking far more than we'd originally bargained for.

Chapter Eighteen
Imogen

Kameron's truck was exactly how I'd imagined it. A new-ish Toyota Tundra, recently vacuumed, with un-scratched leather seats. If I opened the glove box, I was sure I'd find it meticulously organized.

If there was one thing I'd learned about Kameron in the last few weeks, it was that he could be a very organized person, when it came to certain things. He liked to think he was a chaotic, messy person, but he wasn't really. He was prone to being overwhelmed just like the rest of us.

"How far is Laketon from here?"

"About an hour and a half," Kameron said as we began rumbling down the gravel road.

"That's not bad," I said, settling into the comfortable seat. I reached behind me to dig my Kindle out of my bag, just in case I needed it. I didn't want to read right away, which I almost always did on longer car trips where I wasn't driving. I wanted to talk to Kam.

"It's mostly back roads until we get closer to Laketon, so it's scenic, too."

"How often have you made the drive?"

Kameron's jaw twitched, and I knew I'd asked the wrong question.

"Not as much as I should have," Kameron murmured. I turned towards him, resting my head against the headrest and giving him my full attention.

"Tell me about her," I asked gently. "I know you're anxious about this, and if it would help, I'd like to know more about her."

"What do you want to know?" Kameron asked, and I recognized the question for what it was. This was another thing I understood about Kameron Miller: open-ended questions were the opposite of helpful when he was struggling with his anxiety.

"What did she do for work?"

"Before she met my dad, she worked in nursing," Kameron said. "That's how they met, actually. At the hospital. My dad was a paramedic at the time and she was working in the emergency room. It was always funny to ask them how they met, because depending on who you asked, you'd get a different story."

I giggled, thinking that was one of the cutest things I'd ever heard. I also remembered Kameron talking about how his parents had a love story for the ages.

"How would your Dad tell it?"

Kameron's expression softened as he dove into the waves of memory. "He would tell everyone he knew that the first time he'd dropped off a patient at that hospital, he was a brand new paramedic. Had no idea what he was doing. When he rolled in the patient, my mom was working at the nurse's station, and she immediately started asking him what the hell he was doing. He could barely stutter out a reason for being there. She rolled her eyes and took over the patient's care, and he walked back out to the ambulance, completely besotted."

"And how does she tell it?" I asked, enraptured.

"Apparently, she has no memory of their first meeting, though she did admit it was possible they arrived during a rush and she simply wasn't paying that close attention to who was arriving. Several months went by, and my dad went back to school to continue his education and training. He wanted to work his way through the ranks and try out new roles within the world of emergency medicine. My mom continued working in the emergency room, and one night, they met again. But this time, my dad had been hitting the gym, had more job experience, and was more confident in himself."

"Let me guess," I said, my grin widening as I anticipated the ending. "She looked up from the nurse's station, was struck by your father's killer jawline, and immediately fell head over heels in love with him."

"Something like that," Kameron said, laughing. "He asked her out on a date that day, and the rest is pretty much history."

"That's a beautiful story," I said wistfully. "I always love hearing first date stories from couples who have been together forever."

"Yeah," Kameron murmured. "I always thought they'd be together forever."

I pressed my lips together, letting the silence descend between us. I stared at Kameron's side profile, fascinated by the way the early morning sun filtered through the window and highlighted the contours of his face. I wanted to reach out and stroke his cheek, but I didn't want him to run us off the road from shock.

"I'll never ask you directly," I murmured, "but if you ever want to talk about your Dad, you can."

"My Dad was the best person I knew," Kameron said, tightening his grip on the steering wheel. "He was the class clown, and always wanted to make people smile. He'd bend over backward and crack a hundred different jokes, spend hours researching and orchestrating the most elaborate pranks just to make us smile. He helped me with my homework, even when he was half asleep and barely coherent after working a twelve hour night shift."

Kameron inhaled deeply.

"I never saw my parents fight. I'm sure they had their disagreements, but I only ever saw them look at each other with the purest love. When they found out Lilliana was pregnant, she decided she wanted to be a stay at home mom, and my dad was overjoyed. This was his dream. A loving marriage, a kid on the way, and a job he loved doing. They had it all."

Kameron paused again, and I felt the weight of what he was about to reveal before the words formed fully.

"My dad spent his entire life working in emergency medicine. Two decades of his life devoted to saving people, to healing others, to being the person people cling to on the worst day of their life. And every day, when he came home, he opened his arms wide and hugged my mom and I. He showed up for everyone, no matter how tired or worn down he was. He buried his trauma and experiences so deeply they were embedded in his very bones. He never let the cracks show. And it killed him.

"My dad took his own life, but I'll never believe it was because he wanted to leave my mother and I. She never let me read the note he left, but I know it was because of his demons. Looking back, I can see my father's evolution with a clarity I didn't have at thirteen. I can see the slump of his shoulders, the lines in his face, the ghosts in his eyes. I can see how he gave so much of himself to everyone and didn't reserve an ounce of that care for himself."

"And that's why you created Winding Road," I said, not surprised to feel tears welling in my eyes. "To show others how important it is to let those experiences out with people who understand what you've gone through."

"Yes," Kameron said, wiping a hand off on his jeans. I reached for his hand without thinking, linking our fingers together. Kameron let out a shuddering breath, and my chest tightened with how badly I wanted to hug him. To pull him close to me and let him know how grateful I was that he shared this with me.

"I'm in awe of you," I whispered. Kameron briefly glanced towards me, and his expression sent my heart tumbling. It was only a second, maybe two, but the admiration and gratitude in his eyes had me ready to abandon every stupid rule I'd ever made about relationships away and claim this man as mine forever.

"You're the first person I've ever told all of that to," Kameron said, shrugging his shoulders as if it was no big deal. "Connor and Lucas know the basics, but I've tried to keep my past out of my friendships. I prefer it that way."

"I get it," I murmured. Because I did. Despite what plenty of people on the internet think, you didn't have to reveal every part of your trauma to people, even the people you're closest to. Some things can remain unsaid or unexplained. It doesn't make you a liar, or a bad person—it makes you someone who has experienced life-altering trauma, and everyone has their own ways of dealing with things.

"Even Lucas doesn't know the full story with Jacob," I said, turning my attention from Kameron and back to the highway before us. "He knows the general idea of what happened, but he's my friend. And I wasn't ready to share that with him. I don't know if I'll ever want to, to be honest."

"And it would be fine if you never did," Kameron said softly. "For the record, I'm not entirely sure why I told you. It just felt right to do it."

My chest filled with an emotion I dared not name. "I feel the same," I said, though the words sounded strangled.

What lay between Kameron and I was becoming increasingly difficult to navigate. We had explored the romantic side of things, without labeling what we had, and without revealing said situation to our closest friends. It felt deceptive and like the right thing to do all at the same time. It was confusing and anxiety-inducing and also thrilling. It was a jumble of immense highs and deep lows and the rightness of it was getting harder to ignore.

Kameron squeezed my fingers, bringing me back to the present moment.

We didn't say anything else for the rest of the drive.

Everything that might still need to be said was communicated through touch alone.

We arrived at the nursing home, and I was taken aback by how nice it was. I had an image in my mind of nursing homes being places of grief and suffering, but there were flowers in every color of the rainbow blossoming in window planters, and gorgeous flowering shrubs lining the walkway. It was lovely and inviting in a way I hadn't expected it to be.

"Ready?" I asked Kameron as he put the truck in park and turned off the ignition.

"As I'll ever be," he said. We exited the truck, and I followed him up the path to the front door. Once buzzed in, we checked in at the front desk and received our badges.

"Kameron Miller," a warm, gentle voice called out. Kameron turned towards the hallway and waved at the middle-aged blonde woman walking towards us. "It's been far too long."

The woman pulled him into a hug before turning her attention to me. "You must be the assistant."

She waggled her eyebrows, much to Kam's chagrin, and I couldn't help but smile.

"I'm Imogen," I said, extending a hand towards her. "Imogen Phillips."

To my surprise, she took my hand and then pulled me in for a hug. I let out an "oof" of surprise but returned the hug. If Kameron was comfortable with her, I felt like I could be, too. She released me and I tucked a stray curl behind my ear, suddenly feeling out of place.

"This is Gail," Kameron said with a gentle smile. "She's the director here, and a longtime family friend."

"It's wonderful to meet you," I said. Gail gestured for the two of us to follow her.

"She's in the common room with some of the other residents," Gail said.

"How has she been today?" Kameron asked as we walked.

Gail smiled as she looked back over her shoulder. "She's having a good morning. She wasn't fully lucid upon waking, but I wouldn't be surprised if your presence helped her return to the present moment."

We rounded a corner, and my breath caught at the wall of windows overlooking the mountainside. There were several tables and various seating arrangements. Some had board games or books laid out. We approached a woman sitting in the chair overlooking the mountains beyond. Kameron's breath hitched, and I knew that this woman was Lilliana.

"Hi, Mom," Kameron said gently. The woman didn't turn to face him, but I could have sworn her posture relaxed slightly at Kameron's presence.

Kameron took the empty seat beside Lilliana. I hung back, perfectly happy to stand nearby as emotional support for Kameron.

"It's Kameron," he said. "I'm going to sit with you for a bit."

"That's fine," Lilliana said, turning to face him. "You look familiar."

Kameron's expression shuttered briefly, but he kept a gentle smile on his face. Gail squeezed my shoulder gently, and I nearly jumped out of my skin, having forgotten she was there.

"I need to head back to my office for a meeting, but let me know if you need anything," Gail said. "I hope your visit goes well. It was lovely to meet you, Imogen. Kam is a wonderful man, and I'm happy he's found someone to share his time with."

"Oh, we're not—"

But Gail was already walking away, and whatever retort I had died on my lips. I had a suspicion denying my growing feelings for Kameron would have been futile anyway, based on how protective Gail seemed of him.

I turned my attention to Kameron and his mom, watching as Lilliana reached out a hand to stroke his face gently. My heart leaped as her eyes widened.

"Kameron," she repeated, her eyes scanning his face. "My boy. You're my boy."

Kameron's lips trembled as he smiled. "Hey, Mom."

"My goodness," Lilliana said, sitting back in her chair and looking Kameron over. She shook her head a few times, as if trying to clear the last of the fog from her head. "You've been in the gym."

Kameron let out a wet laugh and nodded.

"I try to stay in shape."

"I remember," Lilliana murmured. "Do you still have the farm?"

"Yes," Kameron said, and my heart sped up. She was here with him. I'd hoped she would be lucid even for a few minutes of our visit, and she was. "Things are going really well. Amazing, actually."

"And your friends?"

"Connor and Lucas still work with me," Kameron said. "Connor got married recently, to a girl from his hometown that he's loved his entire life."

"That sounds dreamy," Lilliana said, smiling wistfully. "I remember those early days of love. How perfect everything seemed. How easy it was to believe the dark days would never come."

The expression on Kameron's face crushed something inside me.

"I don't want to talk about that," Lilliana said quickly, shaking her head almost violently. "I don't want to."

"That's okay," Kameron said, and I saw the fear flash in his eyes as he reached out for his mom's hand. He squeezed it gently. "We don't need to talk about that."

Lilliana nodded, but I could tell she was rattled. Even the memory of her husband was enough to shake her.

I realized then why Kameron was so anxious about this. His anxiety went well beyond simply visiting his mom—it was how earth-shattering the loss of his father was for her. He had said it in so many words, that his father's death broke his mother. He'd told me in detail about the ugly days after the funeral, where Lilliana wasn't able to properly care for him.

"That girl is staring at us," Lilliana whispered, and I pressed a hand to my mouth to stifle a mortified laugh. Kameron glanced over his shoulder and his beautiful eyes met mine.

"Well, this is actually a girl I wanted you to meet," Kameron said, gesturing for me to step closer.

Lilliana's eyes widened in sheer delight. "Kameron Miller, are you bringing a girl home?"

Kameron's face flushed. "Mom."

"Forgive me," Lilliana said, tilting her head in my direction. "This is the first time he's ever brought a girl home to me, so you'll have to excuse my shock."

It suddenly felt like the floor was going to fall out from under me.

"Surely this isn't the first time," I said.

"It is," they replied simultaneously. Kameron grimaced while Lilliana was positively delighted.

"Come, sit and talk with me for a minute," Lilliana said. "Kameron, might you fetch us both a cup of tea?"

Kameron glanced between us briefly. "Are you sure that's—"

"Oh, for the love of everything, go," Lilliana said. "Before this ends."

Kameron's jaw dropped slightly as I inhaled sharply.

"You know," I said as I sat down. "About your memory."

I winced, feeling like an idiot for saying that. I wasn't well versed in dementia care, but I did know that each case was different. Some people were aware of their gaps in memory, but others weren't. As things progressed, most individuals lost track of their memory gaps, until lucidity became increasingly rare.

"Memory is a strange thing," Lilliana said. "It's strange what we remember, and what we don't. But let's not talk about me. Let's talk about you."

"My name is Imogen," I said, wringing my hands together nervously. "I live in Watford, a small town close to Winding Road."

"Watford, Watford. . . I'm sure I've been that way before," Lilliana said.

"I met Kameron during the Founder's Festival last year. The Winding Road nonprofit was the main sponsor, so Kameron and I worked together to help the festival organizer with everything. Earlier this year, he offered me a job to help with some administrative work on the farm."

"Oh," Lilliana said, raising her eyebrows to show her intrigue. "And when did you figure out that my son was the most handsome young man you'd ever laid eyes on?"

I choked on a laugh right as Kameron re-appeared with two cups of tea. He handed one to each of us before pulling one of the smaller chairs over to our little corner and settling in behind us.

"I'm not sure," I said honestly. When had I first realized that I was interested in Kameron? I'd known from the beginning that he was attractive—there was no way for anyone in their right mind to deny that—but I couldn't place exactly when I'd started wanting more.

"Don't torture her, Mom," Kameron teased.

"Well, what about you? When did you first realize?"

"There was a party last fall. The five of us were meeting each other for the first time, and when Imogen walked in the door. . . I couldn't take my eyes off of her."

My lips parted as my heart galloped in my freaking chest. I remembered that night, but that was also the *first* time we'd met.

The knowledge that Kameron's eyes had been on me from that very first night had butterflies fluttering to life in my stomach.

"How romantic," Lilliana said. "It reminds me of. . . of. . ."

Kameron leaned forward, concern etched into the lines of his face as Lilliana turned away from him.

"You need to go," Lilliana said, and a lead ball of emotion quickly replaced the butterflies in my stomach. "Thank you for coming, but you need to go. Please. I can't talk about it. I don't want to talk about it."

I quickly waved the nurse standing near the entrance to the common room over, sensing that things were about to go south.

"I love you, Mom. It's okay."

Lilliana looked back at him, but gone was the delight that had been there just minutes before. She looked hollow now. A ghost of who she'd been.

Kameron stood to leave, and I placed my teacup on the table before chasing after him. We took off our guest badges and signed out before Kameron practically ran out of the door into the parking lot.

"Kam, wait," I said, chasing after him. When he turned around, devastation written into his features, I did the only thing I could—wrapped my arms around his neck and hugged him tightly.

He clung to me, and his shoulders shook with the force of his emotions. I buried my face in his neck, inhaling the earthy scent of his cologne.

"I'm here," I whispered. "I'm not leaving."

I felt the truth of it in my bones. I wouldn't leave him. Even if our romantic feelings for one another faded, even if whatever relationship we had between us fizzled out, I wanted him in my life.

Whatever that looked like.

"Let's go home," I murmured. "A snuggle with Bass will do you good."

Kameron sniffled and pulled away from me, wiping his red cheeks and shaking out his shoulders. He turned his face away from me, and I linked our hands together, a silent reassurance that he didn't need to turn away from me.

"Let's go home."

Chapter Nineteen
Kameron

I shoved down on the "for sale" sign one last time before wiping my hands on my jeans and stepping away to admire my handiwork. It was several days after our trip to Laketon to visit Lilliana, and I'd never been more grateful for the distraction of being busy. Imogen had gone back and forth on whether to list the house for sale.

After many conversations with Abbie and Kelly Sakis, she'd finally made the choice to list the house and see what happened. If she didn't find a buyer she felt comfortable selling to, she'd keep it. And if they found a buyer, she would figure out what her next steps would be.

Kelly had suggested adding the sign, not because there was a ton of foot traffic, but because it would look nice for listing pictures.

Imogen hugged herself tightly as she looked at the sign. Her cheeks reddened, and I sensed her tears were about to fall long before they actually did.

I walked over to her, replacing her arms with mine as I hugged her tightly.

"You did good."

Imogen nodded and sniffled, rubbing her nose with the back of her hand.

"I know, this is the most attractive thing you've ever seen," Imogen said, laughing through her cries. "God, I'm a mess."

I pulled back from the hug so I could hold her face in my hands and smiled.

"You're always beautiful," I said, and meant it. Imogen rolled her eyes, but I saw the gratitude shining in them before she turned away.

"Why is it that men always say that?" Imogen said, sticking her hands in the pocket of her jeans before striding back up the driveway.

Because this is what it's like to be in love, I wanted to say. *You're always beautiful because I care for you so deeply that the rest of the world fades away when I look at you.*

I might be losing my mind under the pressure coming at me from a thousand different directions, but my feelings for Imogen were the one thing that hadn't faded in the last few weeks.

The late afternoon sun descended over the mountains as we returned to the farmhouse. Imogen headed towards the kitchen to stir the slow cooker chili we planned on having for dinner, and I grabbed my laptop from my bag so we could continue working on the presentation. I'd pulled the financial information from our various bank accounts and she'd been the one to put all of that information into beautiful graphs that elevated our slides, and would make it easier for me to explain during the presentation.

A few hours later, dusk fell over the landscape, and I closed my laptop. Imogen stretched her arms out above her head and sighed contentedly before walking to the slow cooker to examine the chili. I followed her, placing my hands on her hips. It had been hours of working, and while I was focused on crafting the presentation that would make or break my career, I was also distracted.

"It needs another fifteen minutes," Imogen said, sprinkling some shredded cheese on top.

"I can think of several things we could do to pass the time," I said, moving closer to her. I slid my hands down her sides, painstakingly dragging my callouses down the sensitive skin, looping my thumbs in the belt loops of her jeans to pull her back against me. She let out a needy sound that sent a bolt of desire through me.

Crazy. She made me crazy with want. Having her this close to me was dizzying. There had been so many moments the last few weeks where I'd had to slow down and pinch myself. That I wasn't dreaming.

I leaned down to press a kiss to her shoulder, and she shuddered.

"Your mind is permanently in the gutter."

"When you're around, yes," I said. "Can't blame a man."

Imogen made me reckless. Reckless in a way that meant I would go to her come hell or high water if she asked me to.

She turned around in my arms, her eyes meeting mine.

"We need to finalize things for the grant presentation," Imogen said. I said nothing, tilting her face away from me so I could press a light kiss to her jaw. She ran her hands up and down my chest before settling on my forearms.

"You are so distracting," she muttered, and I kissed her. I kissed her like it was the only thing I wanted to do, and in so many ways, it was. I'd felt happier and more fulfilled over the last several weeks than I could remember being in recent history.

And it wasn't because of the Warrior's Grant, or the strides Imogen was making with getting the word out about Winding Road.

It was because of *her*. Because of what we had between us.

I'd known I wanted more the first night we'd slept together, where I'd woken up to her beside me, looking at me like I was the only person in the freaking world. What had started as a shameless crush was now something real. Something I obsessed over.

I was falling. And that terrified me. Not because I feared my feelings, but because I knew Imogen feared hers.

Not that I blamed her. Escaping an abusive relationship like the one she had with Jacob left scars on a person. I didn't expect her to easily bounce back from that.

There were some scars that never healed completely. Out of everyone in the world, I knew that intimately, as she did.

"Oh Imogennnn!" came a sing-song voice from the front foyer. Imogen and I jumped apart like we'd been burned. Imogen swore loudly, pressing a hand to her chest.

"Who is that?" I whisper-yelled. Imogen's eyes were wide as she looked from the dining room table set for two back to me. Bass's head popped up from where he was sleeping on the couch. He bared his teeth in a snarl before he began barking in earnest.

"It's Kevin," she whispered back, and my heart sank.

"What the hell is Kevin doing here?" I asked incredulously. "Did he say anything to you about coming over tonight?"

"No, he didn't," Imogen said, and there was genuine fear in her eyes. "I have no idea why he's here, but—"

Kevin Phillips rounded the corner, looking frazzled himself. I didn't know the kid well, but I could tell by the fake smile on his face that something was wrong. He mouthed *I'm sorry* to Imogen before stepping to the side. A middle aged White woman stood in the entrance to Imogen's kitchen, looking entirely displeased by what she saw. Her white button up was cleanly pressed without a wrinkle in sight, and she was wearing dress slacks.

Honest to God business professional slacks, in the heat of summer.

"You have a dog now?" Kevin said, cocking his head in disbelief as his eyes landed on the animal behind him. Bass was still primed and ready on the couch, showing his teeth towards Kevin and the mystery woman.

My fingers twitched at my sides as I regarded the woman. I wanted to step in front of Imogen to shield her from whatever terrible energy was spilling out from this woman, or put my arm around her shoulders and drag her close to me.

"Well, this is quite a surprise. The last time I found you in a compromising position in this kitchen, it was a woman between your legs."

And I knew in that moment that this woman was Imogen's mother.

Chapter Twenty

Imogen

This was my worst nightmare come to life.

Kevin snapped at our mother, immediately jumping to my defense, but Carmen held up a hand with a firm shake of her hand.

"And you are?" she sneered at Kameron. My chest caved in even further.

"I'm Kameron. Imogen and I work together at Winding Road."

Carmen's eyes darkened, and I wanted to shake Kameron for revealing that piece of information that my mother would almost certainly latch onto. This was what she did; she twisted people's words and extrapolated them into something they weren't. She would weave all manner of stories in her head about Kameron and I. I desperately cycled through scenarios in my mind, trying to find one solution where I could pull Kameron to the side and tell him to keep his damn mouth shut.

There was no winning an argument with my mother. Based on the hatred simmering in her eyes as she looked at me, I knew it wouldn't matter what I said or did tonight. She'd already made up her mind.

"I seem to recall an earlier conversation with Kevin this summer. You wouldn't be Kameron Miller, the executive director of the Winding Road nonprofit? Surely someone in a management position such as yourself wouldn't willingly enter into a relationship with someone who reports to you."

Kameron stiffened by my side, and that was the moment I knew our perfect bubble we'd been gliding in the last few weeks was well and truly popped.

"It's a bit more complicated than that, ma'am."

"It always is."

There was no mistaking my mother's distaste, and I had never wanted to escape a situation more in my life. I dared a glance at Kevin, who was looking at his shoes, shaking his head, as if trying to comprehend the gravity of this situation.

My mother had barely addressed me during the entire conversation, and yet she still made me feel like I was the smallest person alive.

"We were just about to have dinner," Kameron said, giving my mom a polite smile. "You could join us?"

Oh, hell no.

"Actually," Kevin stepped in, finally finding his courage, "I know it's terribly rude to ask you to adjust your plans, but we were hoping to have dinner as a family."

"No," I said, shaking my head. "Mom, I'm sorry, but we already have plans. You should have called. I would have been more than happy to make time for us to do the whole happy family thing."

I was wrong to make a sarcastic remark based on the way my mother scoffed.

"You can see this man anytime you very well please, given the fact that you work together." She pressed her lips together in a thin line. "I'm only here for a few days. I would hope you'd prioritize family time over your current fling. What with everything that happened the last time you isolated yourself from your family and focused solely on your partner."

Kameron's body stilled completely, and red clouded my vision.

It had been well over a year since I'd had to see my mother in person. One blissful year of being able to ignore her texts and calls, all of the attempts she made to get me to see her side or believe that she truly was just looking out for me. A year of crying to my therapist and trying to forget about the way she cast me aside when she learned of my return to Watford and subsequent divorce. My mother was not a religious woman. She didn't shame me because she thought some religious text somewhere frowned upon divorce. It was more cut and dry than that.

She looked down on me because she'd always wanted to wield her power over me. I was the outcast middle child, always caught in the tension. Cassie was the perfect oldest daughter, always overachieving at everything she did, and Kevin was their only boy, so he was instantly viewed as the golden child and didn't have to lift so much as a finger.

"I can't do this," I muttered. I could feel my brain shutting down the longer Carmen stared at me. I turned to Kameron as tears welled in my eyes. "Can I walk you out?"

Kameron didn't need to see this. I didn't want him to see this part of my life. My mother being in town had the potential to ruin everything. This thing with Kameron was new and delicate, and I didn't want my mother's darkness anywhere near it. She had a way of poisoning beautiful things; especially things that outshined her.

Kameron, thankfully, didn't push me on this. He put his hand in the small of my back, and I wanted to cry. How like Kameron to want to comfort me when it was my fault that our evening was ruined.

I opened the front door and stepped out onto the porch, eager for Kameron to get in his truck and leave.

"Im, talk to me. I'm here for you," Kameron said when we paused at his truck.

"Please go," I said, my eyes welling with tears, unable to meet his gaze.

"No," Kameron said, shaking his head. He opened the door and threw his laptop bag into his passenger seat. He reached for my hands, giving me a reassuring squeeze. "There's no way in hell I'm leaving you here with her, not after everything she said."

I didn't have the heart to tell him that my mother's display in the kitchen barely scratched the surface of what she was capable of.

The front door banged open, and Kevin appeared.

"I'm so sorry Imogen. She showed up at the store, and I didn't know what to do."

"So you brought her here for me to deal with?" I said, unable to stop the bite in my tone. "Nice one, Kevin."

"I didn't mean—"

"We'll talk about this later," I said, shaking my head. I didn't have the energy to debate with Kevin about why bringing our mother here was the worst possible solution to the problem. There was no circumstance where I was the solution to my mother's emotional problems. If anything, I was the one person in the world that would make things far worse.

"I'm not leaving," Kam said, doubling down. "I'm happy to sit on the porch and let the three of you have a conversation, but I'm not leaving you alone here."

"I'll stay with her tonight," Kevin said, wrapping an arm around my shoulders.

"But—"

"Go," I shouted, cutting off Kameron's protest as I pressed the heels of my palms to my eyes. I couldn't do this with him right now. This was the problem with letting myself get tangled up in Kameron—he was light. He was good. He didn't need this crap right now, not when he was so close to securing a life-changing grant for Winding Road, something that would allow him to continue to spread that light into the world.

"I have a lot of respect for you, Kam, and I know you mean well, but this is a family thing. Your presence here will not be helpful. I can't manage my mom, Imogen, and your emotions about how Mom treats her. Let me handle this tonight. Okay?"

I finally mustered enough courage to meet Kameron's eyes. Never had I seen such sorrow, such pain on his face than in this moment.

As if my asking him to leave had cut deeper than I realized.

The minute dinner was over, I practically sprinted for the master bedroom and shut the door. I washed my face, scrubbing until my cheeks were raw, as if it would help ease the sting of my mother's words. Kevin had tried his best to keep the conversation light and unrelated to anything important, but my mother, true to her nature, somehow swung the conversation back in her favor anytime we strayed too far.

I threw my phone on the bed in frustration, sitting down on the edge of the mattress and grabbing two fistfuls of my hair. I let out a silent scream of rage. I was furious. I was beyond pissed that I was having what had promised to be a beautiful night with someone I cared for ripped away and replaced with dealing with my narcissistic mother instead.

I sat there for a long time, alternating between biting my fingernails and rubbing my temples to ease some of the ache throbbing there.

With shaking hands, I eventually reached for my phone, unsurprised to see two text messages from Kameron there.

God, I felt terrible that our night had ended this way. Nothing about this situation was fair. I knew Carmen had a narcissistic streak, but showing up unannounced and demanding that everyone change their plans to accommodate her was a new low, even by her standards.

Kam

I'm so sorry this is happening. Call me tonight?

I'm here for you.

I typed out a quick reply.

Me

I'm sorry our evening got highjacked because of family drama. I'll call you soon.

I navigated to my contacts, my finger hovering over my sister's number.

Throughout the dinner conversation, I couldn't shake the suspicion that Cassie might have had an inkling about my mother's visit. The way my mother talked about Cassie suggested she had seen her more recently than I previously believed.

I hit the call button and prepared myself for the worst.

"Hello, Cassie Phillips speaking."

"Did you know she was coming back here?"

There was a long pause. The damning silence told me everything I needed to know.

"Why," I whispered. "You know how awful she is to me and you couldn't find two minutes in your day to pick up the phone and give me a head's up that she would be here?"

"I didn't know for sure," Cassie exclaimed. "I didn't want you to panic over something that might not happen. She was in Seattle a few weeks ago. Said that she'd had an awakening or whatever about her relationship with her kids. She wanted to talk, make amends."

"And you believed her?"

Cassie sighed heavily, and I tightened my grip on the phone.

"She's our mom, Imogen. We went to dinner together and talked things over. Our relationship isn't magically perfect again."

"She is horrible, Cassie," I said. "You know this. You were there. Not that you ever did anything about it, because you were always the golden child, but you know firsthand what she's capable of when she's angry."

"Like I said," Cassie said, voice clipped, "I'm not discounting the mistakes she's made. I know your relationship has never been the best, but she's our mom. I know it might not be complicated for you, Imogen, but it is for me."

I wanted to curl up into a ball and never leave my room again. It was so like Cassie to do this—to defend Carmen, to try and insulate herself against the way our mother lashed out emotionally.

Cassie was always the favorite, with her honor roll grades and high-powered career aspirations. Kevin was my parents' only son. Everyone had their place in my mother's grand plan for her picture perfect family. If there's one thing I knew my mother loved without a doubt, it was the perfectly curated corporate image of her family. People loved supporting a family-owned business, even if she never deigned to visit us more than once or twice a year. There were no birthday or holiday cards.

There was only crap like this, where Carmen showed up with no regard for what other people might have going on. Hell, she didn't even have the decency to respect the fact that this was my house now, and had been for years. She walked in here like she owned the place, and expected me to change my evening plans to accommodate her.

I was exhausted. I'd worked so hard to put distance between myself and my parents these last few years. But somehow, they managed to keep a grip on my life. It was foolish to forget that.

"I don't want to hear from you again," I murmured. Cassie inhaled sharply and said my name, but I quickly cut her off. "I really thought our relationship would improve once you were out of Watford. You always hated it here, and I foolishly thought that maybe you'd wake up when you made it big, that you'd be able to see that I never needed you to be perfect in the way mom and dad did. I never wanted anything from you but your presence in my life. I wanted a sister. I wanted a friend. And you fought it every step of the damn way."

Cassie said nothing, and for once, I was glad for the silence. It felt like there was ice forming on my heart, in my veins. I felt numb in a way I hadn't in a very long time.

"Bye, Cassie. I hope you find whatever it is you're looking for."

I hung up and blocked her number. It wasn't the most mature thing I'd ever done in my life, but in this moment, I didn't care. I had something good. I was falling in love with a kind man, a good man. A man who cooked me dinner and flirted with me and made me smile and laugh like it was his paid job. A man who texted me to make sure I was okay.

It was like my family could sense when things were going well for me. It's like they knew I finally had something for myself, that I was finally enjoying the success I'd worked so damn hard for, and it didn't matter.

How much more of this could I take?

Hadn't I suffered enough?

Those thoughts did nothing to ease the ache in my chest.

Chapter Twenty-One
Imogen

I walked into Blackbeard's the next morning with my head held high. Carmen had asked me to join her for coffee this morning, and I begrudgingly agreed. I still didn't have a clue why my mother was in Watford, and I really didn't care to know.

I was just grateful she didn't spend the night at the farmhouse. There was a last-minute cancellation at the campsite, and Kevin had driven her to her cabin, saying he'd drive her into town tomorrow for our coffee meet up and any other activities she wanted to take part in.

The only reason I was even entertaining this conversation with my mother was out of a misplaced sense of duty to give my family every chance I could to right these wrongs.

"Hello," I said, sliding into the seat across from her. "Did you order already?"

"I did," Carmen said, folding her hands in her lap. "Thank you for meeting me."

"I'm here," I said, not taking the bait. I scanned the QR code on the menu to order my coffee. Scrolling through the menu on my phone also made a great excuse for why I wasn't looking her in the eyes. "What did you want to talk about?"

"I'm sorry, Imogen."

I was momentarily stunned. Out of all the things I'd expected to come out of my mom's mouth during this conversation, an apology was not one of them.

"Um. . . okay," I said, shifting uncomfortably in my seat as I placed my order for my usual oat milk latte and cheddar scone.

One thing I realized about my mother was that she always had an angle, and it was always a self-indulgent one. My mother didn't do anything in this world that didn't protect her standing or advance that standing.

"How are things at the farm?" Carmen asked, flashing me an awkward, tight smile that had me cringing a little from second hand embarrassment. I knew she wasn't talking about the homestead.

"Winding Road has several businesses all housed in the same place. I'm actually handling more of the administrative tasks for the non-profit. Lucas, Kameron's close friend, mostly handles the farm and for-profit side of things."

My mother let out a disinterested hum, and my shoulders tensed.

"Administrative work?"

I clenched my jaw. "Yeah. I've been revamping their website with pictures I've taken around the property. I'm also in charge of their social media. We're trying to expand our reach, since the new barn venue just opened up. We're trying to get our name out there. So far it's going well. We've had several inquiries for weddings in the next year."

"That sounds right up your alley."

A blonde woman I didn't recognize arrived with our drinks and food, and I was grateful to have something else to do with my hands.

"Wow, that was almost a compliment," I said, taking a sip of my coffee. My mother sighed, putting her face in her hands.

"Come on, Imogen, I'm trying here."

"Let's cut the crap, Mom, shall we?" I said, tired of playing the small talk game. I didn't want to be here any longer than I had to be. "Tell me why you're really here."

"I wanted to see my children," she huffed. "Why does that make me a criminal?"

Here we go.

"It doesn't make you a criminal, but it does make me question your intentions. The last time we spoke. . ."

A lump formed in my throat as I recalled her words. Carmen's eyes flashed with something that looked like regret.

"I'm more sorry than you can understand about the things I said on the phone that day. When Abbie called to say you were back in Watford, and without Jacob, I. . . granted, assumed the worst."

I scoffed.

"What you actually assumed was that your no-good daughter had cheated on her husband with another woman," I said.

My bisexuality was not something I advertised. Not because of the people in Watford, or because of the biphobia in the media, but because I knew myself better than anyone else. I didn't need to advertise my sexuality because it was mine. It wasn't up to anyone else, and I didn't need other people's input into it. I knew who I was.

Now it was my mother's turn to shift uncomfortably.

"You can't blame me for suspecting that something like that might have occurred," my mom said, and it felt like she slapped me across the face. "Especially after the string of girls you dated in high school."

She spat the word girls as if it was something dirty, something to look down upon.

This is how it had always been with my mother. My mother would never dare to look me in the eyes and spew anything outright hateful, but she would toe the line of disrespect. She walked right up to the edge of too far and hovered there. The only thing that gave away her distaste for my dating history was her facial expressions and the tone of her voice.

I'd heard far worse from her as a teenager.

But after everything that had gone down with Jacob, after everything that man put me through, looking at this woman, entertaining her thinly veiled vitriol, made me sick.

"Jacob almost killed me that night," I said, quietly seething. All of that anger and frustration I'd tried to bury came bubbling back up to the surface as I looked at my mother, the one person in the world who was supposed to love and protect me, the one person who looked at me and saw a problem child. A mistake. The lowest of the low. "Did

Abbie tell you that? Did you even try to listen to what she had to say?"

The tendon in my right elbow ached, as if remembering the distant echoes of an injury long healed. I instinctively wrapped my arm around myself, cradling my elbow, protecting myself from whatever blow came next.

Carmen at least had the decency to look pained.

"I didn't—when she called, your father was in the middle of signing a massive contract, and our attention was elsewhere. I *am* sorry, Imogen, that we didn't stop to understand."

Oh, my father. As little as I'd seen my mother in the years since they'd left Watford to build a shinier, bigger life in Los Angeles, I hadn't seen my father in person once.

All's well that ends well. My father and I were never close. That had been my choice. Cassie, Kevin and I were trophies to him, rather than children. We were to be seen and not heard, constantly carted off to booster events and town council meetings, showed off wherever and whenever it was necessary for my father to be seen as successful.

I blamed my father for shaping my mom into the woman she was now. I blamed him for never answering my questions about his side of the family. My Nana had reached out many times to try to connect me with my Black relatives, and he'd shut her down every time without fail.

All my life, I'd heard stories about their great love story, how the great Grant Phillips had come to town, invested an obscene amount of money into Watford's infrastructure, and gave the town the push it needed to become the bustling small town it is today. He swept Carmen off her feet; or so they told me. She was head over heels for him. But neither one of them were cut out to be parents in the way the three of us needed.

"I'm sorry," Carmen repeated, reaching for my hand. I jerked away, ashamed to find that tears were stinging my eyes.

"You keep saying that. But you can't actually believe that showing back up in Watford unannounced and saying 'I'm sorry' without any meaning is going to help us have a relationship," I said. It took everything in me not to let my face fall and to keep my expression neutral.

I silently chided myself for letting myself get wrapped up in the delusional idea that Cassie had been right. Somehow, I'd been willing to let bygones be bygones, if my mother could produce even a scrap of evidence that she'd done the internal work to heal our relationship.

Hell, when I'd walked in and seen her sitting at this booth by herself, looking so painfully out of place in a town she used to know so well, I had pity for her.

It was all an act. Just like it always was. This little tour she was doing with her children wasn't about us at all. It wasn't about celebrating our accomplishments or fixing the mistakes of the past.

It was about drumming up sympathy points among the people she hurt the most.

My father might have given my mother the life she always dreamed of as a small town girl—the fancy galas, and more money than she could ever hope to earn on her own as an actress. She'd thrown all of her dreams out the window in exchange for security in a man who had swept through town when she was barely nineteen. She'd become what he wanted, and left everything else behind.

My Nana had been heartbroken. Carmen's decision to leave Watford had devastated her, and yet she'd stepped up to take care of her grandkids when my mother decided the Los Angeles spotlight wasn't something she wanted for her children.

Watford was a safe place for us, but not for our mother. Watford was good enough for us, but not for her. My Nana had never gotten over it, even though she put everything she had into ensuring we had a beautiful childhood. Our mother visited every month, but never for long, always citing a new initiative or opportunity.

"Do you know why Kevin stayed in Watford when you left for L.A.?" I asked quietly.

Carmen shook her head. "I assumed it was because he wanted to tie up loose ends. I figured the two of you would say your goodbyes."

"It's because he finally had the chance to breathe without you and Dad breathing down his neck," I snapped. "It was because he was exhausted, being your prized show horse. The two of you only ever saw him as your male heir, like it's not the 21st fucking century where people don't give a crap who takes over the family business."

"Don't speak to me like that," Carmen said sternly, shoving a finger in my face. "I'm taking a lot from you right now, Imogen, hoping we can work past this."

"Did you and Cassie have a conversation about how difficult it is to grow up biracial in a small town?" I said. As much as I didn't want to bring this up with her, I needed to. I needed her to hear it from me.

"We were raised in a small town that is predominately White, and our *parents'* actions actively prevented us from being in touch with our Black relatives. We were raised almost entirely in White spaces, and as much as Nana loved and cared for us, we were kids who deserved to know our family. Our *entire* family. Do you even have a concept of what that was like for us?"

Carmen's face fell. For once, she had nothing to say.

Whatever was left of my resolve dissipated.

There was no salvaging this.

"I'm leaving," I said, sliding my coffee mug towards the center of the table and rising to stand. "I'm done with this."

"Imogen, don't walk away from me," Carmen said, snagging my wrist when I tried to walk by.

I snatched my arm back.

"What?" I said, exasperated.

"I heard you're selling the farmhouse."

The hair on the back of my neck stood up as I looked back to my mother, unsure of what she would say next.

"I am," I said. "It's time for me to head down a new path."

"Hm."

Carmen's distaste was palpable, but I couldn't bring myself to care.

My grandmother had been more of a mother to me than Carmen was. She had given me the farmhouse because she knew out of everyone, I was the most likely to need it. I had needed it, but I had also cherished it. I cherished my memories with her and with my friends within those four walls.

"I don't give a damn what you think about me, or my life," I said. Carmen was rattled in a way I'd never seen before. For a minute, she almost looked scared. Something about it empowered me to make this moment count, because I knew I wouldn't have this conversation again.

"I don't want to hear from you," I said. "I don't want to talk to you, I don't want to see your face, and I don't want anything to do with you. Don't call, Carmen. I mean it."

I left my mother there, staring disbelievingly into her coffee cup. I knew as truly as I knew my name that I would never speak to her again. And my life would be better for it.

Chapter Twenty-Two
Kameron

I hadn't heard from Imogen in over a day.

I constantly checked my phone, staring at the text message she sent saying she would call me. On some level, I could recognize that it was silly and juvenile to expect her to call me back quickly. We were both adults, and Imogen was clearly not expecting to be ambushed by her mother in the way she was that night.

She had every right to want some time and space for herself to work through things.

But as someone who cared for her, it was damn hard to sit by the phone and wait for her to come to me.

Which is exactly how I found myself at Watley's diner, finishing up a delicious meal of chicken and waffles. It had become a minor obsession of mine in the months since I'd visited Watford that first time. Connor convinced me to try it, because I'd been burned before. Comfort food was only comfort food if it was done right.

And Lonnie Watley knew good and well what he was doing with these. I was grateful for whatever stroke of fate made Lonnie switch his allegiance from the east coast to the west coast.

I was halfway through my meal, scrolling through articles, when a woman approached my table. At first, I didn't look up, hoping that she would move along.

"Hi," she said. I looked up. She had long blonde hair and striking blue eyes, and carried herself with an easy grace.

"Sorry?" I asked, patting my mouth with my napkin. She smiled.

"You're one of Connor and Abbie's friends, right?"

"Yes," I said slowly, still not understanding. Outside of my little circle of friends, I didn't know many people in Watford, and I didn't particularly care to.

The woman smiled. "I'm Skye."

"Hi, Skye," I said, my brain finally catching up. "I'm assuming you work here?"

"Oh Lord no," she said, smiling. "I work at Blackbeard's with Phillipa and Kyrie."

"Ah," I said. "So, what brings you here?"

Skye flushed a little at that, and I realized my mistake before she even opened her mouth.

"I'm sorry," I said, trying to cut her off as nicely as possible. "I don't want you to get the wrong impression. I'm seeing someone."

Skye, to her credit, didn't balk. She simply shrugged and let out a small sigh.

"You miss one hundred percent of the shots you don't take," she said, flipping her blonde hair over one shoulder. I let out a small laugh.

"I say that all the time. And I'm flattered, really, it's just. . ."

"You're seeing someone else," Skye said, raising her eyebrows suggestively.

"Something like that," I said. "It was nice to meet you, though."

"I'm sure I'll see you around," Skye said, giving me another small smile before heading towards the door. She opened the door to leave, and a man shuffled in after her, sliding past her.

"Oh, excuse me," she said before stepping out onto the street.

I looked up to meet Lucas's steely gaze. *Crap.*

"What was that?"

"She wanted to introduce herself," I said. "I didn't hit on her, if that's what you're asking."

Things with Lucas had been tense lately. Between the stress of his long and seemingly unending divorce from his wife and my stress over the Warrior's Grant, we bickered more than we got along. I also knew good and damn well that Lucas suspected things had escalated between Imogen and I. He was fiercely protective over her, and most days I was grateful for that, but today, my patience was already thin as ice.

"Just feels weird to see you talking with another chick when Imogen's mom is back in town."

I glared at him.

"Don't insinuate that I'm not doing anything to support her."

"Yeah," Lucas said, stroking his chin in mock contemplation. "I heard from Kevin that you were at her house the night Carmen showed up."

Damn Kevin. Out of all the people to catch Imogen and I on a compromising position, he was not the person I'd have picked. He didn't have the discernment for what should and should not be shared with other people, which meant I needed to tread carefully and figure out what Lucas knew before I spoke.

"I was," I replied curtly. "Imogen asked me to leave, so I did."

"Why were you at her house?"

I scoffed and set my fork down. So much for enjoying the rest of my meal in peace.

"We were working on the grant presentation, Lucas, just like we have been for the last three weeks. We're getting down to the wire. We need every minute we can get to prepare. And why the hell are you standing there lecturing me about what I'm doing, when you're running off to Seattle every week without so much as a word?"

Lucas pressed his lips into a tight line, and I barreled on.

"Look, dude, I don't know what the hell is up with your ex-wife. Frankly, I don't think I need to know the full story. But don't start treating the people around you like shit. If she was really that awful, the way most of us think she was, the best payback you could ever give her is to rise above it. Take the high road and all that. But at the bare minimum, don't take your crap out on other people. Got it?"

Lucas blew out a long breath.

"Yeah, alright."

I nodded in acknowledgement. "We're here for you. But don't come in here guns blazing like we're your enemy. You know I'm here if you want to talk things out."

"I know," Lucas sighed. "It's just ugly. I never wanted to be in this position. Having this entire process drug out while she drains me of everything I have is a reminder of how bad I got my heart broken. It's pretty ridiculous, and I don't enjoy talking about it."

"Getting your heart broken isn't ridiculous."

Lucas gave me a wry smile. "No. But making a series of bad choices while trying to prevent the inevitable is."

A pang of sympathy struck me as I looked at Lucas. He hid things behind a suave, humorous personality most of the time. He was a man most people looked at and made an immediate judgment on, without looking behind the curtain to see the kind of man he truly was. But really, he just wanted love like the rest of us.

Whatever his ex-wife had done, it had messed him up badly. I had my suspicions, but I also knew better than to push him on this. Lucas would come to me when he was ready to talk.

That's how it had always been between us.

"Anyway," Lucas said, shaking his head as if to clear his thoughts. "I thought we could go to the Roadhouse for a few hours. It's been a long time since I played a game of pool against a formidable opponent."

I laughed. "You would consider me a formidable pool opponent? I'm honored, Morales."

Lucas waved a hand dismissively. "Yeah, well, I can't ask Connor, because he won't set foot in the place unless he's contractually obligated. So you're the only one left."

I considered this for a moment and then shrugged.

I could use the distraction.

I should have known that Lucas was harboring a secret skill set: the ability to wipe the floor with me when it came to pool.

I groaned in frustration as he landed yet another perfect hit, the blue '2' ball landing in the corner pocket with ease.

"Don't be mad, get good," Lucas teased, and I rounded the table, attempting to line up another shot.

"The last time I played pool was in the barracks," I said, pulling the cue back before tapping it forward lightly. The angle was good, but I didn't put enough power behind it, and the ball stalled out just before it landed. I cursed under my breath.

"You're a little rusty," Lucas said, brushing past me to line up his shot. I had half a mind to call it, knowing it would tick Lucas off. He only had two more balls to land, and this game would be his. Just as Lucas was lining up his next shot, he looked past me over the pool table.

"Do you know that guy?" he asked, voice low so just the two of us could hear.

I turned to look at the guy in question. He was a newcomer to the bar, still hovering near the doorway a few feet away. Definitely current or former military, with the way he was standing.

"No, I don't."

I was immediately on edge. The guy was fidgety, looking around like he didn't know where he was, scanning the patrons as if searching for someone in particular. His behavior was way outside of the baseline, even for a place like the Roadhouse. I was immediately cautious.

"Let's keep an eye on him," I told Lucas, who nodded in agreement. We continued our game of pool. Lucas won, and the guy eventually took a seat at the bar. He was still glancing over his shoulder, occasionally taking out his phone to flip through messages, but at least he wasn't making it everyone else's problem.

One of the men at the bar turned to face him, surprised etched into his features. Before I could make a full assessment, the man shook his head, and then returned to his beer.

There was definitely something shifty about the guy, but I couldn't put my finger on it. Lucas and I retired to the bar to get ourselves some water, allowing the people in line to have a turn at the table. The guy gave me a once over.

I turned to face the man then. I wasn't usually confrontational, but I was getting annoyed with how this man seemed to be laser focused on me.

"Do I know you?"

The man shrugged and slouched back on his stool, sticking his hands in his pockets.

"No. But you know Imogen Phillips, so I'm sure you've heard plenty about me."

Slowly, the pieces of the puzzle snapped into place.

"What the hell are you doing here?" Connor's voice rang out, and everyone, including the bartenders, paused, waiting for the blow. I hadn't seen him come in.

My gaze snapped to Connor's as he walked towards us, anger burning in his expression. Abbie wasn't far behind, and her gaze was stormy, too. Connor kept Abbie behind him, one arm thrown out in front of her protectively. The man regarded Connor briefly, giving him a mocking wave before he turned back to me, a faint sneer twisting his lips.

"I'm Jacob. Nice to meet you."

Someone else came in behind Connor and Abbie, but I wasn't paying attention.

Instead, I turned to Jacob, and lunged for him.

Chapter Twenty-Three
Imogen

T he best place for a girl to get some peace and quiet was at Forest Grove Books.

Mari always welcomed me with open arms, and today was no different. I strolled through the doors after the conversation with my mother, inhaling the deep and grounding scent of faded paperback pages and the new summer candles on display. I waved hello to Mari, who was working behind the check-out desk, before making a beeline for the thriller section.

I had been so stuck on romance for the last couple of months and had barely ventured outside the genre, but after everything that had gone down with my parents and Kameron I needed an escape. Reading a domestic thriller about other people's screwed up lives seemed like a great way to get out of my head for a bit.

I settled for a romantic suspense novel, because I was still a romance girl at heart, and took a seat on one of the green velvet loveseats at the front of the store. Greystone, Mari's cat and the unofficial mascot for the bookstore, came to sit at her perch beneath my feet.

A few minutes later, Mari came by to give me some tea.

"Oh, you didn't have to do that," I said. Mari just gave me a smile.

"For one of my best customers, it's only fair. How are you doing, Imogen?"

I turned to look at the older woman and just shrugged my shoulders.

"Same old, same old."

"Have you heard from your family recently?"

I pressed my lips into a thin line. Of course Mari would know that my mother was back in town. I honestly didn't know if my mother had come in loud and obnoxious, wanting everyone to know that the great Carmen Phillips was back in town so that she could shove her so-called success in everybody's face, or if she had kept a mostly low profile.

People definitely saw us that day at Blackbeard's Coffee, but other than that, I didn't know much about what my mother was up to now that she was back in town. But I knew how people in Watford talked.

"Has she been by to speak with you?" I asked.

Mari shook her head. "Good Lord, no, she wouldn't put herself in the line of fire like that."

I let out a surprised laugh. "You two didn't end things on good terms?"

Mari frowned.

"It's safe to say that many women have found solace in the aisles of Forest Grove over the years, including your mother."

My jaw dropped open. Out of all the stories I'd heard about my mother over the years, I never imagined that she came here often.

"I've had a lot of wonderful conversations with girls like you and Abbie, sitting where you are right now. Your mother, however, is a reminder that no matter how much you talk to someone, try to make them see reason. Sometimes they're not able to see anything beyond themselves."

I swallowed tightly.

"Yeah," I whispered. "My mother is a complicated woman."

Mari chuckled. "That's putting things lightly. I've made my peace with not knowing everything about her and the decisions she's made. But enough about her. How are you doing?"

Just as I opened my mouth to tell her about Kameron, because Mari was probably the only person in my life right now that I could confide in about our weird "situationship" and trust that it wouldn't leave this room, my phone buzzed in my pocket.

I pulled it out to check the notification, surprised to find I had a missed call from Abbie. I glanced back to Mari, who had retreated back to the checkout counter. I looked back down at my phone, frowning as I hit the redial button.

"Where are you?" Abbie asked quickly, picking up after the first ring.

"I'm at Mari's place, reading."

"You need to get to the Roadhouse."

I sat forward, closing my book, using my thumb as a placeholder. "What, why?"

Abbie swallowed audibly. "Just get here, please."

Abbie broke off the call. My skin was clammy as my nerves kicked in. Abbie and I didn't call each other often. We much preferred text and sending podcast-style voice memos. I grabbed one of the free bookmarks from the side table and slid it into place.

"Leaving so soon?" Mari asked.

"I just got a weird call from Abbie," I said, frowning. "Could you hold this for me? I'll come by to pick it up tomorrow."

Mari took the book from my outstretched hands and nodded.

"Of course. Hope everything's alright."

"Me too," I said, giving the older woman a tight smile before I retrieved my bag and opened the door, stepping out into the crisp mountain afternoon.

The Roadhouse was just across the street, and I was surprised to see Abbie hovering in the doorway with her arms crossed, talking heatedly to Connor.

"Hey," I said. "What's wrong?"

Connor's expression was unreadable, but Abbie was fired up.

"I need you to know that we're here for you, and we're not going to let anything bad happen to you."

Alarms blared in my mind as I turned to Connor.

"What is she talking about?"

"Jacob is here, Imogen."

I couldn't help it. I laughed. I laughed for what felt like several minutes before it finally passed. Abbie and Connor were still looking at me with twin grim expressions, and I threw my hands up in the air.

"That's a sick joke, but a good one," I said.

Abbie ran a hand down her face.

Deflection is good. If I continued to deflect with humor, then maybe, just maybe, I could ignore the growing dread forming in my stomach.

"He's really here, Imogen," Abbie said. "Connor and I just saw him go inside. At first I thought I was mistaken, but. . ."

"It's him," Connor confirmed, and my gaze switched to him.

"But he's in California," I said, and Abbie took my hands in hers.

"You don't need to go in there," she said. "I called you because I was freaking out, but Connor pointed out that the last place you need to be is here."

I looked to the entrance to the Roadhouse, focusing on the bubbling vinyl dictating the hours and the faded rug that covered the steps.

"Who else is in there?"

"Lucas. And. . . Kameron."

The alarm bells rang louder.

I pushed through the two of them.

"Wait," Abbie said, pulling me back behind Connor. "Let him go first, okay?"

I nodded my head as the buzzing in my ears grew louder. Connor and Abbie descended the steps first.

"What the hell are you doing here?" Connor yelled, throwing a hand out in front of Abbie defensively.

I came around Abbie's side just in time to see Kameron lunged for Jacob.

The shock of seeing Kameron's face contorted into anger quickly overran the shock of seeing Jacob.

Jacob let out a laugh.

"You think this is a fucking game?" Kameron shouted, shaking Jacob harder. Jacob let out a low laugh that had every cell in my body screaming that we needed to get away.

Kameron leaned in closer, sneering as he tightened his fists in Jacob's shirt. "You think hitting women is funny, huh?"

"Oh God," I whispered, my breaths coming short and fast. I was going to be sick.

"Nah," Jacob said, looking Kameron in the eyes. "It just makes what comes after more fun."

Abbie inhaled sharply, but the words barely cut me. Jacob had said so much worse over the course of our relationship.

The next five seconds happened in slow motion, like my brain was trying to force my eyes to look away and failing miserably.

Kameron raised his fist.

"Kameron!" Abbie shouted, and it was the sound of her voice, angry and desperate, that made time speed back up.

Kameron whipped his head towards us, fist still posed to strike, and something in me broke.

It was the image of Kameron with his fist raised, eyes blazing with anger, combined with Jacob's awful laugh, that made me shut down. I gripped Abbie's arms, silently begging her to get me out.

I need your help.

Memories of the night I left my husband slammed into me. Me, cradling my broken arm, stumbling up the stairs to Abbie's condo, barely coherent as I begged her to let me in.

I didn't know where else to go.

It was all falling apart.

Connor immediately stepped into action. Abbie guided me towards the exit, my chest rising and falling rapidly with the bone-deep panic that threatened to take over.

"I've got you, Im," Abbie whispered. "I'm here. You're safe."

You're safe.

The room spun around me.

I was never safe.

I would never be safe again. Jacob made sure of that.

Kameron—

I lurched forward, feeling like I was going to be sick.

"Imogen!"

I distantly heard Kameron's voice calling out to me over the cacophony of the bar, but I was barely cognizant of walking. I couldn't find the words to make him understand. To make him understand, I couldn't handle seeing him like that—brutal and fierce in the most threatening kind of way.

Only Abbie's tight grip on my arm, her whispered promises of getting back to her place safely, kept me upright.

I was never safe.

It had all been a lie. I had constructed this new life on unstable ground. I would never truly be free of the death grip Jacob held on my life. He would always find his way back.

This is why you promised.

I willed that voice to be silent and focused on Abbie's floral perfume and the rustling of distant wildflowers.

I wasn't there anymore. I was home. I was *safe*.

I repeated it over and over to myself as I focused on what I could feel and see.

Anything to forget the look in Kameron's eyes when he raised his fist.

Chapter Twenty-Four
Imogen

I woke up the next morning in the guest room of Abbie's condo. The morning light filtered in through the blinds. I sat up in bed, rubbed the sleep from my eyes, and stared at the phone on my nightstand. Someone had plugged it in for me.

Kam

> I am so sorry Imogen.

> Please call me when you wake up.

Well, it could have been worse. At least he didn't have a laundry list of excuses why he'd broken his pacifist ways and punched Jacob Kilpatrick in the face.

Even if the bastard deserved it.

I groaned, flopping back against the pillow.

I was the worst kind of hypocrite.

I used to have dreams about enacting all manner of revenge plots on Jacob. Everything from turning his ass in to the Marine Corps—I never took pictures of the abuse, so they would have sided with him anyway—to telling his mother, who had always hated me for taking her son away from her.

Needless to say, none of those plots ever panned out.

Kameron had the opportunity to do what I wish I'd gotten to do.

Kevvy Kev

I just heard about what happened at the Roadhouse. I'm here if you need me.

I groaned again. At least there was no mention of Kameron. But then another, far more alarming thought flashed through my mind.

If Kevin—who was not in attendance last night—had heard about what happened, the entire town of Watford no doubt had too. Word traveled fast, and a bar fight would soar to the top of the gossip list.

My stomach lurched at the implications of that.

If there was a video of Kameron's actions last night, and it was posted on social media and the Warrior's Foundation somehow saw it, they might pull Kameron's chance to interview for the grant.

"Shit," I whispered, throwing the covers back and grabbing one of Abbie's cardigans from the closet. I'd never been more grateful for her insanely excessive collection of Taylor Swift cardigans than I was right now.

Leave it to Jacob to ruin everything we'd worked so hard for these last few weeks.

The sight of Kameron angry with his fist raised flashed before my eyes and my stomach turned over. I stumbled to the bathroom across the hell and puked my guts up. I prayed Abbie wasn't awake yet. The last thing I wanted was for her to feel like she needed to take care of me now, too.

I rinsed my mouth out and brushed my teeth with one of the spare toothbrushes, and headed into the kitchen.

Abbie was making eggs in the kitchen, and Connor was sitting on the couch, reading a book.

"Have a seat, babe. Here's your coffee," Abbie said, flipping the egg and extending a cup of coffee to me. I took a seat on the couch opposite Connor, pulling the cardigan around my shoulders, trying not to look and feel out of place.

"Is it okay if I'm here?" Connor asked me so quietly I thought for a moment I'd imagined it.

My heart squeezed at the sincerity in his eyes. If I needed him to, he would leave. Somehow, he knew that being around another guy after being triggered on the level I was last night might not be the best thing for me.

But Connor didn't have a mean bone in his body when it came to the people he cared about. I felt safe around him, if for no other reason than knowing that Abbie would absolutely lay his ass out if he ever did something out of line.

I hated myself a little for ever doubting the care this man had for Abbie, and by extension, her inner circle.

"Yeah," I said, giving him a small smile. "I'm sorry for making things weird for everyone."

Connor grimaced, but it quickly faded to a smile when Abbie came and delivered us each a plate of bacon and eggs.

I set my mug down on the coffee table and took the plate from her outstretched hands.

"You didn't make things weird."

Abbie kicked Connor's leg under the coffee table as I took a sip of my coffee.

I raised my eyebrows, and Connor sighed.

"How are you feeling, Imogen?"

The bite of eggs I swallowed felt like ash in my mouth.

"How am I feeling?" I repeated, trying to find the words. "I'm feeling like my ex-husband who abused me for years is back in town for reasons I don't want to know. I'm feeling like my mother is also back in town because God hates me. I'm feeling like I watched the only person I've had a crush on in recent history punch my ex in the face, and then I had a panic attack in the bar, because I'm spiraling into thoughts about how men are violent and I was stupid for ever thinking I had a chance for a normal life and a normal relationship."

Connor blinked a few times, and even Abbie looked taken aback.

Way to go, Imogen.

"I'm sorry," I said, pinching the bridge of my nose. "Thank you for letting me crash at your place last night, and for breakfast. I'm going to head home."

"You know Kameron didn't—"

"You should talk to him," Connor cut her off gently. Before I could stand to leave, Abbie turned to whisper something I couldn't understand. Connor shook his head placatingly. "I know what happened last night was probably shocking.

Kameron doesn't often get mad or show that side of himself, except for when it comes to the people he loves."

The people he loves.

My stomach lurched again. "I—"

"You don't have to say anything," Connor said gently. "I'm just saying you should give him the chance to talk it out. Especially with the trip to Seattle."

I groaned in despair. I'd almost forgotten about Seattle.

This was the worst possible timing for everything to break down.

"You are still planning to go to Seattle for the grant presentation, right?" Abbie asked, casting me a wary glance.

My answer was immediate.

"Yes," I said. "Of course I'll go to Seattle. But I'm not talking about last night. Thank you both again for letting me stay the night and for taking care of me during my. . . episode." I waved a hand dismissively. "But I'd prefer to just let the past be in the past. There's no sense in rehashing it."

Connor looked about as convinced as I felt about the whole thing.

"What about Kameron?"

My heart squeezed.

"Kameron and I are friends," I said, even though the statement felt like I was stabbing myself in the chest.

We were friends, but we were more than that too.

Connor and Abbie looked at each other, an entire conversation shared in a single glance.

This is exactly what I had been afraid of this whole time. Things were messy and awkward, and it was my fault. And the worst part was they didn't even know the truth. They didn't know that Kameron and I had been exploring things. They didn't know about the conversations we'd had.

It was my fault for entering into something with Kameron that was never defined. I couldn't categorize my relationship with Kameron in an Excel document. I couldn't fit what we had between us into neat little boxes. And now that those boxes were overflowing with everything I couldn't manage, my friends were being affected.

This tension would spill over into the grant presentation.

And if Winding Road lost their chance at the Warrior's Grant because of last night, I would never forgive myself.

Chapter Twenty-Five
Kameron

It had been a long time since I'd allowed myself to get that angry.

I normally kept my feelings pretty close to my chest and didn't let other people bother me. But the sight of Imogen's ex-husband sitting at the bar, like he didn't have a care in the world, unraveled something in me.

I knew now why he was so fidgety. It's because he knew people at the bar would recognize him and he was trying to keep a low enough profile that someone didn't start something before he had the chance to talk to Imogen.

But someone *did* start something, and that someone was me.

And I had never felt more like a piece of shit in my life than when I turned around to see Imogen standing there, face sunken and void of feeling, looking at me with that haunted expression, like I was a monster.

Like I was the villain in her story.

Jacob deserved to get punched in the face. I refused to sit here and say that he somehow deserved redemption, or the chance to explain himself. He didn't.

But that choice on how he deserved to be punished for his past actions wasn't up to me, and I shouldn't have taken it upon myself to do that.

But damn if I still wanted to.

I'd let Jacob go as soon as Connor told me Imogen was watching. Jacob had just stood there and laughed, calling me every name in the book, saying I was weak.

I couldn't care less what he thought of me. I knew what kind of man I was.

My only concern was Imogen.

Imogen hadn't answered my texts or my calls from last night, though I couldn't blame her. I wouldn't want to talk to me either.

I was the world's biggest idiot.

When Connor finally came back after spending the night at Abbie's apartment, I immediately asked him how Imogen was feeling.

Connor just gave me a look, as if to say, *you're a fucking idiot.*

"I know I'm an idiot," I said, throwing my hands up in defense. "But I need you to tell me how she is. She didn't answer my calls, and I'm losing my freaking mind here."

Connor slung his keys on the bar top with a sigh.

"She feels like shit, Kam. I don't know what you want me to say."

Whatever hope I had that things were salvageable was quickly dissipating the longer I looked at Connor. He slumped his shoulders forward in defeat.

"Did she say anything to you?"

Connor shook his head.

"Not really. I left pretty quickly after breakfast. I wanted to give her and Abbie some space to talk things out. She's still planning to go to Seattle."

I let out a long sigh of relief. In the aftermath of what happened at the bar, I had completely forgotten about Seattle. Not having Imogen there would be devastating. I needed her administrative help, yes, but I needed her there for moral support.

I couldn't imagine giving that massive presentation that I was so nervous about, that meant so much to Winding Road and was so important for our stability in the future, without her there. She had been such an integral part of this process.

And selfishly, I needed her there for me, because she was the one damn thing in this world that could calm me down with nothing more than a brush of her fingers against mine.

Not that I had a right to ask her after the events of last night.

"That's good," I said, trying to remain optimistic. If she was still up for Seattle, there was a chance we could talk things out. There was a chance I could apologize.

Connor just shook his head.

"She doesn't want to talk about last night."

"She doesn't want to talk about last night," I repeated, trying to process the words. She couldn't just go back to normal after last night.

Connor shook his head again, frustration making his body stiff.

"You're a freaking idiot, Kameron. You're an *idiot*, going after Jacob like that. What the hell were you thinking?"

"I know, I know," I said quickly. "I wasn't thinking. When I saw him there and realized who he was, I lost my mind."

"Yeah, you did lose your mind," Lucas said, appearing from the hallway behind me. I whirled to face him.

"Jesus Christ, I thought you were still sleeping."

"Yeah, well, the two of you talk really loudly," Lucas said, trotting over to the coffee pot to pour himself some caffeine.

"What am I supposed to do?" I said, looking to Connor for guidance. Connor just shrugged.

"I gotta be honest, I don't know. Abbie knows Imogen better than me, but I remember what Jacob was like in high school. I don't know why he's back in town, but I have to assume it has something with trying to talk to Imogen."

"Well, that's not going to happen," Lucas said, and I nodded my head in agreement.

"I agree," Connor said.

"Okay," I said, closing my eyes and pressing my fingers into my temples to ease the ache forming there. "So we all agree Jacob doesn't come anywhere near Imogen."

Connor and Lucas nodded their heads in agreement.

"I need to talk to her," I said. "But I don't want to spook her anymore than she already is. I don't know what the hell to do."

Lucas and Connor shared a rare glance.

"I have an idea," Lucas said after a sip of his coffee. "Let me talk to her."

"Are the two of you still planning to come to Seattle?"

"I will be," Lucas said before jerking his chin towards Connor. "Big Man over here is sitting this one out. Something about Abbie having an appointment in Brighton."

I nodded. I had kind of expected Connor would stay behind.

"As much as I hate to say it, we'll just have to wait and see how things shake out over the next couple of days," Connor said, reaching out to squeeze my forearm.

Sitting around and waiting was the last thing I wanted to do.

But if Imogen was truly as triggered as I thought she might be by the events of last night, I knew she needed her space.

I trusted that Lucas would encourage her to come to me when she was ready.

Chapter Twenty-Six
Imogen

"**A**re you sure you're going to be okay?" Abbie asked as she idled in my driveway. I hopped out from the passenger seat and grabbed my meager bag of yesterday's clothes from the backseat, since I was now wearing Abbie's. I gave her the most reassuring smile I could muster. Bass bounded up the front steps of the farmhouse and whined at the top step, begging me to open the door.

"I'm good. Thank you again for last night. Sorry I freaked out on you."

Abbie let out a small breath, and my heart sank. In my panic I hadn't stopped to consider how she was feeling about having to play babysitter last night. That familiar shame slithered through my veins, oily and ink black, a stain that covered everything in my life and made it impossible to live somewhat normally.

"You don't need to apologize, Im," she said, and I noticed then how exhausted she looked. I wanted to ask her why, but I was scared to.

This is what always happened. Things would be good, and something would come along.

I feared her next words would be a criticism. Not of my reaction to Jacob's presence, but how I reacted to Kameron. What he did.

Because the truth was, I knew that the two things were separate. I rationally knew Kameron wasn't Jacob.

That was the nature of being triggered by past trauma—it wasn't a random reaction.

Your body has been told one story, over and over, so when it encounters that story again, the same plot points play out—even if it's been years since it happened.

"Hey," Abbie said, reaching through the driver's side window to squeeze my hand. "I'm happy to stay with you."

I squeezed her hand back and shook my head. "Thank you. I appreciate it. But I think I need to be alone for awhile."

There was so much crap I needed to sort through now that the haze of last night was finally clearing. Jacob. Kameron. This weird overlap in my head that shouldn't even be there, much less affecting me in this way.

"Okay," Abbie said, pulling her hand back. "Call me if you need anything. I mean it, Imogen. Don't sit there and be in the bad place."

Unshed tears sprung to my eyes, and I forced them back, opting for a shaky laugh instead of a full on sob.

"I promise I'll call."

I turned towards my house, letting out a shaky breath as I fumbled in my pockets for my keys.

I could do this. I had survived worse things. Yes, my abusive ex-husband was back in town, and the man I was definitely falling in love with had punched him in the face, but I was fine. It was fine. Maybe if I repeated it enough times, it would be a reality.

The first thing I did when I got inside was to lock the door behind me. I then checked every window, every screened door, the back porch. I carefully secured every entrance point. It eased my anxiety only slightly.

Once I was certain I had locked every entrance and there was no possible way Jacob could get in here and catch me unprepared, I made a beeline for the bathroom. I took my time in the shower, cranking the temperature up to scalding hot as I went through my painstakingly long wash day routine. By the time I had my hair towel dried with my curl cream, I pulled on my comfiest PJ set and put the kettle on so I could spend the rest of the day in bed reading with a hot cup of tea. I'd find a new fantasy series that I could spend the day binging and escaping into.

Kam

I'll be here when you're ready to talk. I'll give you all the space you need. But don't shut everyone else out, okay?

Let Lucas and Abbie be there for you.

Right. Weeks ago, I'd adjusted my do not disturb settings so that Kameron's text came through. I'd told myself it was so I didn't miss any important work-related texts, but the truth was far more complicated and messy than that.

And those two messages from him hit me like a punch to the gut. He had to be losing his mind, trying to figure out what the future was going to look like. Despair threatened to pull me under when I remembered Seattle was *this week-end*. The presentation that could very well determine the future of Winding Road was just days away, and Kameron was spending the time he should be rehearsing texting me reminders about sorting my crap out.

God, I'd colossally fucked this entire thing up.

I spent the rest of the morning and early afternoon wishing I could sink into the couch and avoid all of my problems. I drank tea, read my book absentmindedly, stared at the wall. I didn't want to think about Kameron, or the terrible way things ended. I didn't want to consider the notion that I would never be able to fully move past the abusive relationship that had tore me down in a way I couldn't recover from.

Which is why I was stunned when the doorbell rang. My stomach pitched. I wasn't ready to face Kam. I hadn't responded to his texts because I couldn't let myself go back to that night. I was fighting tooth and nail to keep my wits about me, and Kam—

He'd always had the ability to see right through me. Which is exactly why I was keeping him far away from me.

I slid my feet into my slippers, pulled on my robe, and splashed some cold water on my face before I answered the door.

My knees went weak with relief when I saw Lucas standing there, alone, with two iced caramel crunch lattes from Blackbeard's. My favorite guilty pleasure.

"Hey Im," he said. "Can I come in?"

I nodded and stepped aside, not trusting my voice.

We made our way to the living room. I took up residence in my usual spot, pulling the navy chunky knit blanket Abbie'd gotten me for Christmas two years ago up to my chest. Lucas pulled out two coasters and set a latte on each, pushing one towards me. I reached for it gratefully, taking a large sip.

"Your ex is a piece of shit," Lucas said once we were settled.

I couldn't help it, I laughed. This was why Lucas and I had become so close. Abbie and Connor had doted on me, asking about my feelings and telling me everything would be okay. And while I appreciated them and the care they had for me, I was barely holding it together. I *needed* Lucas's humor.

"You're telling me," I said, grateful for the distraction.

"I almost wish Kameron had beat the guy to a pulp."

I closed my eyes and fought to keep my breathing even.

"You didn't actually think I'd come here and us not talk about it."

"Lucas."

"Imogen."

I opened my eyes and found Lucas staring back at me.

"I *can't*," I whispered.

"Can't or won't?"

Ouch. Lucas came to play hardball, and I knew there was no weaseling my way out of this conversation. This was Lucas. If I couldn't talk to him about what I was feeling, there were few people on the planet I could.

"You have me there."

"What are you afraid of?"

Everything. All of it. The whole fucking thing felt too big for me to hold. And it wasn't just the incident at the bar. I could compartmentalize that event; I could distill my feelings about it down to a neat set of boxes on a spreadsheet and go on about my life as if nothing about it had hurt.

"I should also tell you that I know," Lucas said.

"Know what?"

Lucas gave me a wry grin. "Come on now. That was a weak attempt and you know it. Let's cut the crap. You love him."

I averted my eyes.

"There's no sense in denying it."

Love. Kameron. In the same sentence.

Of course I'd thought about it. My body knew it. It was in the way my body leaned into his nearness, the way my hand always seemed to find his, even when there was no reason for us to be touching each other. My very bones knew it. It's why I'd been so shocked and scared at the bar. If I didn't love him, I never would have reacted so severely to seeing him lose control.

"I'm scared to ask you how you figured it out."

Lucas laughed and shook his coffee, ensuring the milk was evenly dispersed—having an unbalanced ratio of milk to espresso in his lattes was a pet peeve of his.

"I've had my suspicions for awhile, but I didn't have any hard evidence to support my conclusion. Until the night at the Roadhouse. Because after Kameron launched himself at Jacob, everyone else was looking at the two of them, but I was looking at *you.* I saw your trembling hands and the way you clutched Abbie like she was your lifeline. At first,

I thought you were looking at Jacob, but then I realized you were staring at Kameron. And I knew in that moment exactly what kind of narrative you'd written in your head."

"I've never seen him angry," I whispered. "I know it sounds so stupid and naive of me, but I think I'd convinced myself he never got angry."

"Everyone gets angry, Im," Lucas said. "But Kameron would *never* lay a hand on you. Ever. God, he'd fling himself into space before he ever touched you out of anger."

"I know," I said. "I believe you."

"You don't have to believe me," Lucas said. "I want you to let Kameron explain, in his own words. Do I have your permission to invite him over here tomorrow? It's the last day we'll have together before we have to leave for Seattle, and I'd really prefer *not* to be stuck with two brooding lovesick idiots in the car."

"That's rude, Lucas," I replied, teasing. Lucas rolled his eyes and finished his coffee, setting the empty plastic cup down on the coaster.

"What's the verdict?"

"Okay," I said. "He can come over tomorrow."

"Thank God."

"What would you have done if I'd said no?"

Lucas rubbed at his chin as he considered. "Honestly? You saying no didn't cross my mind. Because I know how you feel about him. You just needed someone to lay out all the data points. I had confidence you'd come to the right conclusion."

"It doesn't make you feel weird?" I said. I fiddled with a stray piece of yarn on the blanket. Bass let out a massive yawn and stretched his paws out on the couch, rolling belly-up so Lucas could pet him. "That all of your friends are in relationships with each other, I mean."

Lucas quirked an eyebrow in my direction and shook his head. Bass whined when Lucas stopped petting him, and took it upon himself to crawl into Lucas's lap, pressing his nose into Lucas's side in an impressive guilt trip. Lucas sighed and resumed petting him.

"If that was the reason you guys felt like you had to sneak around at the farm, I'm sorry to inform you I wouldn't have cared," Lucas said. "But watching you two try to hide it from everyone was very entertaining, so thank you for that."

I laughed. "Thanks. Always so supportive."

"I love you both," Lucas said, all hint of playfulness and teasing vanishing from his voice. "Kameron is one of the best men I've ever had the honor of working with. And he loves you. He would give you the world on a silver platter if he could. Hell, if you asked him to, he'd probably make it happen."

I tried to laugh, but it came out as a strangled cry. Lucas patted my leg, and I rolled my eyes. Lucas had always been one of those people who ran for the hills as soon as the tears started flowing.

"I've got to head back to Winding Road. I'm sure Kameron is doing some serious brooding, and I live to annoy him."

"Be nice," I said. "He's got a lot going on right now."

"I know how to handle him," Lucas quipped.

Twenty minutes and an astronomic meltdown from Bass later, Lucas was rumbling down the gravel driveway, headed towards town. Bass whined at the front door.

"He'll be back another day," I said, reaching down to scratch between his ears. Bass inclined his head towards me, pressing his face against my palm. He whined again.

"Let me guess. You're not mad about Lucas leaving. You're upset because your Dad isn't here?"

Bass yipped and wagged his tail. My fingers stilled in Bass's fur.

"He'll be here tomorrow," I said, shaking my head to clear the anxious thoughts before they fully took root in my mind. "He'll be here tomorrow, and everything will work out how it's supposed to."

I'd never envisioned having children, and I'd certainly never seen myself as a particularly maternal individual. But my words seemed to comfort Bass, based on the way he flopped belly side up and demanded more tummy scratches before bolting off in the direction of his toy basket.

Everything will work out how it's supposed to.

That sentence became my mantra for the rest of the day.

Chapter Twenty-Seven

Kameron

I wasn't accustomed to having so much anger and frustration I didn't have a place for.

I'd taken to skipping rocks off the dock like a teenager.

I'd spent the better part of my adult life learning about the neuroscience behind anger and trauma. I knew on an anatomical level how anger manifested and why certain experiences were so difficult to move past. I'd taken that knowledge and built a place where people like me could come to learn those things, and use it to change their life.

I knew all of that, but the situation with Jacob had humbled me by reminding me I was still human.

I'd let Imogen have her space yesterday. I'd texted her and then forced myself to mute my notifications, so I didn't stare at my phone all day. Lucas had texted me early in the day to let me know he was going to attempt a visit with her in the morning, and it had taken everything in me not to blow up his phone with a million questions about how things were going.

I'd taken all the horses for long rides through the forest surrounding the farm, trying like hell to get the image of

Imogen's horrified expression out of my head. The image would haunt me for a long time.

When that didn't work, I'd grabbed my fishing gear and come down to the docks. I hadn't caught anything—hadn't even gotten a bite. It was like the fish could sense the self-hatred and steered clear of me. I'd been out here for over three hours when someone else finally joined me.

Lucas, of all people, came to stand beside me on the dock, letting out a low whistle when I skipped a stone more than twice.

"You're getting good at that."

"Don't be a dick," I warned. "I'm not in the mood."

Lucas shrugged. My gaze drifted towards the fold out chair and insulated lunch bag tucked under his arm. He unfolded the chair and sat down, rifling around in the bag and pulling out a sandwich.

"When were you going to tell me about Imogen?" Lucas said as he unwrapped his lunch. My next throw faltered, and I cursed under my breath.

"Excuse me?"

"I've been pretending not to see the way you two have been making heart eyes at each other over the last three months. I've also been ignoring the way you spend all night in the tiny house, only to sneak in the back door early in the morning and pretend like you've been there the whole time. There's little else for you to do at Winding Road when there isn't a cohort, so the only logical explanation is. . ."

He waited for me to fill in the blanks, but I refused, pressing my lips into a tight line. I didn't have the wherewithal to withstand yet another Lucas lecture—not about my flaws, not about the farm, and certainly not about Imogen.

Not after everything had fallen apart. My sanity was hanging on by a thin thread.

"You're too smart for your own good," I muttered.

"Heard that one before," Lucas said, taking another bite of his sandwich. He took another tin foil-wrapped sandwich out of his bag and offered it to me. I narrowed my eyes at him.

"If you came to berate me, I'm not interested."

"Jesus, you're moody."

Something in me snapped. I whirled to face him, finally letting that anger bubble over.

"If you want to ask me a fucking question, *Morales*, then ask it. But don't waste my time."

"Oh, we're finally going to kick it Sergeant Miller style? Lay it all out there," Lucas said right as I opened my mouth to speak. He leaned forward in his chair, eyes blazing with that familiar fire. "I'm not scared of you."

My jaw twitched, and I clenched my fists at my sides. Lucas had always been the wild card. He and I were both squad leaders in the Marine Corps, and every time our unit went to the field, he was always the person leading the machine gun squad attached to ours. He was always asking questions and pushing for answers I didn't have. If anyone had a criticism of the way things were going, it was Lucas.

It had made me respect him more back then, because behind his "deflective asshole" persona, I saw a kid that genuinely cared about what was happening.

That was then, though. The dynamic had long since shifted between us, and I didn't have the emotional energy
to shepherd Lucas through another long-winded explanation of why human relationships were complicated, fickle
things.

"I'm good."

"For someone who knows as much as you do about anger
and frustration, you fight it more than anyone else I know.
You fight it so hard until it boils over and causes you to act
in a way you never would if you'd just acknowledge the very
human reality that we all get pissed off sometimes."

I gave Lucas a weary glare, sighing heavily and letting the
pebble in my hand clatter to the dock.

"It's not fair," I muttered. "That's it. It's just not fucking
fair."

"What's not fair?"

"That Imogen can't let herself have anything good in life
because that low-life son of a bitch stole her spark."

It felt damn good to say it out loud. Lucas took another
bite of his sandwich.

"No one would have blamed you if you'd broken the guy's
jaw."

"Believe me when I say I wanted to."

Connor and I had many conversations about violence in
the months after we'd left the Marine Corps. He and I were
similar in that way; we'd both had traumatic experiences
involving the loss of male figures in our lives, and while
my father was a brilliant man who'd never once laid a hand
on me, he still fought his own demons. I'd watched my
father lose his temper plenty of times. I'd watched how that

despair ate at him. And after his death, I'd watched that same despair eat away at my mother. I'd never know if my father's death sped up Mom's decline, but I had my theories.

"But you didn't," Lucas said, his voice lighter than before. "You had an opportunity and justification, and you didn't."

"She thinks I did," I murmured, staring at the calm surface of the lake before us. "She's built an entire story in her head about what happened."

"Explain it to her, Kam. She'll understand."

"That's the thing though," I said. "Domestic violence recovery isn't linear. There's a chance whatever ship we were on has set sail."

Lucas pressed his lips together. "I think you should let Imogen make that call."

Lucas was right. I knew he was right, but letting Imogen make that call meant baring myself completely before her, letting her see into my past and into my head in a way I had never let another romantic partner do. It meant admitting my fears were real, tangible weapons to be used against me.

And more importantly, it meant admitting to myself that this was no longer a silly crush.

My feelings for Imogen were as real as my fear of losing her was.

"Which is why I went to talk to her yesterday."

My head snapped towards him.

"How is she?"

Lucas's soft smile told me I'd passed some kind of unwritten test.

"She's okay. She wants you to come to the farmhouse."

"Today?"

"If you're okay with that."

Oh, *crap*. This was what I wanted, but the weight of the conversation we needed to have was crushing. We'd both have to come to the table willing to lay it all out there. I'd never allowed myself to be that vulnerable with another person. Not when it mattered this much.

Imogen Phillips meant everything to me.

"Life moves fast," I said, unable to find any other words to describe the feeling of panic clawing its way up my throat. I took the foil-wrapped sandwich and glanced towards the sky. It was already early afternoon. I needed to get a move on if I was getting to Watford before nightfall.

"That it does," Lucas said. "Sometimes we all need to be told to get our shit together."

I let out a small laugh. "Yeah, well… You and Connor need it more than me."

Lucas' smile turned into a smirk as he stood to help me gather the fishing tackle and cooler to bring back to the house.

"Keep telling yourself that, Sarge. Maybe one day you'll believe it."

Chapter Twenty-Eight
Imogen

The morning after Lucas's visit, I turned my phone on do not disturb, and went for a walk around the homestead.

It had been weeks since I'd taken the time to walk the grounds. I thought back to all of the times I'd run through these fields, back when they were overgrown with wildflowers and native grasses. My Nana had given us full rein of the place as kids, and we'd run wild. I picked wildflowers, climbed trees, scaled the hills, and imagined a world that was kinder; softer.

This place would always have a piece of my heart. My childhood has been beautiful because of this place. All of the crap with my mother aside, I'd remember this place fondly. It was the place where I found my love for reading, and for exploring.

I entered the barn and smiled when I saw Kevin hard at work. He'd just finished mucking out the cow stalls when I approached him.

"Hey," I said, scratching Betty between the ears. She let out a low moo of approval, and I smiled. "Anything I can do to help?"

"Can you grab the feed buckets?"

I nodded and did so. We filled both of the pails before setting off for the chicken coop.

"Haven't changed your mind about selling the place, have you?"

I shook my head as we tossed the food out for them.

"No. It's time to let go."

Kevin nodded once. We watched the chickens peck at the feed for a few minutes before Kevin grabbed the egg baskets and handed one to me.

"By let go, I can also assume you mean everything that happened with your marriage?"

I blew out a breath. Kevin and I's relationship was complicated, as bonds between siblings often are. He didn't know the full details of what happened with Jacob, and I had every intention of keeping it that way. He knew enough; that Jacob hadn't treated me well, and that I would bear the mental and physical scars of that time in my life forever.

"I'm still working on that, but yes," I said. "It's time to move forward. I've spent a lot of time mulling over the past. I'm tired of it stealing my future."

"What's your next step?"

I pressed my lips together. That was the question of the hour.

"I think. . . I think I'm going to Winding Road."

The corner of Kev's mouth twitched, and I knew he was fighting a smile.

"You think, or you know?"

I rolled my eyes.

"I haven't exactly asked to keep my job, and depending on how things go in Seattle, I might not have one in a few weeks. But I'll do everything in my power to make sure we get this grant."

"We?" Kevin asked. I opened my mouth to respond, but when I glanced his way, he was laughing.

"Shut up," I said. Kevin stuck his tongue out at me, and Pam immediately squawked with indignation. She was always there to defend my honor, bless her heart.

"You're a pain in my ass, you know that?" Kev said, jerking a thumb at Pam. I smacked his arm playfully.

"Don't talk to her like that," I said, smiling.

"She's a menace," Kevin said. "You know Kyrie wants to keep the chickens, right? She's been begging me to let her have them."

"That sounds good to me," I said, reaching into one of the nests and putting three eggs in my basket. "I'm hoping the livestock can stay local. We're pretty much at capacity at Winding Road, but I'm hoping I can find some other folks in town to take the herd."

We settled into a comfortable silence as we finished collecting the eggs and cleaning out the henhouse. By the time we returned to the barn and finished washing the equipment, the early morning sun cast a beautiful orange glow over the fields beyond.

"I'm your brother, so I don't want details, but I will say. . . I can tell Kam makes you happy," Kevin said. "Happiness looks good on you."

"Aw," I said, grinning. "I think that might be the nicest thing you've ever said to me, Kev."

"Yeah, yeah, don't get used to it," Kevin said, waving a hand. "You can head back to the farmhouse. I've got the rest of the chores handled."

"You sure?"

Kevin nodded and headed deeper into the barn. He paused before he reached the last stall, looking over his shoulder and calling out to me.

"Go get him, sis. Stop overthinking it."

I smiled the entire way back to the farmhouse.

Because of the chaos of the last few weeks, my pantry was looking pretty barren. I didn't have anything for spaghetti or chili, which were at the top of my go to's. The only thing I had enough ingredients to make a full spread out of was breakfast food. "Brinner" was a perfectly acceptable "I love you, I'm sorry" meal, right?

Kam

Hey. Lucas just talked to me. I'm on the way.

I glanced at the stove clock, cursing under my breath when I realized I didn't have enough time to dwell on it.

Me

Okay. See you soon

Kam

He sent the last message like an afterthought he couldn't keep to himself. My heart practically tripped over itself as I ran towards the bathroom to shower and change clothes. As soon as no longer smelled like the barn, I cranked the oven on to preheat.

I let myself drown in the calming rhythm of cooking breakfast. I lined a baking sheet with foil and baked the bacon, the way my Nana would on the mornings when she didn't want to deal with the extensive clean up involved with pan-frying. I made too many pancakes because I'd never figured out a batter recipe that yielded a reasonable amount. It was either too much, or too little. The straw-berries in my fridge were still good by some stroke of luck. I had tea and coffee and fresh creamer.

I wasn't as destitute as I'd originally thought.

I was focusing too much on the logistics of this—I *knew* I was, and yet I couldn't help myself from rearranging the table runner three times and wiping down the kitchen island once more for good measure after all the food was staged.

The doorbell ringing was my saving grace. I readjusted the color of my yellow sweater and smoothed out the wrin-kles in my jeans. I could do this. I walked calmly and eagerly towards the door and took a deep breath before opening it.

"Hi," I said, and the sight of Kameron was a shock to my system. His black hair and beard were both longer, and he looked more undone. He was so put together, so restrained in his usual day to day, but this Kameron—*this* Kameron looked like a man who'd been tortured by his own thoughts for the last two days.

We had that in common, it seemed.

"Hi," he replied. He looked me over, but there was no heat in his gaze. He was assessing, cautious—like he was checking me for recent injuries and new scars. The gesture set a fire in my chest, stoking all the feelings I'd tried to keep dormant to life again.

"Come in," I said, and stepped aside to allow him entrance into the farmhouse. He kicked his boots off at the door. Bass barked in the living room, releasing a low growl as he came sprinting towards the door. The growl transitioned to extensive tail-wagging when he noticed Kam.

My heart squeezed as Bass launched himself at Kam. Kam let out a laugh and eagerly petted the little rascal, a smile of pure joy on his face.

"I missed you, buddy," Kam said. His eyes met mine, and I smiled.

"The last time we tried to have dinner here, we were rudely interrupted," I said as I walked towards the kitchen. "I thought we could have a do over?"

I winced as the words sounded less like a statement and more of a question. I'd never been the most confident person in the room, but there was so much we needed to talk about.

"And I didn't really have food in the house, but I had enough to make breakfast, so I hope pancakes, bacon, and eggs work for you?"

I was rambling, and afraid of turning around to see whatever emotion might be written on Kameron's face. He'd always worn his thoughts and emotions on his sleeve in a way so few men did—equal parts restrained, observant, and eager. I leaned against the kitchen island which was overflowing with the breakfast spread. Kameron kept his distance, and I finally looked up to meet his eyes.

"You didn't have to cook," Kam said, and there was a warmth in his tone that put me at ease. "Really."

"I wanted to," I admitted. "There's so much I want to say, Kam."

He swallowed tightly at the sound of his name on my lips. I tracked the movement. He was restrained, his posture more formal. Standoff-ish, but not in an aggressive way.

He was guarding his heart. I couldn't blame the man for that.

"I need to explain myself first, if you'll allow me. I've been going out of my fucking mind thinking that your entire perception of me has changed, and I just—" he ran both of his hands through his hair.

"Okay," I said, grabbing both of the plates I'd pulled from the cabinet and handing one to him. "Food first, then talk?"

Kam nodded and took the plate gratefully. When we were both seated at the kitchen table with overflowing plates, we spent a few minutes eating. Abbie would laugh if she could see us, only because she always made me eat something before or during a disagreement. I was prone to forgetting to eat, and when I did, our discussions quickly became heated when they didn't need to be.

I chuckled at the memory, slapping a hand over my mouth when I remembered I wasn't alone.

"Sorry," I said sheepishly. "I'm thinking of all the times Abbie made me eat when I tried to start a fight. Most of the time I'd forget what we were supposed to be arguing about after I had a snack."

"Are we going to fight?" Kam said. There was a teasing lilt to his voice that made me shiver.

God, I'd missed him. I'd missed him so much more than I'd allowed myself to consider before this moment.

"I wasn't planning on it," I said. "Certainly not now that I have pancakes."

"They're delicious. Thank you for this. It's been ages since I had breakfast for dinner."

"It's one of my specialties," I said proudly.

"I learn more about you every day," Kam said quietly. I put my fork down and bit my bottom lip.

"Kam, I'm—"

"You don't need to apologize," Kam said, holding up a hand. "I need—I *want* you to have the facts about what happened with Jacob before we go any further. And I need you to know that the ball is in your court, Imogen. If you want to end this, I will walk away and we'll never talk about it again. I will be whatever you need me to be. But I want you to have all the facts before you make that choice."

My mouth went impossibly dry, but I nodded, encouraging him to say what he needed to say.

"I didn't hit Jacob."

All of the air seemed to vanish from the room. I picked my fork up again just to have something to do with my hands. I stabbed at one of the strawberry slices and avoided Kam's gaze.

"I wanted to. I'm not going to sit here and pretend like I didn't want to. But I didn't. It's important to me that you know I chose not to."

I speared another strawberry slice onto the fork as my mind spun around in circles.

"Okay," I said. "That's—that's good."

Good? Jesus, I needed to get a grip.

"I get angry just like everyone else," Kam said. "But I don't like it. I don't like the feeling of being pissed off, the way it makes me act towards the people I love most in my life. I'm still working on figuring out how to release that anger on a more regular basis, so what happened with Jacob will *never* happen again."

"Has it happened before?"

"No," Kam said. "The only time I've ever put my hands on someone else is when the Marine Corps told me to, or when someone asked me to touch them."

My cheeks flushed. I finally dared to meet his gaze, and there it was. Every single thing he had left to give me was written on his face, etched into the corded muscles of his chest and arms. He was laying every card out on the table for me to decide.

It was a long few minutes before I found my words. Kam was laying everything out, and it was only fair that I did the same. That's why I'd wanted him to come here, and the fear I'd harbored about this conversation was quickly dissipating, replaced by a current of excitement.

"I don't know how I didn't see it before."

I watched Kameron's face and smiled when his features shifted, signaling my words had hit home.

"Your focus was elsewhere," Kam said, fighting to keep his voice even.

"No, it wasn't," I said, putting my fork down and pushing my plate away from me. "I was trying too damn hard to create a new reality that I kept missing what was right in front of me. That's the nature of trauma sometimes, isn't it? You spend all of this time fighting for your life, and when you finally break free, you're flailing. Because even though that person was awful to you, they became a structural part of your life. And when you leave them, or they leave you, the floor falls out from under you, because somehow they became part of your foundation, even when you didn't want them to."

Kam stayed silent. I fiddled with a loose thread on my sweater while I figured out where to go next.

"I've spent most of the last few years with my head in the sand. Not because I wanted it there, but because I felt like that was my only option to keep myself safe. I've been running since I met you, running from the way your presence makes my heart beat faster, the way my mind stills when I'm in your arms. But now I'm realizing that my brain lied to me. I'm not safer on my own. I'm safer with *you*. Because of how you make me feel. How you take care of me without even meaning to. I gravitate towards you, and I'm tired of pretending like I don't."

Within seconds, he was standing, making his way to me. He wrapped his gloriously thick arms around my waist and picked me up. I relaxed into him instantly, and my body sang with the nearness of him, of how right it felt to be in his arms. He turned us around, so I was sitting on the kitchen counter. He stepped between my legs and my very blood hummed with the sensation of *him*.

"You can't fit what we have in a neat box on your spreadsheet," he murmured. His palms were face down on my thighs, squeezing gently. The touch was delicate and grounding and everything I'd ever wanted, ever *needed*. "You can't explain the depth of my feelings for you through any kind of rational, scientific thinking. Because my love for you isn't rational. It's a storm, Imogen. It's a damn wildfire that encompasses every fiber of my being whenever you're near me. It's the way my heart pounds when I hear your laugh, and the way I want to make you make that sound every day for the rest of my freaking life."

My lips trembled as I fought to keep my tears at bay, and still he pressed on. This was it. This was the moment where everything came together after all this time.

"I love you, Imogen," he said, though I barely heard the words as he spoke them over the sound of my beating heart. "I have loved you for months."

"Since the kiss on the dock?" I said as I wrapped my arms around his neck. He shivered as my nails grazed the sensitive skin.

"Before," he answered immediately, pulling me even closer so our bodies were flush against each other. His hands moved to my waist, squeezing gently. "Long before that day at the dock. Long before that night at the tiny house. Long before I let you bring a random dog into my house and make him part of our family."

Upon hearing his name, Bass let out a contented sigh from where he was sleeping on the couch.

"I still can't believe you let me do that, knowing that dogs aren't your favorite."

"I can," he said, raising a hand to stroke his knuckles down my cheek. I didn't flinch, didn't even hesitate as I leaned into the touch, laying my hand over his. "Because that's the effect you have on me. You make me crazy, Imogen Phillips. And I love you for it."

"I didn't plan you," I murmured, slightly bewildered by how perfect the moment was.

Now it was his turn to laugh. He tilted my face towards his, gazing into my eyes the way I'd imagined a hundred times before. There were no secrets left between us. We were both stripped down to the core of our beings and it still felt so damn right. Nothing had ever felt like this, like the damn cosmos had aligned to give us this, like we'd met at precisely the right time. It was otherworldly.

It was *everything*.

"I know you didn't," he murmured. "But it happened. And I for one am so damn glad it did."

"Are you sure you want this?" I said, wrapping my arms around his shoulders again. "Everything we talked about that morning at the tiny house, about kids and marriage. . . all of that stands. I need you to understand that I'm not going to change my mind. I don't want you to accept it now when we're young and free and wake up twenty years from now hating me because I can't give you what you want."

"What I told you that morning stands, too," Kam said, smiling. "No kids, no marriage paperwork. Just you and me and wherever we want to go next."

"And Bass," I reminded him.

"And Bass," he agreed, and then paused. "How do you feel about getting another dog?"

I gasped in mock outrage, and his smirk widened to a grand smile.

"Do you think Bass would do well with siblings?"

He shrugged, and pulled me in closer. "There's only one way to find out."

I kissed him then, wild and open, unable to bear another second without his lips on mine. He met my advances step for step, wrapping my arms around my waist once more and lifting me from the island. I wrapped my legs around him as his hands traveled to my ass, keeping me upright as he walked us down the hallway towards the bedroom.

This is what I wanted every day for the rest of my life. This handsome, strong, kind man, taking everything I gave him and giving as good as he got.

No matter what happened with the Warrior's Grant this weekend, I knew we'd be okay.

Because we'd face whatever came next together.

Chapter Twenty-Nine
Imogen

The next day, we spent the entire car ride in our own worlds. All three of us had different ways of handling travel. Lucas took up residence in the passenger seat, citing his motion sickness as justification for why he needed to be up front, and I sat in the back, perfectly content to gaze out the window as the rural Washington mountains gave way to highways and cities. When I got bored, I flipped open my e-reader and continued binging the fantasy series I'd started weeks earlier. We stopped for lunch at a gas station where we could both refuel and eat chicken nuggets.

Lucas let out a low whistle as we walked into the lobby of the hotel hours later, and I was inclined to agree with him. The hotel was hands down the fanciest establishment I'd ever been in.

"Before you thank me, I didn't choose this hotel," Kam said. "The Warrior's Foundation did."

"They're so wining and dining us."

I shot Lucas a glare and rolled my eyes. "They want us close by, goofball. The foundation building is only a block away. They're keeping tabs on us."

"Fine by me," Lucas said, still taking in the vaulted ceilings and plush carpets of the lobby space. It was very new age and modern, with vintage accents sprinkled throughout in the form of a velvet armchair or an abstract painting. It looked exactly like a hotel I'd expected to find in a place like Seattle, the epitome of vintage elegance, perfect for someone who loved the eclectic and moody rather than dreary beige tones.

Kameron left Lucas gawking in the middle of the lobby, and I awkwardly found a seat, determined to keep my distance from the train wreck that was Lucas Morales. He looked like such an outlier in this plush hotel with his black beard, flannel, and worn in jeans and boots. He never failed to amaze me.

"I didn't take you for an art buff," I said teasingly when walked towards me, still regarding the large artwork in the foyer.

"I'm not," Lucas said, rubbing his chin with his thumb and forefinger. "I'm mostly trying to figure out how they got it up there in the first place," he said, gesturing to a massive painting on the right wall. Large, overlapping brushstrokes dominated the canvas. The artist had chosen mostly earthy tones that reflected the Washington forests. It was the kind of painting that housed a different interpretation for every person who looked at it.

The illustration brought me a small sense of comfort. It felt like there was a small piece of Watford hanging in the hotel. If I was a believer in some kind of higher power, I would have taken that as a sign of good things to come.

"We're all checked in," Kameron said, returning to us. I grabbed my duffel bag and stood, gesturing for him to lead the way to the elevator. Lucas fell in line behind us, and I rolled my eyes when I noticed he'd been staring at a woman from across the lobby. The man wasted no time. Lucas had already regaled me with tales of how it was "slim pickings" in Watford, and he was ready to hang out in a bigger city for a while.

"What's the sleeping arrangement?" Lucas asked, not deigning to look up at either of us while scrolling on his phone.

"Imogen and I are sharing a room," Kameron murmured. Lucas made a gagging noise.

"Good," I said, and Kameron's gaze heated. I couldn't stop the smile that took over my face, and I decided I didn't want to.

The elevator doors opened, and I eagerly stepped into the hallway of our floor, grabbing the keycard from Kameron's outstretched hand. Kam handed Lucas his keycard. His room was a few doors down from ours.

"I swear to God, if the two of you wake me up with your sexual escapades tonight, I'll commit a homicide."

"It's a good thing my lawyer sister lives here them," I quipped. "Sounds like we'll need her services."

My breath caught when the full meaning of my words set in.

Cassie. I hadn't so much as thought about trying to meet my sister while I was in town. I couldn't remember the last time I'd come to Seattle. I'd want her to visit me if the roles were reversed.

Then again, Cassie had never yielded her pride and come home to Watford to visit any of us.

I didn't need something else distracting me this weekend. Not when there was so much on our plates.

"The same goes for you," Kam shot back. "And for the love of God, do *not* be late tomorrow. Go have fun, but don't be late."

"Wouldn't dream of it," Lucas said before retreating into his room.

Kam opened our door, gesturing for us to step inside. I walked past the bathroom and the entryway table, my eyes widening at the spacious layout and modern amenities. There was a plush king size bed in the center of the bedroom space, overflowing with fluffy pillows and lush blankets.

"If it's okay with you, I'm going to see if there's a gym in this place," Kam said. He dropped his duffle bag on the floor and grabbed his gym clothes.

I raised my eyebrows. "You want to work out? Now?"

Kameron gave me a teasing grin. "Lifting heavy weights is how some of us work through our stress and anxiety."

"Ah," I said. "Of course."

"And, me going to the gym means that you have the room for yourself to listen to your music and shake it out."

Heat rushed to my cheeks.

"How in the world did you know I do that? You know what, don't answer that. I bet Abbie told you."

"I saw you," Kam murmured, and a fresh wave of heat flushed to my cheeks. "It was after we'd finished one of our grant proposals. You were stressed about whether or not it was good enough, and after we hit submit, you headed back to the tiny house. A few minutes later, I realized you'd left your water bottle on the kitchen table, and I wanted to return it to you. As I made my way down the hill, I saw you dancing through the kitchen window. You had your headphones on and you were dancing with your eyes closed like no one was watching. I admittedly watched you for longer than I probably should have, and I realized you were working through something, so I just. . ."

"You set the water bottle down on the porch," I murmured, rubbing my hand along my arm. "I'd thought I was going crazy when I saw it there, but it was just you."

Kameron rubbed the back of his neck and shrugged. "Yeah, it was me."

Something warm spread throughout my body, a homey feeling that overpowered my apprehension about the grant presentations.

"Thank you," I whispered. Kameron took a step towards me, and I tilted my face towards him out of instinct. Kameron's hands cupped my face as he kissed me, and my God, I didn't know how I'd gone two whole days without his hands on me.

I let out a small breath as we pulled away, my eyes closing of their own volition as I focused only on the feeling of Kameron's hands against my skin.

"You dance it out, I'll get a gym session in, and then we'll order room service and go over the grant presentation a thousand times in a futile effort to alleviate our shared anxiety."

I chuckled as I stepped to the side.

"Sounds like a plan, lover boy."

"What happened to cowboy?"

"Lover boy fits you better," I said, pressing a kiss to his cheek. "Nicknames are supposed to evolve."

"I guess I'll have to work harder to come up with one for you."

The idea of Kameron giving me a nickname sent a wave of heat through my body. This was what it was supposed to feel like. This awareness of someone, the ache when they weren't around, the anticipation of seeing them again.

"I'll hold you to that," I said, my voice slightly breathy.

Kameron simply winked and ducked into the bathroom to change. I quickly grabbed his phone and scrolled to his contacts, writing down the number I needed on the hotel notepad. I returned his phone to his duffle bag so he wouldn't be suspicious.

As soon as he left the room, I grabbed my phone and dialed.

"Hi Gail," I said. "My name is Imogen Phillips. We met a few weeks ago—"

"Imogen!" Gail said, sounding positively delighted that I'd called. "Of course I remember you. How are things? Is Kam alright?"

The hint of concern in her tone made me smile. I was glad Kameron had people in his life who looked out for him outside of our little group.

"He's good. We're actually in Seattle this weekend. The judges selected Winding Road as a finalist for a monumental grant that could sustain us for a long time, and we're here for presentations so they can make their final decision.

"That's wonderful," Gail exclaimed. "Can I do anything to help?"

"Actually, there is. This whole process has stressed Kameron out immensely. I was thinking it would be nice if. . ."

I dove into explaining my idea. Kam had support from the people closest to him, but given how monumental this presentation was in the life of his nonprofit, I wanted to honor his father's legacy.

Luckily, I knew just what that was, and Gail was thankfully on board.

"I'm tearing up," Gail said. "I'll get right on this. Can you send me your email?"

Once the logistics were in place, I sat back and waited for Gail to send me what I needed.

I also phoned Abbie and Lucas, and gave them the rundown on what I needed from them. Abbie had immediately jumped on it, and I knew Lucas wouldn't be far behind based on the text I received less than an hour after I'd called him with the request.

Lucas Morales

This is a really good idea, Im. He'll appreciate it more than you know. Let me know if you need help editing.

It would be a quick turnaround between receiving the files and the grant presentation tomorrow, but I'd stay up all night if it meant I got it done.

I could only hope Lucas was right, and that Kam would appreciate it the way I thought he would.

Chapter Thirty
Imogen

The Warrior's Foundation building was a skyscraper like any other, but walking through the doors, my heels clacking on the marble floors, I felt completely out of place. The lobby boasted a long, cascading waterscape and custom made light fixtures from a prominent local artist. I'd never dreamed of the city life, certainly not in the way my sister or my friends had.

Being back in Seattle was a reminder that I didn't want this life.

I adjusted my laptop bag and headed for the security desk.

"Hi, I'm Imogen Phillips. I'm with Winding Road Recovery. My executive director is presenting to the grant proposal board today."

I didn't know where this confidence was coming from, though I suspected it had something to do with the thrill of waking up next to Kameron this morning. He'd gotten an early start at 4 a.m., wanting to get a run in before he showed up early for the preliminary meet and greet with the two other nonprofits. I didn't dare question it as the security guard checked my I.D. against their logs and then handed me a temporary badge.

"The boardroom is on the third floor," the woman said, gesturing towards the elevators to our left. "There's signage along the way."

"Thanks," I said, flashing her a smile.

I hung the badge around my neck and made my way to the elevator, pressing the up button and stepping back to wait. When they opened, Kameron was standing in the elevator, arms crossed over his chest. I stepped inside, biting the inside of my cheek to keep from smiling.

"There you are," Kameron said, smirking as the doors shut behind us. "I've been looking for you."

"I told you I planned to be here at late," I said, smiling. "Presentations don't start for another hour."

"Yeah, well, I just threw up because I'm so nervous, and seeing your face an hour earlier would have done me a world of good."

"I'm here now," I said, reaching for his hand and linking our fingers together. Kameron's wobbly, excitedly nervous smile made my heart stutter. The elevator doors opened, and we exited together. I reluctantly let go of his hand now that we were around other people.

"So, what's the plan?"

"We got an overview of the Warrior's Foundation and their mission this morning. We have a few minutes of reset time before the brunch hour starts."

I grimaced. "Surely they're not making you mingle with the other organizations competing for the grant?"

"All in the name of community," Kameron said, quoting part of the foundation's mission statement. I sighed.

"Have you talked with the other executive directors?"

"Not yet," Kameron said. "We're the only nonprofit here that deals directly with veterans. One nonprofit advocates for teenagers and young adults facing cancer, and the other works directly with children rescued from the sex trafficking industry.

I let out a long breath.

"Both are good causes," I said.

"They're *all* good causes," Kameron said as we started walking towards the large glass doors that led into a large conference room. "That's what makes the nonprofit grant process so grueling. I don't envy the selection committee. This grant is a big deal, and any of the three nonprofits could change hundreds of lives with more support."

Upon entering the room, men and women in suits immediately surrounded us. I felt slightly underdressed in my white button up, knit cardigan, and slacks, but I also wouldn't be at the front of the room for the presentation. I'd be in the room, but towards the back.

"You must be Kameron Miller," one gentleman said, extending a hand to Kam. "I'm Jackson Smithfield, executive director of..."

Jackson immediately launched into his elevator speech about the nonprofit he worked for and their mission, all while guiding Kameron towards the refreshment station.

Kameron briefly looked back over his shoulder at me, and I gave him a small wave of encouragement.

He only had to survive small talk for this next hour. When the presentations finished, we would be free to go. I'd never been more excited about the prospect of heading back to the tiny house. I'd be ready to hibernate for a week after the amount of socializing I'd need to do today.

I turned to walk towards the outer rim of people when I bumped into a familiar body. Lucas had finally deigned to show up.

"Really? This is the day you decide to show up late?"

"I had a late night," was all Lucas said.

I wanted to strangle him, but I politely refrained from messing up his beautifully pressed button up.

Kameron's loud laugh reached my ears, and I turned toward his voice, watching with amusement as he made a beeline for the water station. I pushed past the throng of people to get to him, knowing Lucas could stand on his own. He was far better at mingling than either of us was.

"Hey," I said. Kameron turned to face me and I saw the panic etched into the sharp lines of his bearded face.

Without considering where we were or who was watching, I slid my fingers into between his, squeezing firmly. A reminder of everything we'd shared the previous night.

"You've got this."

"You'll be in the room, right?" Kameron asked, his eyes searching mine. I smiled and nodded.

"I'll be towards the back, following along. Specifically, I'll be making sure the slideshow is matched to what you're saying."

Kameron let out a small laugh and leaned closer to me, our chests brushing. If anyone was watching—and someone undoubtedly was, given how packed the room was—I knew we looked more like lovers than we did coworkers.

"Imogen? Is that you?"

I turned to face the woman, and my heart stopped when I saw her face.

No. It couldn't be.

"I'm sorry, I must have missed your name," I said, quickly scanning her chest for a name tag, even as my heart lurched in my throat. It couldn't be her.

She laughed too brightly and waved a hand dismissively.

"You're so funny," she said, and my stomach heaved. Definitely her. "My name is Claudia. Technically, I suppose I'm your ex-sister-in-law, but I'm here representing the Kilpatrick Collective."

Kilpatrick. I was going to be sick.

"Right," I said, still keeping my neutral smile plastered on my face. "You all work with children who have been rescued from sex trafficking."

Jacob's sister. Jacob's sister was *here*.

She didn't know.

I was certain she didn't know, because if she had, I can't imagine she would so brazenly approach me and re-introduce herself like we'd ever been close.

She was older than us. I'd met her once when she came to visit Jacob at Camp Pendleton, and it had been a brief interaction. Jacob had been eager to get rid of her—for reasons that were painfully obvious to me now.

"Correct," Claudia said, as if my remembering the basic gist of her nonprofit meant I'd passed her quiz. "This opportunity is so crucial to reaching more families. Our work is so necessary in this day and age. There are many organizations that focus on logistics of rescuing survivors, but few that focus on supporting the intense recovery that comes after the rescue."

I fought to keep my expression interested. I'd envisioned this brunch hour as a place where people could network, and not as a sales pitch for our various nonprofits. It felt competitive in a way that made my skin itch. Every nonprofit was important. We all served different communities, and there wasn't a hierarchy. Any of the three nonprofits represented today could do amazing work with the money and support bolstered by the grant.

Claudia and I hadn't been close. We could barely be considered acquaintances. But this. . .

Anger swelled in my chest, swift and violent.

I knew the world existed in various shades of gray. I knew nothing was ever black and white, and nowhere was that more obvious than in the decisions people made. Claudia's brother was capable of such horrible things, and yet here she was, leading a nonprofit that saved women from a life of horrors.

It was sickeningly ironic.

Several long seconds passed, and I realized Claudia was expecting a response. Right—this was a conversation, and it was my turn to talk.

But all I could do was stare at her.

Kameron had stayed silent up to this point.

"Kilpatrick," I murmured, and his eyes widened as the words sank in. I gave him a small nod to say yes, that Kilpatrick. Kam pressed closer to me, wrapping a hand around my shoulder. I'd never been more grateful for his comforting presence than right now.

"We're all here representing nonprofits that help people. In that sense, it's a competition. But you don't have to come after other nonprofits to build yourself up, Claudia," Kam said.

God, he was perfect.

"I wasn't saying—"

"I know it wasn't your intention, but we're telling you that's how it comes across," I said, politely interjecting. I wanted the final say in this conversation not because of the principle of it, but because I was about to walk away from this situation entirely and I didn't want her to misunderstand my meaning.

"There are many valuable causes in the world. We should lift each other up, even in the sometimes cutthroat world of grant proposals and securing funding for those causes. I wish you the best of luck today. And I truly mean that. No matter what the results end up being."

I gave her the most genuine smile I could muster and pulled Kameron's hand down to link his fingers with mine again.

"Excuse me. I need to spend some time with my team before our presentation," I said.

I pushed past Claudia, keeping my hand in Kameron's, mentally counting the steps until I made it back to Lucas, who was gawking beside the breakfast table.

"That might just be the hottest thing you've ever done," Kameron whispered in my ear, and I bit my lip to keep my smile at bay.

"Same could be said for you," I replied.

"Winding Road? We're ready for you," a woman called from the door, ducking back inside the hallway after her announcement.

I smiled at the two men and shimmied my shoulders. I couldn't do a full-on "dance it out" session, but I could do something.

"Let's do this thing," I said, and stepped into the board-room.

Chapter Thirty-One
Kameron

I'd given a lot of speeches in my time in the military, but I'd never felt more confident in my delivery.

I strolled to the stand, and proceeded to confidently and calmly present my case for why Winding Road deserved this funding. I elicited laughs from many of the committee members, and I'd received several nods of acknowledgement and understanding as I read through some testimonials from previous cohort members.

I clicked to the last slide, which showcased a picture of Lucas, Connor, and I, kneeling in front of our most recent cohort of veterans.

"The work we do at Winding Road has brought more to my life than I could have ever dreamed," I said. "I even met someone I've grown to love and care for very much, and she traveled with me to be here today."

I gestured to Imogen, who had been hovering in the back of the room throughout the entire presentation. There were tears in her eyes, and her smile was blinding as she waved to the committee members. To my surprise, she also stepped towards the podium. My heart lurched in my chest, and for a moment I wondered if I'd forgotten a slide.

"Hi everyone," she said as she stood beside me. "If you could turn your attentions back towards the screen, there's one final piece of the presentation, in the form of a video essay. This was meant to be somewhat of a surprise for Kameron, so you'll forgive his confusion."

There were several chuckles as I stepped to the side. Imogen plugged in the USB and brought the video up, tapping the spacebar to begin the video as we stepped away to watch.

The video started with some b-roll footage Imogen had taken of Winding Road, including some cameos from Chesty and Reckless. Then it panned over to Connor, who briefly explained his sobriety story and how Winding Road had saved his life.

It hit me like a ton of bricks, seeing my best friend sitting on the front steps of the farmhouse with Abbie next to him, his hand in hers. The love written on her face as she listened to his story had me reaching for Imogen, professionalism be damned.

This was my mission—reuniting families, reconnecting loved ones, and helping people realize that they could rise above their struggles, if they had the tools to help them.

"Oh my God," I murmured as the scene shifted again. Imogen took my hand, linking our fingers together and squeezing gently.

Next was Lucas, who talked about how Winding Road was a place people came to not only to find healing, but purpose. I chuckled when I realized Imogen had managed to green screen him into the pasture.

"Had to keep the continuity," Imogen whispered. I was still too shocked to answer, but I gave her fingers a squeeze in response.

After Lucas's clip, the scenes transitioned away from Winding Road to a montage of pictures of a young family.

It took me a moment to realize who the family was.

My shoulders shook with the force of my emotion, and my tears fell freely as we watched.

Imogen must have reached out to Gail. She was the only person, other than my mother, who had pictures of the three of us from before my father's death. Watching the slideshow of my childhood play was surreal. Pictures of us at Christmas, on vacation, at my father's work parties.

A childhood—*my* childhood—forever immortalized in the grainy lens of an early 2000s camera.

A lifetime forever changed by one man's absence.

Text explaining my Dad's service and his death played alongside the photos.

And at the end, there was a video of Lilliana, sitting in the nursing home in Laketon, telling the audience about Patrick, and why a place like Winding Road was so important for first responders and their families.

"I love you, Kam. I'm so proud of you. We both are."

I choked on my next breath, unable to bear the emotion of it. That Imogen had put this together, that my mother had been lucid enough to take part, that Gail had kept those treasured memories hoping one day I'd be strong enough to look at them again—it was *everything*.

There wasn't a dry eye in the room as the video faded.

I turned to Imogen and enveloped her in a tight hug.

In many ways, the video was meant to drive an emotional punch that left a lasting impression on the selection committee. I knew we'd succeeded there.

But for the five of us that knew Winding Road so intimately, it was more than that. It was an acknowledgment of the pain of the past, and an invitation to step into a new future.

Winding Road would survive whatever came next, because the team of people behind the mission knew how valuable it was.

We would *never* stop fighting to change the story that was written too often among first responders, veterans, and their family members.

We would never stop.

Chapter Thirty-Two
Kameron

The Warrior's Foundation had promised us a brief wait while they deliberated. On day three, we'd all gathered in the Winding Road farmhouse, ready to receive the news. Abbie and Imogen were baking cookies in the kitchen, while Connor and Lucas lounged on the couch with Bass running laps around the living room.

My chest tightened at how perfect the scene was. After my dad died, I'd struggled with finding and making friends. Even in the Marine Corps, I'd tried to keep a healthy professional distance between myself and the people I worked with. I never dreamed I would have a family like this.

More than anything, I hadn't dreamed I'd have a woman like Imogen to call mine. As if she heard my thoughts, she looked at me over her shoulder and blew me a kiss. A moment later, my phone rang, and I almost jumped out of my skin. All conversation ceased, and all eyes landed on me as I fished my phone out of my pocket.

The caller ID showed a Seattle area code, and a lump formed in my throat.

"Good morning. Is this Kameron Miller?"

I damn near dropped the phone, despite the fact that I'd been expecting this call.

"Yes, it is."

"This is Candace, from the Warrior's Foundation. We wanted to let you know we made a decision."

Imogen appeared at my side and squeezed my hand encouragingly. I focused on the feeling of her skin against mine as I waited for the final domino to fall.

"The main grant you applied for, the Warrior's Grant, will be going to another nonprofit."

My grip on the phone tightened. Connor and Abbie were clutching each other, waiting with patient ears, and I shook my head, making a "cut the camera" motion underneath my neck. Abbie's face fell, and Connor's expression turned stoic.

Abbie immediately turned to whisper to Connor, no doubt discussing the next steps and how we were going to come back from this. Imogen had already muttered "freaking Claudia" under her breath. I untangled my hand from hers and began pacing around the living room, grasping for words that didn't convey how utterly crushed I was in that moment.

"That said, everyone on the selection committee was inspired by the Winding Road story. We would like to work with you in a more intimate capacity."

What?

I paused my steps, fumbling for the right words to remain professional and not an asshole. But another offer of funding outside of the Warrior's Grant was a curveball I hadn't expected or rehearsed for.

"I don't follow."

"Winding Road serves a population that needs this work. There are relatively few nonprofits that focus on healing the effects of PTSD and traumatic experiences holistically. This is something our foundation has been at the forefront of researching for the last decade. We're fascinated by the idea of having a front-row seat for a case study on how for-profit and non-profit programming might coincide, as with the two subsections of Winding Road Farm and Recovery."

There was a brief pause as Candace shuffled some papers in the background. I sucked in another short breath of air.

"The Warrior's Grant included a monetary stipend and resources, and this mentorship—should you wish to accept it—would include those things and more. We'll send all the details to your email, including the contract. Take a few weeks to think things over and review the contract with your lawyer. If you have questions, or if you'd like to sit down for a conversation with someone you'd be working with, let me know. I'm happy to arrange it."

"It's an honor," I said, my throat closing up as a new well of emotion rose in my chest. "Thank you for seeing the value and vision in Winding Road. It means more than I can express."

"What?" Imogen whisper-yelled. She looked ready to combust. "What's happening?"

"You're more than welcome, Mr. Miller. We look forward to hearing from you. We'd like a formal decision by the end of the holiday weekend."

"Thank you," I said, not knowing what else to say. Thank you wasn't powerful enough to describe how meaningful this gift was. This was more than I could have hoped for.

Imogen's phone dinged with a new email, and her face lit up as she briefly read the subject line. Her gaze snapped to mine as I exchanged closing niceties with Candace before.

"Is she serious?" Imogen said. The excitement and wonder in her eyes made me weak in the knees.

We'd done it. Not in the way we'd originally planned, but we'd done it.

"I think so," I said, still slightly dizzy from the emotional roller coaster I just got off.

Imogen let out a whoop of excitement as she launched towards me, hugging me tightly.

"Wait, what's happening? Explain yourselves!" Abbie cried. "Are we celebrating or crying?"

"They gave the grant to someone else, but they extended us another offer. It's funding and mentorship, the same as the Warrior's Grant, but it sounds like it will be more personalized. They really see potential in us," I said, not fully believing it, even as I wrapped my arms around Imogen and buried my face into her shoulder. The comforting scent of her perfume mixed with the fresh mountain air enveloped me.

"This is really happening," I said. "Am I actually getting everything I want?"

Imogen's laugh was bright and beautiful as Connor, Abbie, and Lucas came over to swarm us in a big group hug.

"There's no one else in the world who deserves it more, Kam," Lucas said, and for once, I believed him.

Epilogue

Fairy lights twinkled above me as I gazed at the farmland before me. A gentle breeze blew past, bringing with it the smell of wildflowers and wood chips and late summer nights. The crickets chirped in the tall grasses beyond my farmhouse porch. Glassware clinked as Connor and Kameron brought silverware and plates to the table.

This would be the last time we gathered together on my back porch. After two months of the house being on the market, I'd finally found a buyer who wasn't a developer. This house would become a home for a young family that wanted to move to Watford to start their life over. They were excited at the prospect of renovating an older home; of giving something historic new life.

I couldn't think of a better way to close this chapter of my life. To know that this house and all of its memories would live on in the form of a new family brought me a joy I couldn't explain.

"If everyone's here, we can eat," I said. "Everything is set."

"I'll call them out here," Connor said, poking his head inside the farmhouse and calling for everyone to come outside for dinner.

Kameron came to stand at my side, wrapping an arm around my waist and pressing a kiss to my uncovered shoulder. I shivered involuntarily. Everything was different now, and I reveled in the beauty of it.

"It's the perfect night for a family dinner," I said. "I still can't believe how nice it is to have everyone in one place. I'd always dreamed about having this kind of friend group, but considering this time last year we were mostly strangers, it feels. . ."

"Dreamlike," Kameron said. "It feels like it's been a whole lot longer than a year."

"We do have a strange setup though, considering some of us knew each other long before the rest of us."

"They had a head-start," Kameron agreed, jerking his head in the direction of Connor and Abbie as they stepped onto the porch. Connor offered Abbie his hand to help her down the tiny half step, and while she rolled her eyes at the gesture, she still accepted it. Kevin and Kyrie stepped out afterwards, followed by Lucas.

Kyrie walked over to me first and enveloped me in a crushing hug. The girl used to get on my nerves, but even I could admit she was growing on me. Kevin had taken over most of the operations of Watford General Store since Abbie and Connor had been married and Malcolm had been focused on his recovery. Throughout it all, Kyrie had matured a lot.

Some of that had to do with getting older—I knew as well as anyone that there could be a big difference between the person you were at eighteen and the person you were at almost twenty.

Whatever the reason was, Kyrie was spending more time thinking and discussing her future options. She was working on finalizing portfolio pieces to finally submit some of her art to trade shows. It filled me with joy to know that her future options focused on what she wanted. She didn't see Kevin as a means to get her out of Watford.

Selfishly, I was glad she didn't seem to be making many of the mistakes I did in my eagerness to leave this small town.

I returned her hug and gestured for her to have a seat next to Kevin. I sat at the head of the table, with Kameron to my left, and Abbie at the other end of the table. Kevin, Kyrie, and Connor were seated on the right bench, with Kameron and Lucas on the left. There was a plethora of food before us—namely, a lush salad with fresh greens with what was going to be the final yield from my homestead. There was also an overflowing home style broccoli and cheddar casserole, and golden rolls baked to fluffy inside, crispy outside perfection.

"Before we eat, Abbie and I have an announcement," Connor said, almost sheepishly. That was when I noticed Abbie's hand draped casually over her stomach. "Since we have everyone here, we wanted to let you know—"

I screamed as the dots connected in my head. Kameron jerked next to me, letting go of my hand like it was burning as I leaped towards Abbie.

Connor didn't seem phased by my complete overreaction and opened his mouth to continue. "Abbie's—"

"Pregnant," I sobbed as I reached my best friend. I took her hands in mine. "Right? You're pregnant? That's why you've been quiet these last few weeks?"

Abbie's eyes welled with tears as she nodded, pulling me in for a hug. "Sorry for that, by the way. There were some concerns in the first trimester, but things are good now. I'm sorry for not telling you earlier, we just—"

I sobbed again, squeezing her tighter. "I'm glad everything's okay. I'm so happy for you. Oh my *God*, Abbie. You're going to be a mom. This is amazing."

"Congratulations," Kameron said. I released Abbie and turned back to the table, where Lucas was shaking Connor's hand like a weirdo and Kameron's eyes were misty.

"Do you know what you're having?"

"We haven't decided if we're finding out yet," Connor said, reaching for his water glass. I let out a horrified gasp.

"How? Why? I'd go insane," I muttered.

"Some of us actually like surprises, you know," Abbie said, her eyes shining with amusement as she leaned into Connor's side. "A baby is admittedly sudden, even for us. We're obviously excited, but having the gender be a surprise feels like the right thing. I don't know how to explain it."

"Well, regardless, we're throwing you a baby shower."

"Please do," Connor said as he passed out the plates so dinner could be served. "Because if you don't, we're not having one."

I gasped again.

"Well, you're in luck. You're going to have the best baby shower ever. One, because I'm your best friend and I wouldn't allow anything less, but two, because you're looking at Winding Road's newest event planner and coordinator," I said, gesturing to my body and shimmying my shoulders. "The Warrior's Foundation agreed with Kameron's assessment that our focus should be on solidifying the farm side of things before pursuing further expansion on the nonprofit. They recommended hiring a full-time event coordinator, and since I was already in a similar position. . ."

"As if I would have given the job to someone else," Kameron teased, accepting an outstretched plate from Connor.

"Hey, some people have a problem with nepotism."

"But everyone loves love," Abbie said with a frown.

"I rebuke that," Lucas chimed in. I rolled my eyes.

"Ignore him," Connor said, shaking his head. "He's been glued to his phone since the three of you got back from Seattle."

"And?" Lucas said defensively.

"And you're being weird about it," Connor said with a pointed smile. Lucas grumbled something unintelligible under his breath.

"Who are you texting that has you smiling like that?" I asked, leaning my chin into my hand and waggling my eyebrows. Lucas scoffed, but I didn't miss the pink tint in his cheeks.

"What's it to you?" Lucas muttered. "And for the record, we're not actively texting."

"You're waiting for *her* to text *you*?"

Oh *God*, this was too good. I was never letting him live this down.

Lucas didn't reply, so I pressed forward.

"Is it a girl you saw in Seattle?"

Lucas's silence was all the confirmation I needed.

"What's her name?"

"Nope. Nuh-uh."

"What!" I exclaimed, crossing my arms over my chest and sitting back in my chair. "A first name seems innocuous enough."

"I know how you work, you sneaky fiend. I'd tell you this chick's first name and you'd have a full FBI file on her within twenty four hours. Not playing that game."

I pouted but left it be. As much as I planned to tease him relentlessly about keeping this from me, I was secretly glad Lucas was getting back out there. If anything, he needed the distraction. What would hopefully be his final court date regarding his divorce was coming up quickly.

"I sense that your boyfriend is moping."

I shook my head to clear my thoughts and looked towards the sliding glass door, where Kameron was in the kitchen washing dishes.

"Love ya," Lucas said.

"Mhm," I said, standing to head inside. "Don't stay out here too late."

"I won't, *Mother*."

I rolled my eyes and slid open the door, stepping inside before pulling it behind me. I headed right for Kameron, who opened his arms wide without missing a beat of his conversation with Kevin, who was watching a football game on the TV. I wrapped my arms around his waist and let out a heavy sigh of relief and happiness.

"This is my favorite place to be," I murmured, the sound muffled against his shirt. Kameron hummed low in his throat and wrapped his arms around me, giving me a tight squeeze.

"Well, this is my favorite place for you to be. Wait, scratch that. Second place. No, third. Maybe fourth. . ."

"You're dirty," I said. Kameron leaned down to whisper in my ear.

"I never said anything about sex. Who's dirty minded again?"

I lifted my head from his chest and scowled at him.

"Are we going to be alone in the house tonight?"

"That depends," Kameron said. "Do you want us to be alone in the house?"

"I always want to be alone with you," I teased. "In all seriousness, my social battery is going to be drained after this amazing and demanding night. I'd prefer if it was just us tonight."

"Say no more," Kameron whispered, kissing my forehead before stepping away from the sink. He began to politely bark orders at the masses, telling them to wrap up whatever they were doing and head for the door.

"It's only 8 p.m.," Kevin whined. "We just got here."

"You've been here for two hours," Kameron pointed out. "Dinner is over, and there's an introvert here who needs recharging. You'll see her again tomorrow."

Abbie appeared from the hallway and turned towards Connor, who was already handing over her shoes.

"Does this recharging involve—"

"Don't finish that sentence, Abbigail Collins," I practically screeched, my cheeks flaming. Abbie giggled, damn her.

Once everyone was gone and the front door was locked, I wrapped my arms around Kameron's waist and sighed contentedly.

"I get you all to myself," I sighed happily. "It's the best part of my day."

"The best part of my day is doing this," Kameron said before picking me up and hauling me off towards the bedroom.

I giggled despite myself, but the sound quickly ceased when Kameron gently laid me down on the bed and crawled on top of me. I held his face in my hands, pressing a gentle kiss to his lips as his fingers drew gentle circles into my hips.

"I love you," I whispered. "More than I ever thought I could love another person."

Kameron's answering smile could power a million suns.

"You have my entire heart in the palm of your hand, Imogen Phillips. I couldn't love you more if I tried."

Acknowledgements

Two books? In a year? Who is she?

This wouldn't be possible without the love and support of so many people. I'm so grateful to everyone who has been part of my author journey so far.

To my husband and son, I love you both to the stars and back again.

Mom and Dad, thank you for everything. But most of all, thank you for loving and supporting me unconditionally, for encouraging me on the bad days, and for feeding my toddler peanut butter crackers during grandparent time so I could do all the things.

To my in laws, thank you for all of the weekend play dates with your favorite grandchild, the love and encouragement, and takeout (seriously, thank you).

Eve, thank you for *everything*. I cherish our friendship more than I can express in words.

Emily, you're the best. Thank you for letting me borrow your brain to fix plot holes and for encouraging me to follow my intuition when it came to the ending of this book. I can't wait to read your book one day (putting this in the acknowledgements of my book so we can look back when you're a bestselling author).

Angel: being able to experience motherhood *and* girlhood with you is a gift.

To Steph and Katrina: you guys are the best writer friends a gal could ask for. Thank you for being there through the good times and the bad, and for sharing your wisdom about all things writing and publishing.

To all of the bookstagrammers and booktokers who help me spread the word about my stories: y'all are the absolute best.

A special thank you to Jayla for your time and effort in sensitivity reading.

And lastly, to you dear reader, for coming along with me for yet another book. Without you, I wouldn't be able to do what I do, and I'm endlessly grateful for your support!

If you loved Imogen and Kam's story, please share with a friend, and leave a rating and/or review on Amazon and your favorite review platform. Ratings and reviews are so important for indie authors!

At the end of his enlistment, Lucas chose to leave the active duty life—and memories of his failed marriage—behind. He joined his best friends in launching a veteran nonprofit in the Washington mountains, but he can't shake the feeling that something is missing. Lucas must decide whether to return to active duty and finish what he started, or find a civilian path and purpose that is entirely his own.

Neither expect to see each other again. But when they find themselves attending their close friends' baby shower, they both come face to face with the one-night stand who just might change everything.

As they navigate old scars and new beginnings, Cassie and Lucas must decide if they're willing to take a chance—on healing, on love, and the possibility that some detours are meant to lead you exactly where you belong.

About The Author

H allie Anne writes romance stories with complicated characters working through tough problems and the love they find along the way. She lives in the Carolinas with her family. When she's not writing, she's curled up with a cozy blanket, a cup of coffee, and a romance book. Connect with her on Instagram at @hallieanneauthor, and join her Discord server for behind-the-scenes snippets and exclusive online events!

Sign up for my newsletter
to stay up to date!

Join Hallie's Heartstrings

S ick of the constant social media scroll? Me too. That's why I created a Discord server where we can hang out and connect on a deeper level—without being buried by the algorithm.

Join the Discord server